# PRAISE FOR THE BERT AND NAN TATUM MYSTERY SERIES

## DOUBLE MURDER

"A double dose of delight! A boisterous mystery with more twists than a double pretzel."

—Carolyn Hart, author of the *Death on Demand* and *Henrie O.* mystery series

"A lively mystery."

—*Publishers Weekly*

"Deftly plotted and wickedly amusing."

—Joan Hess, author of the *Claire Malloy* and *Maggody* mystery series

## DOUBLE EXPOSURE

"A nice little twinset."

—*Booklist*

"A wryly chipper style."

—*Kirkus Reviews*

"Easy, breezy fun . . . This story bounces along."

—*Publishers Weekly*

## DOUBLE CROSS

"Should keep reader interest high."

—*Library Journal*

"A good, fast read, complete with appealing touches of local Louisville color."

—*Booklist*

Books by Barbara Taylor McCafferty and
Beverly Taylor Herald

DOUBLE MURDER

DOUBLE EXPOSURE

DOUBLE DEALER

DOUBLE CROSS

DOUBLE DATE

Published by Kensington Publishing Corp.

# DOUBLE DATE

**BARBARA TAYLOR McCAFFERTY**
**AND**
**BEVERLY TAYLOR HERALD**

KENSINGTON BOOKS
Kensington Publishing Corp.
http://www.kensingtonbooks.com

*Dedicated to our sons,*
*Paul Young,*
*Chris Taylor,*
*and*
*Geoff Taylor,*
*our personal computer gurus,*
*who make cyberspace, bytes, and e-mail*
*more accessible to their*
*computer-unfriendly moms*

In memory of
Anna Herald Harris
(1922–1999)
who made the word *mother-in-law*
rich with kindness, thoughtfulness, and fun

## ACKNOWLEDGMENTS

The authors would like to express double thanks to Mark Wolterman, the winner of the Double Easy Contest on our Web site at www.mysterytwins.com, for giving us a great name for Nan Tatum's kitten. Mark won a complete set of autographed DOUBLE novels for helping us come up with a name.

We also continue to be doubly grateful to Bill Love of WKDQ-FM in Evansville, Indiana, for sharing his expertise and advice.

# Chapter One

## Bert

They say what doesn't kill you makes you stronger. If that's true, I figure by the time I'm seventy, I ought to be able to lift a house.

And if I keep having weeks like the ones I've just had, I might be able to lift a car by my next birthday.

I, no doubt, started growing stronger by the minute right about the time I hung up my phone last Sunday and turned to face my twin sister, Nan. Nan Tatum is my twin's full name, and if that name sounds familiar to you, I'd be willing to bet that you live somewhere near Louisville, Kentucky. Nan is the afternoon disc jockey on WCKI-FM Country Radio here. Having listened to her for free all my life, it's sometimes hard for me to believe that there are those in "Radio Land" who will pay Nan to talk. For several hours a day yet!

To be brutally honest, I confess there have been times when I would've paid her to shut up. Quite a few times this last week, in fact, I would have shelled out the big bucks to get Nan to close her mouth for just five seconds. I'd have particularly liked to push her MUTE button on those far-too-frequent occasions when she's told me to "get a grip."

Evidently, to hear Nan tell it, one should never let a little thing like murder get on one's nerves.

True, this wasn't the first time that Nan and I have ever run across such a thing. After having the misfortune of solving a twenty-five-year-old murder mystery that was written up on the front page of the Louisville *Courier-Journal*, Nan and I were all but stalked for a while there. *Lord.* It seemed as if everybody and their grandmother within a one-hundred-mile radius of Louisville had an ages-old murder in their family that hadn't been solved. It had been pretty sad to listen to. And even worse to get involved in. No matter what Nan says.

Of course, now that I think about it, I don't know why I'd be surprised that Nan would be so blasé about everything. Nan was pretty laid-back right from the beginning. That Sunday afternoon when I hung up the phone and started quizzing her, Nan hadn't even bothered to look up from the newspaper she was reading.

Nan and I often spend Sunday afternoons together, wading through the fat Sunday edition of the *Courier*, eating whatever is easiest to make for dinner, and more or less getting caught up on what's going on in each other's lives. We alternate between our apartments, getting together at Nan's place one week and mine the next. On this particular Sunday, it was my turn.

Whose apartment we meet at really doesn't much matter. I rent one half of a duplex that Nan owns in Louisville's Highlands area, so it's not as if either one of us has to drive across town or anything. All we have to do to get together is head next door.

Most Sundays, it's a nice, comfortable routine. Unless, of course, I happen to get a really disturbing phone call. One that makes my voice shake after I hang up. I had to swallow a couple of times before I could trust myself to speak. "Nan," I asked, "is there anything you've neglected to tell me? Anything that perhaps you meant to let me know about, but you forgot to mention?"

One of the bad things about being identical twins is that it's almost impossible to pull anything over on a woman who has the same face as you do. Stretched out on my couch, with the Arts & Entertainment section blanketing her lap, Nan looked up from the article she'd been reading with the wide-eyed, innocent look that I myself have used on numerous occasions.

"Anything I've forgotten to mention?" Nan repeated. "Nope, nothing comes to mind, Bert."

That's right. Nan and Bert. I guess there's no way to get around it, so I might as well admit it—our mother named us after the older set of Bobbsey Twins. Mom managed to do this even though the Bobbseys were boy-and-girl fraternal twins, and Nan and I had turned out to be identical twin girls. From what our dad has told us, Mom took one look at me, lengthened the name she'd already picked out to Bertrice, and then promptly started calling me Bert for short.

If the whole Bobbsey thing hadn't been so tacky, I probably would have admired Mom's ingenuity.

"What makes you think I've forgotten to tell you something?" Nan gave an uneasy glance to the telephone I'd just hung up. "Who was that on the phone?"

"That was Elsa," I said. "You know, Elsa Watkins, the receptionist at OfficeTemps?" OfficeTemps is the temporary agency I work for. Ever since my divorce three years ago, I've been a walking, talking contradiction in terms—a *permanent* temporary. That's the kind of career you end up with if you've spent all your adult years raising two children, have zilch job experience, and then one day your husband leaves you for his twenty-something secretary. Oh my, yes, I'd say my entire life could be summed up in just two words: *poor planning*.

Nan frowned. "Elsa Watkins? Don't think I've ever had the pleasure." Her eyes wandered back to the newspaper on her lap. Nan had indeed met Elsa—more than once, as a matter of fact, on a couple of occasions when Nan and I had decided to meet at the office to go to dinner or shopping. As I recall, Nan had been put off by Elsa's nonstop chatter. Nan had also not cared for the way Elsa seemed to relish passing on all the latest gossip about anybody and everybody.

Frankly, I didn't care whether Nan remembered Elsa or not. Or even whether she liked her or not. As our daddy used to say, right up until our mama told him to stop talking like a country bumpkin: I had bigger fish to fry.

"Elsa just told me the strangest thing," I said.

Nan tore her eyes away from the *Courier* once again, still doing wide-eyed innocence. In all honesty, I believe I do it better. "OK, Bert," Nan said. "I'll bite. What did Elsa say?"

I took a deep breath. "Elsa said she was thinking about signing up for an Internet matchmaking service—"

Nan's already large brown eyes got a little larger when I said the word *matchmaking*. I hurried on. "—but she was a little leery about doing it. She said she was afraid she might run into some weirdo online." I paused here, watching Nan closely. "In fact, Elsa had just about decided to forget the whole thing when she noticed something."

Nan didn't even blink. "What did she notice?"

I didn't blink, either. "Elsa noticed that *you and I* had signed up. Finding that out made Elsa feel better."

Actually, Elsa had sounded as if she'd felt not just better but totally elated. "That *was* you two, wasn't it?" she'd squealed. "Sure it was! It *had* to be you two! I mean, how many single forty-year-old women twins can there be here in Louisville? Especially where one twin is an office temp and the other one is a disc jockey?"

Elsa had been talking a mile a minute as usual, but I had to admit she had a point.

"As soon as I recognized you two," Elsa had prattled on, "well, I started thinking that if you two girls had the guts to take a chance like that—I mean, if you two aren't afraid that you might be making a date with a serial killer—well, then, I thought, hell's bells, maybe I should give it a whirl, too! I just never would've thought that you, Bert, of all people, would do such a thing. I mean, oh sure, *Nan* might, but, well, my goodness, I always thought you were the sensible one—"

At that moment, the sensible one had been grinding her sensible teeth. "Let me call you back, Elsa, OK?"

"Not to mention"—Elsa had gone right on just as if I hadn't said a word—"aren't you dating somebody? What does he think of all this?"

Once again Elsa had a point. For a little over a year now, I'd been dating Hank Goetzmann, a detective with the Louisville police force. I guess you could say that Hank and I met under less than ideal conditions. Hank had been investigating a homicide that he'd suspected that Nan and I had committed. Having some guy think you're capable of cold-blooded murder is not exactly a turn-on. It had taken me a pretty long time to warm up to the guy.

But warm up, I certainly did. As crazy about him as I am these days, it's hard for me to believe that once I hadn't even liked Hank very much.

It's even harder to believe that Hank had once dated Nan. Of course, that's one of the things that I find sort of amazing about him. Hank has accomplished something nobody has ever done before him. Something, in fact, that before Hank came on the scene, Nan and I had thought was so difficult as to be virtually impossible. Hank has actually pulled off the "Twin Switch." He's managed to stop dating one of us and start dating the other without making either one of us look at him as if he were something we'd found on the bottom of our shoes.

What a guy.

"Or did you two break up?" Elsa had hurried on. Eager as always to hear the latest gossip, Elsa had all but gushed. "So, tell me, what happened? Was he seeing somebody else or did you—"

"Elsa," I'd said, "let me call you back, all right?" I'd hung up before she'd had a chance to say anything more.

"So, Nan," I said now, crossing my arms across my chest, "what do you suppose could have possibly given Elsa the ludicrous idea that you and I had signed up for a computer matchmaking service?"

Nan had the colossal gall to smile at me. Just as if nothing whatsoever was wrong. "Well," she said, "now that you ask, it could be—hey, I'm just guessing here— but Elsa might have gotten that idea because I signed you and me up at the MySoulMate Web site."

My mouth actually dropped open.

I guess up until then I was hoping against hope that Nan would tell me that Elsa was mistaken. As soon as Nan spoke, though, I realized that I should have known. This was not exactly a big departure for Nan. My sister has been joining me to things all our lives.

Even though I'm ten minutes older and, according to a lot of the twin research I've read over the years, I'm supposed to be the dominant twin—nothing could be further from the truth. Nan has always been the leader of this pack. Dominant twin or not, however, she still hadn't wanted to join things all by herself. I guess you can't be a leader unless you have a follower.

For a while there during our senior year in high school, it had seemed as if every single day after school

Nan had been waiting with news of what she'd led me into. In one week alone, she'd joined me to the French club, the debate team, and the glee club. As I recall, I had not been gleeful about any of it.

I was certainly not gleeful now. "You signed us *both* up? And you didn't even tell me. Are you nuts? Why in the world would you do such a thing?"

Nan shrugged. "Now, Bert, don't get your panties in a bunch."

I frowned. Lately Nan has been using a lot of quaint phrases like this one. Of course, it's better than what she used to say. She used to pepper her speech with four-letter words, having saved up quite a few after spending hours on the radio adhering to FCC standards. After people started referring to her as the "potty-mouthed twin," though, she started toning down. Nowadays Nan doesn't curse much at all; instead, she mouths charming little phrases like this one. It's enough to make you long for the good old days when what came out of Nan's mouth was enough to singe your ears. "My panties are just fine," I said. "It's you I've got a problem with."

Nan's eyes had wandered once again to the paper in her lap. "No you don't. You don't have a problem with me or anything else. This is nothing to be concerned about."

"Nothing? You've signed me up with a matchmaking service on the Internet, and you think it's nothing?" I couldn't believe my ears. "Nan, it's dangerous, that's what it is! It's a great way to run into Ted Bundy!"

Nan gave me a look. "Ted's dead, Bert. He sat a little too long in an electric chair. You don't have to worry about running into him." She shrugged, rattling the paper on her lap. "Hell, you don't have to worry about any of it. After all, it's not as if you actually have to go out with any of the guys who contact you—"

I hadn't thought of that. "Oh my God."

"Bert, it's no big deal."

I tried to keep my voice calm. "No big deal? Have you gone completely crazy? How am I supposed to explain this to Hank?" OK, so maybe my voice wasn't all that calm. Unlike what Nan might tell you, however, I was not yelling my head off. I'd merely increased my volume just a bit in order to emphasize the point. Besides which, it wasn't as if I had to worry about the neighbors next door hearing me. I *am* the neighbor next door. "I cannot believe you'd enroll me in a matchmaking service! I don't need to have a match made. I already have a match, thank you."

Nan had the unbelievable gall to smile at me *again.* It was quick, tight-lipped smile, but it was most definitely a smile. "Well, Bert," she said, "I don't happen to have a match myself, thanks so much for reminding me. I guess it won't be exactly a shock to hear that I'm getting very tired of sitting home, feeling depressed, every single Saturday night. So I decided to try this. But I'd like to make this clear, I didn't really sign you up. I just signed myself up twice. That's all."

I believe I came up with the only appropriate response. "Huh?"

Nan had the sort of expression on her face that an elementary school teacher wears when she's explaining multiplication for the first time. "It's like this. First I signed myself up, using my own profile—you know, country-music disc jockey, never married, no kids, the whole bit—but I found out right away that was a mistake."

"What do you mean?"

Nan shrugged again. "The only men who contacted me were guys called 'Lou.' Short for *loser.* I had one Lou who wanted to break into the radio biz, another Lou who wanted me to play on the air a cassette of a really awful song he'd written himself, and yet another Lou who wanted me to rush right over and join him in his hot tub."

"So you decided to sic all these Lous on me?"

Nan laughed. Really. She laughed right out loud, as if all of this were just too silly to be of any real concern.

I love my sister. I really do. Most days I would throw myself in front of oncoming traffic to save her. So the fact that at that moment I wanted to go for her throat really should not be taken as an accurate indication of my sisterly devotion. "For God's sake, Nan, what were you thinking?"

"Well, I was thinking that I might get a lot better results using a more ordinary, run-of-the-mill profile— you know, a profile that says that I just have a regular job, that I'm divorced rather than never married—although I do think that it's a sad comment on our society that women our age who've been divorced are apparently considered far more normal than women our age who've never been married—"

I was in no mood to discuss the problems of American society. I held up my hand. "I still don't understand."

Nan shrugged again. I was getting pretty tired of see-

ing her do that. "Look, I needed to think up a new profile, and yours was the only one besides my own that I already knew real well. I wouldn't have to make up stuff, I
could just sign up again and answer questions as if I
were you. I wouldn't have to worry about the profile
sounding fake, because it wouldn't be fake." Nan
grinned. "It was perfect."

"Perfect," I repeated. In total disbelief.

Nan nodded. "I'll answer responses to both profiles,
and if any of them sound promising, I'll set up a meeting. If it turns out that I really do start dating somebody,
I'll tell him the truth."

I cleared my throat. "It doesn't bother you that you
could possibly be starting out a relationship with some
guy by lying to him?"

Nan grinned again. "A tiny little white lie, that's all.
I'm sure when I explain it to him, he'll understand."
She shrugged yet again. "Besides, I want to see what sort
of men answer your profile, so I'll find out once and for
all if it's my being on the radio that's been my problem."

I'd heard this theory before. Nan thinks that men
meet her with the concept already firmly entrenched in
their minds of her having an OFF switch somewhere.
Whether that's true or not, I do have to admit that
every guy she's ever dated seriously has eventually
reached for that switch.

I was sorry about that. I really was. I'd love nothing
better than my sister finally finding a guy who adored
her. However, I'd prefer her to find him without having
to sacrifice my own relationship. Call me picky. I ran my
hand through my hair. "Nan, if I didn't know better, I'd

think you were deliberately trying to sabotage my relationship with Hank."

Nan actually winced. "You can't really believe that." Then she said the thing that really bothered me. It was at once an admission and a dismissal of the seriousness of the problem. "Besides," she added, "Hank will never find out."

I just looked at her. "How could you possibly know that?" Twins are supposed to be more intuitive than the general population, but clairvoyant? I didn't think so.

"Who'll tell him?" Nan said. "Not me. And certainly not you."

"Who'll tell him?" My head was beginning to hurt. "Anybody who knows us and who wants a date this weekend! That's who! Hank knows a lot of people, Nan, any one of whom could decide to sign up with MySoulMate."

Nan shook her head. "Hank could see our entries on MySoulMate and he still wouldn't know it was us. I didn't use our real names."

"Nan," I said, "*Elsa* figured it out. And Elsa is a secretary. Hank, on the other hand, is a detective. It's his job to put clues together. Don't you think if Elsa can figure it out, Hank could?"

Nan didn't hesitate. "Not necessarily. For Elsa, it was probably just a lucky guess." Unbelievably, Nan's eyes returned to the paper in her lap.

I gritted my teeth. Evidently, the subject had been discussed to Nan's total satisfaction, and Nan's mind had been eased. What a relief for us all. "Nan," I said, fighting the urge to yank that paper right out of her hands, "you could not have picked a worse time to do this."

Nan didn't even glance my way. "I'll say. I haven't had a decent date in six months."

"What I meant to say is: If Hank discovers that I'm on the Internet, looking for a date, of all things, it could ruin everything."

Nan dragged her eyes once again away from the paper. "Everything? What do you mean?"

I had not meant to say anything until Hank and I had come to a definite decision, but it was too late now to back out of it. "Nan, last night Hank mentioned— that is, he talked about—"

I couldn't bring myself to say the word out loud. That would seem to me to be a pretty good indication of just how ready I was to discuss this particular topic. Instead, I used a phrase Nan herself used all the time. "Hank mentioned the *m*-word."

Nan's head jerked up, and her eyes riveted on mine. "Wha-at?"

OK. Now I finally had her full attention.

# Chapter Two

## Nan

With anybody else, I might've tried to conceal my surprise. With Bert, though, I knew it was useless. When you've stared at the same face in the mirror every day of your life, you can pretty much read it like a book. The words *OH MY GOD!* might as well have been scrolling across my forehead. "The *m*-word?" I said. "Really? Hank asked you to marry him?"

Wow. Having dated the big oaf for several centuries one month, I couldn't imagine Hank ever going all gooey and soft and finally popping the question. Not without weapons involved, anyway.

Before anybody gets the idea that I'm being hard on the guy, I would like to submit as Exhibit A the following: This was the same man who'd always whispered "NPDA" every time I'd tried to hold his hand when we were in a darkened movie theater. The first time he'd whispered it to me, pulling his hand away as if my own hand were something unclean, I'd thought that the initials probably referred to some New Police Department Act—no doubt relating to the necessity of a cop keeping his hands free in case he might be called upon suddenly to fire his pistol. At least, I'd thought that until Hank thoughtfully decoded the letters for me: No Public Displays of Affection. It was apparently a rule he lived by.

How cute.

After a few weeks of NPDA, I came up with a few initials of my own: NWJ (No Way, José); HTRJ (Hit The Road, Jack); and, my personal favorite, DLTDHYOYWO (Don't Let The Door Hit You On Your Way Out).

Since Hank has been dating Bert. I've heard him whisper "NPDA" to her a few times, too. Strangely enough, though, Bert has never seemed to mind. In fact, every time Hank has whispered his stupid little code, Bert has always smiled at the ignoramus affectionately, as if his saying such a thing were just the cutest, most adorable thing she'd ever heard in her entire life.

Oh brother.

Sometimes it's hard to believe that Bert and I started out in this world as a single entity. It's easy to believe that she and I are mirror twins, though. A subset of identical twins, mirror twins are even rarer than identical. What being mirror twins means to Bert and me personally has nothing to do with how rare they are, though. What it means to us is that, even though technically Bert and I are identical twins, we are not exact duplicates. We are, instead, mirror images of each other. That means that Bert is left-handed, and I'm right-handed. Our hair naturally parts on opposite sides. We start off walking on the opposite feet. And sometimes, oh, yes, we have the exact opposite reactions to things.

"Well, Hank didn't actually out and out ask me to marry him," Bert was going on. "He sort of pre-asked me."

"Excuse me?" I said. This sounded more like the oaf I'd gone out with. Hank had told me several times during the eons that we'd dated that he thought the *m*-word was equivalent to an obscenity. A word he never said out loud in mixed company. "Bert, did you say *pre-asked?*"

Bert nodded, smiling. Good Lord. Was she actually smiling like a schoolgirl? OK, this proves it. That old saying is simply not so. Love is not blind. And it's certainly not deaf. It's just dumb. Really, really dumb.

"Yes," Bert said, "I think poor Hank wasn't sure that I'd say yes, so that sweet man was testing the waters. Last night he asked me to think about the idea of our getting married, and let him know of any concerns I might have. Wasn't that sweet?"

*Sweet* was not exactly the word I would've used to describe it. *Cold. Impersonal. Clinical.* Those were the words I would've chosen. The way I saw it, Bert was lucky Hank hadn't given her a clipboard with a survey to fill out, listing the pros and cons of matrimony. Staring at Bert with her happy little smile, though, I realized that none of this bothered her in the least.

She really didn't care that a guy she'd been dating

for almost a year didn't have the guts to come right out and ask her to marry him.

Man. Maybe Bert and I really do need to have our DNA checked. Not just to see if we really are identical twins, either. No, we need to check and see if we're from the same planet.

"Hank ended our evening by asking me to give the idea serious consideration. Which, of course, I'm doing," Bert said, a little breathlessly. "In fact, up until now I've hardly been able to think about anything else." She started to smile again, looking a little misty, but then her eyes met mine.

And turned icy.

"Of course, now I have something else to think about, thanks to you, Nan. Now I get to think about my sister putting me on the Internet, looking for a date!"

I rolled my eyes. Bert was making it sound as if I'd signed her up with a pimp. "Bert, you don't get it, I—"

She didn't let me finish. "No, you're the one who doesn't get it! Nan, if Hank finds out, he could think I was running around on him!"

I stared at her, honestly shocked. The thought had never occurred to me. "You? Hank might think *you* were running around on him?" I tried not to smile, but the idea of accusing Bert of infidelity was about as plausible as accusing Mother Teresa of child abuse.

Bert had probably been the last woman in America who was a virgin on her wedding night. Until her divorce a year or so ago, the number of men she'd had sex with could be counted not just on one hand but on one finger. Jake, her husband of twenty-something years, had been Bert's one and only.

Until, of course, she'd found out that she had not been his one and only.

Poor Bert had also found out that she had not been old Jake's one and only several times during their marriage, the last time notable only in that it had involved his twenty-three-year-old secretary, a woman only a very few years older than Jake and Bert's daughter, Ellie.

Even now I could cheerfully kick Jake the Snake in the nuts for the pain he'd put Bert through.

I folded my arms across my chest. "Bert, in all honesty, if Hank really thinks that you would run around on him, he doesn't know you very well. And if he doesn't know you very well, then maybe you two shouldn't be talking about getting married. Not yet, anyway."

I'd say Bert took that little comment well. Her eyes bugged out, the way they might have if she'd just stuck her finger in a light socket. "Oh, so you have a problem with my getting married again, do you?" she burst out. "I was afraid of this. Admit it, Nan. You really do have a problem with it, don't you?"

Once again I stared at her, shocked. Wow. This conversation had taken an ugly turn. "Bert, I do not have a problem with your getting married again," I said. "I think it would be great."

Oddly enough, my voice sounded pretty thin even to my own ears. Good Lord. Could it be true? Was I feeling a little strange about all this?

I took a deep breath, thinking it all over as fast as I could with Bert standing right there, glaring at me. OK, let me see, it wasn't that I had a problem with Bert marrying *Hank*. For God's sake, no. Been there, done that, never want to do it again, would like to forget that I'd ever done it—that pretty much summed up my feelings on *that* subject.

No, now that I thought about it, the thing that was bothering me was pretty simple. It was just that I myself have never been married. *Never.* Not once. Zilch, zippo, goose egg in the marriage department. And now it looked as if Bert—the quiet homebody twin—might be tying the knot for the second time. The way I saw it, the matrimonial score was fast getting to be 2 to 0.

And before anybody starts thinking I should run— not walk—to the nearest shrink, hey, I realize it is not a contest. It is most definitely not true that the woman who dies with the most marriages under her belt wins. Besides, everybody knows that—if there is such a contest—Elizabeth Taylor has already won.

Still, at the risk of sounding more than a little self-centered, I'd have to admit that I couldn't help feeling envious of Bert. And, to be brutally honest, kind of amazed. How in the hell did she do it? A woman who looked just like me; a woman who'd spent a significant portion of her life as a housebound housewife; a woman who'd actually told me in all seriousness recently that there could not possibly be any organized crime anymore because the police would never let such a thing go on. Oh yes, Bert was that naive, Lord love her—and yet, she seemed to know a lot more about getting a man to the altar than I did.

Of course, Bert was ten minutes older than me, so

maybe she'd learned a lot more about men and relationships during that crucial head start.

Bert was now smirking at me. "Yes, sure, I'm stupid. I believe you. I truly believe you're so tickled about the prospect of my getting married to Hank that you've enrolled me in a matchmaking service!"

I unfolded my arms and shifted position on the couch. "If you recall, I didn't know about your marriage possibilities until now, so I don't see how you can possibly think that it could have anything to do with my signing you up." I shrugged. "Besides, the whole matchmaking thing wasn't my idea. Not at first, anyway."

"Oh yeah?" Bert said. "Whose idea was it? What moron came up with this little brainstorm?"

Bert wasn't going to like my answer. "Ellie."

Bert's eyes widened.

It was true. Bert's twenty-year-old daughter, Ellie, had dropped by my duplex on a Friday night a couple of weeks ago, and for the first time in several months, she'd actually sounded enthusiastic about something.

"A lot of the girls I know at U of L have signed up with a matchmaking Web site, and they're meeting some great guys." With straight blond hair and blue eyes, Ellie had obviously inherited her father's Nordic good looks. Most of the time, you'd never guess that Bert was her mother. At that moment, however, with her eyes dancing with excitement, Ellie reminded me of Bert when she was a little girl laughing at something on *The Mickey Mouse Club*. "The Web site is called MySoulMate," Ellie hurried on, "and I really do think that you and I should join."

At the time, I knew that I should've been feeling happy that Ellie was finally cheering up, but to tell you the truth, it was pretty annoying. When you're feeling kind of down yourself, the last thing you want to hear is just how great somebody else is feeling.

Up to that particular evening, Ellie and I'd had a lot in common.

Both of us currently had no man in our life.

Both of us were pretty angry at the last guy we'd dated.

And both of us felt like crap.

If Bert had not been so tied up with Hank, Ellie and I might have been spending our time with her, happily complaining about how rotten men were. As it was with Bert unavailable a lot of the time, it was only natural that Ellie would have started phoning me. "It's really great to have a backup mom," she'd told me.

"It's really great to be a backup mom," I'd told her. I meant it, too. Sometimes Ellie seemed like the daughter I never had. As a matter of fact—as Bert herself has mentioned more than once—occasionally Ellie seemed to be more like me than her mother.

Poor Ellie sure seemed to have my luck with men. More's the pity, I might add. She had recently had a truly awful experience with a guy who'd fast-talked her into confessing to murder for him. Really. No joke. I know it sounds pretty hard to believe, but unfortunately, it's true. To that book Dr. Laura wrote about the ten stupid things women do to mess up their lives, Ellie could add number eleven: confessing to murder for some guy because you think you're in love.

Predictably, it had ended badly—so badly, in fact, that recalling the entire episode has actually made me feel better every once in a while. I know, I know. I'm a first-class schmuck. Occasionally, though—when I've been at a particularly low ebb and kicking myself for how incredibly dumb I've been about men—I have thought about Ellie and actually felt better. Hey, I may have been a total idiot again and again and again, but look on the bright side: At least, I hadn't gone to *jail* for some guy.

Wisely, I have never told Ellie what a comfort she has been to me.

I have told her, however, about how not all that long ago I fell totally head over high heels for this jerk whose kisses made me say, "Wow." This particular jerk kept telling me that I was the only woman in his life, that he and I were made for each other, and that one day when he felt we were both ready, he wanted us to commit to each other forever.

I realize now that it was significant that he, like Hank when I'd dated him, had never actually said the *m*-word out loud. Significant because, what do you know, one night I'd run into El Jerko with a buxom blonde on his arm at what had been our favorite restaurant, The Bristol Bar & Grill on Bardstown Road. Earlier that day, Jerko had told me that he'd be working late, so I'd decided to pamper myself and go out to eat. While I was there, I ordered one of his favorites to go—steak with béarnaise sauce. I'd been planning to go to his office and surprise him.

As it happened, I was the one surprised.

Before Jerko spotted me, I'd watched him lean over and wow the blonde several times with his kisses.

I'd felt ill.

It had helped some to march over to his table and dump the steak with béarnaise sauce right into his lap, but on the drive home, I'd had to pull off a couple of times because I couldn't see the road ahead through my tears.

What was even worse, it had been months and I still missed the guy. And his damn *wow* kisses. I still couldn't walk past my phone without wishing it would ring and it would be him. Talk about the things women do to mess up their lives. I'd actually found myself thinking one day: *OK, he's a cheat and an asshole, but what did I do wrong? Why doesn't he phone and try to make up?*

Dr. Laura would've slapped me. Hell, I wanted to slap myself.

"Come on, Aunt Nan," Ellie insisted that Friday night, "it's high time you and I stopped moping and started living again."

"I don't know, Ellie. Internet dating? It sounds like a great way to meet weirdos."

Ellie actually laughed, something I hadn't heard her do in a while. "Nan, a singles bar is a great place to meet weirdos. The mall is a great place to meet weirdos. The grocery, for God's sake, is a great place to meet weirdos. So what's your point?"

I had to smile, in spite of myself.

"Besides," Ellie hurried on, "you can find out more reading a guy's profile on the MySoulMate Web site than you can in an entire evening talking to him in some smoke-filled singles bar."

I was still skeptical. "Like what, for instance? What could you possibly find out that you couldn't find out just talking to him?"

"You can get an idea how smart the guy is; you can tell if he can actually construct entire sentences; you can see if he can spell—"

I shook my head. "I don't know, Ellie. Whenever I've been thinking about what I wanted in a guy, the ability to spell just never seemed to come up."

Once again, Ellie had laughed. It took her a while, but finally she'd talked me into giving MySoulMate a shot.

I only wished that Ellie were here now to convince her mother. Bert was looking pretty alarmed. "You don't mean that Ellie has signed up for Internet match-making, too? Oh dear Lord. There's no telling who she could meet!"

I gave her what I hoped was a reassuring smile. "Bert, not everybody you meet online is a psycho."

Bert glared at me. "I should think that meeting just one is far too many."

What could I say? Bert always knew how to make a point.

Bert turned now and started to head down the hall toward the back of her duplex. "Come on," she said over her shoulder.

I got up but made no move to follow her. "Come on? Where are we going?"

"We're going back to my study," Bert said. "We're going to get online, and you're going to show me this idiotic Web site. Right this minute."

For a second I just stood there, motionless. And yet, there didn't seem any way to get out of it. Slowly I followed Bert down the hall.

This wasn't going to be pretty.

# Chapter Three

---

## Bert

Let me tell you, there is nobody on God's green earth who can make you crazier than someone with the exact same genes as yours. Mainly because the entire time you're dealing with that person, there's a little voice in your head that keeps asking, "How in the world can somebody who's supposed to be just like me act like THAT?"

Like, for example, it was growing more and more apparent that Nan truly believed that just because she'd listed me on a matchmaking Web site, there was no real need to show it to me. My goodness, no. So what if my very own daughter had also listed herself there? That was still no reason to bother letting me see for myself what Ellie and I were getting into.

I was already at the door to my study. I stood there

and watched Nan walking toward me. If the woman could've moved any slower, she would've been going backward.

"Come on, Nan." I said. "For God's sake, if this Web site is as great as you say it is, I should think you'd want to show it to me."

Nan gave me a weak smile. I believe she'd had the same look on her face back when we were in the sixth grade—right after she'd broken the news to me that she'd accidentally set fire to my diary while she was trying to light a cigarette for the first time. Back then, at the ripe old age of twelve, I had already known that smoking would not be on my list of "Things To Do in This Lifetime." Nan, on the other hand, had found it necessary to give blackening her lungs a trial run.

"Oh, I want to show the site to you, all right. I really do," Nan now said, her voice totally lacking in enthusiasm. "And MySoulMate *is* a really good deal, I'll have you know. For just ten dollars a month, MySoulMate acts as a go-between for single people. And part of that ten dollars goes to research into heart disease."

"Heart disease," I repeated. "That certainly sounds appropriate."

Nan ignored me. "MySoulMate lets you send e-mails to whomever you want, and they can e-mail you back, but you never, ever see the other person's e-mail address. And they don't see yours. MySoulMate gives you an anonymous e-mail address to communicate through. So it's really very safe. Nobody knows your real e-mail address or your real name or where you live, unless you tell them yourself."

I knew a diversionary tactic when I heard one. Nan had come to a dead stop while she talked. "Cut the commercial, Nan," I said. "Get online and show this thing to me."

I sounded testy, I admit, but I didn't even care. Lord knows, I had enough on my mind these days without adding this. Ever since Hank had asked me to think about our getting married, I'd been mentally spinning. I wasn't exactly sure why I was so surprised. After all, we'd been dating for over a year now, so it wasn't as if we barely knew each other or anything. I guess I just thought that Hank had been permanently soured on marriage after his divorce a few years ago.

I can't say I totally disagreed with him, either. In fact, before Hank brought the subject up, I'd pretty much decided that I'd figured out what had been causing the high rate of divorce in this country: marriage. If people just didn't ever walk down the aisle together, they would never have to go through the pain of splitting up. It had seemed simple to me.

Yes, I guess I was a little jaded on the whole concept. I'd been a virgin when Jake and I had gotten married. I'd followed all the rules, I'd been a faithful and loving wife for almost twenty years, and what had it gotten me? A philandering husband and a divorce when I was fast approaching forty.

On the other hand, Hank was not Jake. According to what Hank had told me, it had been his wife who was running around, not him. She'd just walked in one day and announced that she couldn't take being married to a cop anymore. It was too "stressful." She'd assured him that there was no one else, and then had quietly mar-

ried her tennis instructor two weeks after Hank's and
her divorce was final.

Oh my, I had been sure that Hank was soured on
marriage, all right. For sure, he was soured on his ex-
wife. He hadn't spoken to her since he found out about
her marriage. It broke my heart to see the look in his
eyes whenever he spoke of her. In fact, the very last
thing he needed was to find out that I was listed with a
matchmaking service, looking for someone else.

"OK, I'll show you the Web site," Nan said, now
sounding a little testy herself, "but, really, Bert, is it absolutely necessary?"

I caught my breath. "It's necessary, Nan."

Nan was finally going through the door to my study,
but once again she stopped dead still as she listened to
my answer. "I was right in the middle of reading the
paper."

She made it sound as if she'd been in the middle of
heart surgery. I just looked at her.

Nan didn't budge. "Can't you just take my word for
it? I'm telling you there's nothing to worry about. Don't
you trust me?"

Once again I just looked at her. Jake used to say
things like this to me all the time. The first few thousand times he said it, I'd actually felt guilty that I had
not taken everything he'd told me at face value. The
next thing out of my mouth was usually—I'm now
ashamed to admit—something along the lines of asking
his forgiveness for ever doubting his word. Oh, Jake,
how could I? Why do I always think the worst? What is
wrong with me that I am always such a doubting
Thomas?

Uh-huh.

Jake's little ploy had worked like a charm for most of our marriage. Until the day I'd walked in on him and his secretary. That little scene had pretty much opened my eyes. In more ways than one.

These days, whenever people accuse me of not trusting them, I always answer with what I wish I'd said to Jake during all those years.

"Yep, you're right," I told Nan. "I don't trust you." I led the way to my computer.

Sitting on an old, scarred oak desk that I found at a garage sale, my computer is an IBM clone that my son, Brian, gave me last Christmas. Brian is studying computer science at the University of Kentucky, and he is of the opinion that if you don't have a computer in today's world, you really have no reason to go on living.

Faced with that kind of a choice—and in the hopes that one day I might actually be able to understand a word or two of what Brian was saying—over the last few months I've made a concentrated effort to learn how to use the thing. I've actually learned how to send e-mail, how to surf the Internet, and how to balance my checkbook. The biggest surprise was that I actually liked it. So much so that I started encouraging Nan to get a computer, too.

When she'd finally given in and bought a Dell desktop with an internal 56K modem and a Hewlett-Packard color inkjet printer, I'd actually been pleased. For once in my life, I'd finally dragged Nan into something. I'd never dreamed that I was creating a monster.

A cybermonster, to be sure, but a monster, nevertheless. Nan now sat down in my desk chair, turned on my computer, and after waiting a bit for Microsoft Windows to finish booting up, her fingers began to fly over the keyboard, typing in *http://www.mysoulmate.org.*

I didn't even want to think about what the *org* stood for.

I stared over her shoulder, actually feeling a little afraid, as colorful images began to appear on the screen. Oh dear. If you liked hearts, flowers, and the color red, this Web site was a movable feast. And I do mean movable. Something seemed to be moving in just about every inch of the computer screen. Apparently, whoever had designed this Web site had discovered how to animate things, and then gone a little mad. Hearts pulsated, words changed from pink to red, and red rose petals drifted across what looked to be a lace doily background. Occasionally, for no apparent reason, pink balloons floated skyward. While all this activity was going on, the theme song from the *Titanic* movie sounded stridently clear over the computer's speakers.

I stared at the screen, pretty much mesmerized by the commotion. Good Lord. I was fairly certain that I really was in love. I even suspected that Hank might really be my soul mate. So you'd think that if anybody would like this site, it would be me. Yet, as I stood there, watching this amazing display of synthetic romance, the nicest word I could think of to describe this site would be: *nauseating.*

Once the entire page filled the computer screen, a fat pink cupid holding a bow and arrow flew in from nowhere. While the cupid hovered in the middle of the screen, a balloon appeared over his head containing the message: *Hi SoulMate! Please enter your member name and your password below.* Two empty white boxes then magically appeared, outlined in red, on the cupid's plump tummy.

I turned to look at Nan, to see if she found anything at all off-putting about all this, but Nan was busy typing in "CountryMusicTwin" and some word that didn't show up on the screen. When she hit the ENTER key, the cupid shot his arrow.

Perhaps *nauseating* was too kind a description. *Revolting* might have been more accurate.

While the plaintive notes of "Love Is a Many-Splendored Thing" now blared from the computer speakers, another screen appeared listing options: *Create Your SoulMate Profile, Browse the SoulMates, Search the SoulMates.* Nan went for the search option, clicking it decisively with her mouse. In the box that appeared on the tummy of the cupid this time, Nan typed "OfficeTempTwin."

She hit the ENTER button, and the cupid once again let his arrow fly. In a matter of seconds, a profile appeared. Outlined in red and printed over a lace doily background, it looked like a valentine. A valentine that was hard to read. The small type seemed to get lost in the doily.

I leaned closer to Nan and squinted. Good Lord. It was all there. My height (five foot six). My weight (126). My number of children (two). My number of marriages (one). My occupation (office temp). My Associate Arts degree (biology). My divorce (two years ago). My religion was Protestant, my ethnic group Caucasian, and my body type was slender.

Nan had described me with appalling accuracy, except for one thing. Oddly enough, she'd missed my age by five years. In the kingdom of the SoulMate, I was only thirty-five.

Amazing, the miracles a computer can accomplish.

Nan had also given them my hair color (dark brown), my eye color (dark brown), and my diet preferences (varied). According to my profile, I preferred intimate gatherings instead of large parties, liked watching video rentals instead of network TV, and didn't want any more children. Nan had even told them my income level ($20,000 to $25,000).

"For God's sake, Nan, why didn't you just give them my Social Security number and be done with it?"

Nan shrugged again. "Nonsense, Bert, nobody would ever know this was you."

"Except Elsa, the Super Sleuth," I said. "And, oh yes, anybody who happens to know me!"

Nan evidently decided that topic had been exhausted. She changed the subject. "So have you seen all you need to? Do you realize now that this is not that big a deal? That all I want to do is answer the e-mail that's sent to you? And that you really don't have to do a thing?"

"Except try to explain it to Hank," I said. "Nan, I thought we'd agreed that we weren't ever going to do any more switching."

Nan had the audacity to look bewildered. Or, at least, she tried to. "Switching? This isn't switching."

"Every time you and I switch, something awful happens."

Nan crossed her arms over her chest. "It does not. Besides, this isn't switching."

"Nan, the last time we switched, somebody died." It

was true. In fact, it had happened twice. "Now, I may be a little oversensitive, but it seems to me that if people actually end up dead when you do a thing, that's a very good reason never to do it again."

Nan rolled her eyes. "Nobody died because we switched. It was just a horrible coincidence, that's all. Besides, this isn't switching."

I just looked at her. I didn't say a word, but Nan responded as if I had. "This is *not* switching!" she said, a little louder this time.

I took a deep breath, trying not to lose my temper. "OK, Nan," I said, "let's go over this. Are you going to act as if you're me?"

Nan cocked her head to one side and wrinkled her nose. "Well—"

I took that as a *yes*. "Are you going to sign e-mail messages as if you're me?"

"Well, I can't exactly sign my own name, can I? I'm already listed as CountryMusicTwin. The site hasn't come right out and said so, but I do believe listing yourself more than once is not exactly encouraged."

No kidding. "So," I said, "what you're telling me is that you are going to sign e-mail messages as if you were me. Right?"

Nan sighed. "Bert, some of the guys who write you might've actually heard of me. I am on the radio, you know. If I sign my own name, they might make the connection, and—"

I cut her off. "OK, so you're signing my name. And if you go out on a date with some guy who thinks you're me, are you going to answer to the name Bert?"

"Well, sure, on the first date, until I see what he's

like, but I wouldn't keep on doing it, eventually, I'd tell—"

I cut her off again. "Then we're switching. That's all there is to it. And we agreed that we would never, never, *never* do it again."

I leaned over and positioned my fingers over the keyboard.

"What are you doing?" Nan had the same alarm in her voice as the computer HAL had in that scene in *2001: A Space Odyssey* when HAL had asked almost the exact same question: "Dave, what are you doing?"

I didn't even look at her, as I started hitting keys as fast as I could. "What do you think I'm doing? I'm deleting my entry."

"No!" Nan yelped as the computer screen filled with the page showing my SoulMate profile. "You can't!"

I looked over at her and made my voice very, very firm. It was the same no-nonsense voice that Mom had used back when Nan and I were in junior high school and she'd told us that we absolutely, positively could not have boys visit us in our bedrooms. "Oh yes, I can," I said, "and I will. I want to delete this stupid thing before anyone sees it and tells Hank."

"Bert, I can't believe you're being so unreasonable about this."

I couldn't help but stare at her. *I* was being unreasonable? Nan had taken the liberty of signing me up for Internet dating without asking me first, and she thought *I* was unreasonable? "If it's any consolation, Nan, I'm sure I would not have gotten any e-mail, anyway. And I have no doubt that you'll be getting a ton. Surely, one of them won't be a Lou."

Nan frowned. "I'll bet you a Big Mac and fries that there won't be a single keeper in any of my e-mails and you'll have some possibles."

"I'd rather bet on a sure thing—that I am definitely, without a doubt, deleting my entry right now," I said. I turned back to the computer keyboard, but Nan grabbed my arm.

"Wait, Bert—look." She pointed to the screen.

I looked.

There, in the center of my page, a small red heart blinked on and off.

Oh dear.

"Well, look at that," Nan said, sounding far, far too pleased. "Bert," she said, "do you know what that means?"

I had a pretty good idea.

Nan grinned at me, tapping the little blinking heart. "You've got mail!"

Something told me it wasn't from Tom Hanks.

# Chapter Four

## Nan

I've always hated it when people say, "I told you so." It always sounds so smug. Me, I always try to resist the urge.

Watching that heart blink in the middle of Bert's computer screen, I took a deep breath. "I told you so," I said.

Like I said, I always *try* to resist the urge. Sometimes—what can I say?—I fail.

Bert responded to my little comment with a sullen look.

"I knew it, Bert," I said cheerily. "I knew your SoulMate listing would be getting some e-mail. And I'll bet you there's some keepers among them, too."

I moved the cursor over the heart and hit return so that Bert's list of e-mail messages would show up. The screen had barely begun to open when Bert reached past me to click the back key that made the computer screen return to the previous Web page. Her list of male hopefuls disappeared. I didn't even get a quick peek at who had written to her. "Hey!"

Bert turned to face me. "Look, Nan, just because my listing has gotten some responses doesn't mean that yours hasn't. It also doesn't mean that the men e-mailing me aren't Lous, too. Besides, your profile could have some perfectly nice responses by now."

Lord, she sounded like a schoolteacher.

"Come on," Bert said. "Instead of looking at mine, let's look at yours first."

"Fine," I said. "Have it your way, but I'm telling you, if I get any e-mail, it's going to be from one Lou after another." I pulled the keyboard toward me, made a few keystrokes, and then typed in my password. What do you know, the little red heart was beating for me, too.

Bert grinned so wide, it showed all of her teeth. "I told you so," she said, mimicking me. "And I have no doubt that some of the responses you've received are from very classy gentlemen who are every bit as nice as the ones—"

Bert probably would've continued in that vein except that, as she spoke, she was reading the computer screen, just as I was doing. The screen showed a list of the e-mail messages, one message to each line, with the time and date they were sent, the screen name of the person who'd sent them, and the first few words of each letter. There were five messages in all.

The first letter was from KYSTUD. He began his letter in a thought-provoking way: *Hey, baby, how's about a threesome—you and me and Jack Daniels. . . .*

This time I managed to resist the urge to say, "I told you so." Instead, I just said, "A very nice gentleman who calls himself Kentucky Stud. Hmm. Who wants me to come over and get drunk with him. My goodness, he does sound classy, doesn't he?"

Bert said nothing.

The next message was signed LUVMACHINE. It began on an upbeat note: *I been listning to WCKI and if your half as perty as your voice, you must be gorgous.*

Then it took a bad turn. *You being in country music and all probly means you like rasslin as much as I do—*

Bert frowned. "Rasslin? What's rasslin?"

I tried not to smile. "I believe that's how LUVMACHINE spells *wrestling.* Which is why he didn't call himself *ROCKETSCIENTIST.*"

Bert sniffed.

The third e-mail was from IWANTUBAD, whose message had been left blank. He apparently had not bothered to write a letter, preferring, no doubt, to let his screen name do the talking.

Fourth on the list was an e-mail from LONGAND-HARD. I gave Bert a pointed look.

Bert frowned. "Now, Nan, there's no reason to jump to conclusions. Maybe he's just describing how he's been looking for someone to care about."

Have I mentioned that Bert can be incredibly naive? I don't know how she got this way. Maybe she's just a lot nicer person than I am, so naturally she always thinks the very best of people even in the face of abundant evidence to the contrary. Or maybe—since I do happen to know that Bert's favorite cable station is American Movie Classics—during all those years Bert spent at home being a housewife, she watched a few too many classic reruns. Years of watching Donna Reed vacuum her living room day after day in a dress, pearls, and high heels, followed by episode after episode of Mrs. Cleaver saying, "Ward, I'm worried about the Beaver," affected poor Bert's mind.

"Of course, Bert," I said, "you are so right. LONGANDHARD is, no doubt, just trying to let everybody know that he's been searching long and hard for his very own true love. I don't know what got into me. What could I have been thinking of?"

LONGANDHARD's message was not a surprise to me. I can't say the same for Bert.

*Baby, I'm more man than you've ever had. I can do the wild thing all night long. Satisfaction guaranteed. If you think you can handle it, e-mail me your photo. Show me yours, baby, and I'll show you mine.*

Bert's eyes looked like saucers. After a moment, she finally said, "Well, my goodness." She took a deep breath, and then said, "Oh my, Nan, do you really think that there are people out there who actually send photos of themselves to each other? Over the Internet? Without any clothes on?"

I was no longer trying not to smile. I was trying not to laugh. "Well, Bert, I think when they're e-mailing photos to each other, they probably are wearing clothes. In the photos themselves, though, that might not be the case."

Bert's eyes managed to get even wider. "Oh dear" was all she said.

"So are you satisfied now? Do you believe me when I tell you that the only guys who write to me are Lous?" I reached for the mouse, highlighted all the messages, and started to hit the DELETE key when Bert grabbed my hand.

"Not so fast," Bert said. "That last one looks all right." She tapped a forefinger on the bottom message on the list. Sure enough, someone calling himself LUKE was writing me.

That was it. LUKE. I sat there for a moment, trying to figure out what obscene message you could make out of those letters. I couldn't think of any.

Wow. I had to hand it to this Luke guy. Right away he had my attention.

The first few words of his letter began: *Hi, Country-MusicTwin. I was wondering if . . .*

Hmm. With a bland beginning like that, the message could go either way.

Bert must've gotten tired of waiting for me to decode the name LUKE. She grabbed the mouse and clicked on the line. The computer screen slowly filled with Luke's entire letter.

It started off OK. Luke was forty-two, a computer programmer, and divorced, with two kids, both of whom lived with their mom.

I actually scooted my desk chair a little closer to the computer screen. I was that interested.

Until I got to the end of his message.

*I reckon, if we started going out, you'd probably be able to get us free tickets to see all the big country*

*music stars. Faith Hill and Shania Twain are my ab-
solute favorites, but there's practically none that I
don't like a little bit. I'm between jobs right now, so I
got time these days to go to some shows. Being out of
work has been a real learning experience. Made me realize that a man doesn't have to foot the bill for everything on a date. Fact is, I now believe in equal rights
for women 110 percent. Real men don't have to throw
money around to make themselves feel important. E-mail
me soon, OK?*

I pushed my desk chair back. "This guy's name isn't
Luke. It's Leech," I said.

Bert looked disappointed. "Do you think he meant
that you're supposed to pay for everything if you go out
with him?"

OK, she was starting to get on my nerves. Next she'd
be asking if I thought Al Capone might be a gangster.
"Yes, Bert, I believe that's what he meant."

Bert looked back at the computer screen. "Well,
maybe he's just a little poor right now. He sounded very
nice."

I just stared at her. "Very nice? The man wants to see
a few free country music shows, and he wants me to
pick up the check! He doesn't have a job. He's a user!"

"User, loser—my goodness, Nan, you don't give guys
a chance," Bert said, shaking her head.

I swallowed hard before I spoke so my voice didn't
come out as an out-and-out scream. "Bert, think about
it. This guy is a computer programmer, for God's sake.
How in today's economy with every company in the

world getting on the Internet does a *computer program-mer* manage to be out of work? Riddle me that one, Batman."

Bert blinked. "Oh," she said. "My. That *is* odd, isn't it?"

I scooted back up to the desk, deleted Leech's message, and started to type in Bert's SoulMate name, OfficeTempTwin. "OK, Bert, I think I've adequately made my point. My profile does not exactly attract Mr. Right. Mr. Right-Now maybe, but not Mr. Right. So can we please read your messages now?"

Bert responded like the mature forty-year-old woman she is. She grabbed the mouse off my desk, darted away, and held the thing aloft, wordlessly daring me to make a grab for it. Obviously, the poor woman did not recall that I could beat her at arm wrestling and had been doing so ever since, oh, we were in a playpen together. I could pretty much guarantee that I could take the damn mouse away from her. I stood up and faced her, extending my hand for the mouse. "Give it to me, Bert," I said.

"I will not," Bert said, covering the mouse with both of her hands, just like you might hold a live pet mouse. Its little wire tail hung out between her thumbs. "Not until you promise to take my entry off this stupid Web site."

Oh, for the love of Pete.

"All right, all right," I said. "I promise. But, you know, it would only be polite to respond to any men who have written you and at least thank them for their letters. The Lous who've written to me don't really deserve good manners, but the guys who've written to you, well, they think they're writing to *you*, you know. I think it might really hurt their feelings to not even get a polite reply."

I wish I'd thought of this sooner. Appealing to Bert's basic niceness was clearly the way to go. She stood there, thinking it over. Finally she sighed and handed the mouse over. "All right, I guess just writing them back and thanking them for the message won't take all that much time. But, Nan, I want you to delete my profile right after that."

"Sure thing," I said. I sat back down in front of the computer, made a few keystrokes and a few clicks of the mouse, and presto, change-o! Magically, Bert's list of responses was back on the screen. Bert sat down on the edge of my desk chair, next to me, and shoulder to shoulder we read the letters. In all, there were fourteen.

No surprise, Bert's guys were nice. Boy, were they nice. Every single one of them seemed to be nice, run-of-the-mill guys. Emphasis on *run-of-the-mill*. Some sounded so run-of-the-mill, so completely blah, that I could easily imagine them nodding off while writing their own letters. Hell, I had a little trouble staying awake myself. I kept picturing fussy little men in wire-rimmed glasses and clip-on bow ties.

Bert, of course, was murmuring after each and every one, "OK, he sounds nice. Write him, thank him, and then delete my profile."

One in particular, however, did catch my eye. "Look at the fifth one down," I said. "He's a brave one. Instead of using a nickname, he actually signed his own name."

Bert leaned forward. "Hmm," she said. "*Derek Stanhope.* Very classy." She nudged my arm. "OK, write him. Then thank him and delete my profile. Right now."

I clicked on Derek Stanhope's message. It read: *You sound like someone I'd like to know better. How about checking out my profile? If you like what you read, I'd really like to hear from you.*

Next to the message was a small picture of a camera.

"It looks as if he's scanned in a photograph of himself, too."

Bert's eyes widened. "Oh dear. I do hope he's wearing clothes."

I couldn't suppress a smile as I clicked on the little camera. "Bert, if he wasn't wearing clothes, his photo wouldn't be posted by whoever runs this Web site. You can only get away with that kind of thing when you send messages person to person. On a Web site, anybody can see what you've posted. And unless it's a porn site, the people in charge of the site generally frown on that kind of thing."

As I spoke, the computer screen was filling with the profile supplied by Derek Stanhope.

"Porn sites?" Bert said. She sounded surprised.

Oh yes, she was driving me crazy. "Bert, there's tons of porn on the Web."

"Porn? Really?" Bert asked. "I mean, I knew there was some, but a *lot*? Why, my goodness, that's illegal, isn't it?"

To keep from screaming, I leaned forward and concentrated all my attention on the information now on the screen. Age: *Forty-something.* Height: *Six foot two.*

Weight: *185*. Occupation: *Graphic Designer.* Under the heading Marital Status, he'd written: *SINGLE, unfortunately.*

I smiled. That was a nice touch. Adding the word: *unfortunately.*

Under Likes, Stanhope had listed: *Bicycling, Tennis, Swimming, Antiques, Country Music, Traveling here and abroad, Reading, Just sitting and talking.* Under the heading Added Information, Stanhope had written: *Hoping for a long-term relationship with one special person. Someone with whom to share my life . . .*

The lower part of the screen began to fill with the photo that Derek Stanhope had posted with his profile. It took several seconds to load. Tantalizing, the photo started at the top of his head and worked its way down, showing first a full head of slightly curly dark hair, then a wide forehead, dark even eyebrows—not too bushy— and then dark, almost black eyes, staring straight into the camera.

Lord. The man had wonderful eyes. They seemed to look straight through you. And yet, they looked warm and accepting. Tiny laugh lines accentuated the corners.

I was looking into those mesmerizing eyes and almost missed the straight even nose, wide mouth in a slightly self-conscious but amused smile, square jaw, and broad shoulders. Derek Stanhope was wearing a collarless blue shirt with the top button undone, and to be totally honest, he looked far better than a lot of movie stars.

No wonder the man had posted a photo of himself.

Standing beside Bert, I could hear her low whistle. "Wow," she said, still staring at the computer screen. "You know, if this guy hadn't been wearing clothes, I don't think I would've minded."

Oh my, yes, Derek Stanhope was a keeper.

# Chapter Five

## Bert

No doubt about it, Derek Stanhope was very good-looking. A cross between Harrison Ford and George Clooney. I could understand why Nan started wearing that glazed look on her face the second she saw Derek's picture on the MySoulMate Web site.

I could also understand why she started typing a reply to his e-mail message only a little faster than you could say the name *Derek Stanhope.*

What I couldn't understand, though, was how from that point forward Nan seemed to accept without question every single thing this Derek person had to say. It was a little scary. I mean, *I* was supposed to be the gullible twin. Not Nan. She was, after all, the woman who lately had acted so cynical about men that I'd been worried about her. It had actually crossed my mind a couple of times recently to suggest to Nan that she might need to get some therapy or something, to work out all her hostility.

"All men are either users or losers," she'd told me not too long ago. I'd had to admire the way she'd managed to express her anger in rhyme; however, it seemed to me that she was being a bit harsh. Of course, she had been a tad depressed at the time, having just run across her latest boyfriend playing kissy-face with some other woman. In their favorite restaurant, yet.

I guess if that won't make you hostile, nothing will.

And, of course, I certainly understood Nan's feelings. I'd be the first one to admit that I was pretty hostile right after I found out about Jake and his youthful secretary. Eventually, though, you wake up one day and realize that you've got to move on. That it isn't the guy who's hurting you anymore, it's you. You're rubbing salt in an old wound again and again, just by going over the whole horrible mess so much in your mind.

In my case, it had helped to have Jake get dumped by his new girlfriend. In less than a year's time, she'd thrown Jake over for a guy with a bigger wallet. I mean, what could I think, but: *Wow, who could've possibly predicted* that?

And, to be totally honest, it had also helped to have Jake try to come back to me. What had helped most, though, what I will always be grateful to him for doing, was the time Jake tried to come on to Nan.

That had been the biggest eye-opener of all.

Now when Jake comes around, I look at him and can't help but think of that song "You're My Favorite

Mistake." Only, if I'd been singing the song to Jake, the title would've been: "You're My Mistake."

Now that I think about it, I probably should've just been glad that Nan had run across Derek on the Internet in the first place. It had certainly taken her mind off Mr. Kissy-face. In fact, that Sunday afternoon Nan had been so distracted by Derek that she hadn't even put up an argument when I'd reminded her to delete my profile from the MySoulMate Web site. She'd just calmly deleted it, smiling vaguely.

What's more, Nan had not seemed at all depressed and not the least bit hostile once she'd started exchanging e-mail with Derek. In fact, every day for the next week she seemed to have a new Derek wonder to phone me about.

"Derek graduated magna cum laude from the University of Louisville."

"Derek is a runner—he came in second in last year's ten-K Derby Run."

"Derek won three gold Louies at last year's Louie Awards." When Nan told me this last, I tried to ooh and ah like I knew she wanted me to, but frankly, I didn't even know what a Louie was. Nan was all too eager to explain. "Well, Bert, I'll have you know it's a very prestigious graphic design competition held in Louisville every year. It's sort of like winning an Academy Award, only for advertising."

Academy Awards? In Kentucky? By the end of the week, I admit it, I was getting a little tired of hearing about all of Derek's achievements. I mean, what was next? A Purple Heart or the *Good Housekeeping* Seal of Approval?

I kept waiting for the old skeptical Nan to show up and say a few words, but apparently, that Nan had been completely mesmerized by a pair of dark eyes and a sexy smile.

By the following Tuesday I had passed *concerned* and was headed straight for *worried out of my mind.* I realized that in the movies good looks continued to be a powerful motivator, but in real life it was an entirely different story. *Wasn't it?*

Now that I thought about it, it had been in a recent George Clooney movie, coincidentally enough, that a woman detective had fallen head over heels for George after riding around with him for a few minutes in the trunk of a car. The woman detective hadn't even gotten that good a look at him—it had been, mind you, pretty dark in that trunk—and yet, for the rest of the movie, she was risking her career, at the least, and her life, at the most, to save old George and his extreme good looks.

Nan was beginning to remind me of that woman detective. Only Nan didn't even have the benefit of meeting this Derek character face-to-face. All she'd been doing for over a week  was exchanging letters with the guy. In my opinion, a nice ride in a car trunk with him would've been a major improvement in their relationship.

That Tuesday I decided to drop in on Nan's side of the duplex after work, intending to stay only for a few minutes. I just wanted to check in on her, to see if she'd had a lucid moment recently.

Big surprise. Nan was seated in front of her Dell at

the huge walnut desk in her living room, pecking away at the keyboard. I suspected that her rear end had been glued to that chair just about every spare moment since the cybercupid had shot his arrow her way.

Nan barely glanced up when I unlocked and came in her front door. We have keys to each other's apartments for convenience, in case one of us gets locked out or needs to have repair people let in.

Or, oh yes, has to save the other one from a crazed e-mail maniac.

I took off my heavy wool coat, scarf, and gloves and hung them in Nan's front closet. It was early February and the weather in Louisville was typical. Typical for the North Pole. I'd have been wearing one of those furry hooded Eskimo suits if I could have found one that went with black Nine West dress boots.

"Still doing the e-mail thing, huh?" I asked, making myself comfortable on her sofa. There was no need for "Hello, how are you?" This is one of the great things about being twins. You can just start in where you last left off, picking up a conversation from days ago, and you both are still on the same page.

That is, if you call grunting being on the same page. Nan made this really disgusting noise in the back of her throat. Without even turning around, she hit the keys a little harder, smacked the ENTER key, and the computer hummed in reply.

I crossed my legs and leaned back against the sofa cushion. "Nan," I said, trying to sound casual, "don't you think it's a bit odd that you haven't met this guy face-to-face yet?"

"His name is Derek. Not *this guy*. And he works, you know. He's very busy. He just hasn't had the time for us to get together yet." Nan's eyes seemed to take on a strange, dreamy look as she spoke.

I couldn't help but stare. This was the woman who'd once declared that women should think of men like clothes—nice to have when you first get them, but eventually you always realize that you've gotta have a new outfit. "Actually, Derek is really a very, very nice man," Nan went on, "very sweet and very attentive."

I stared at her. Four very's in a single sentence. Wow. They say love is blind. In Nan's case, it was walking into walls.

"He writes me every day—morning and night—sometimes two and three times a day. Derek is so sensitive. Really, Bert, he seems just about perfect," Nan said.

"You mean, as in 'too good to be true'?" I asked.

Nan gave me a look. "No, Bert," she said evenly, "I most certainly do not mean that. Derek is sweet and kind and—and the poor man is a little lonely."

I met her look with a look of my own. "Nan," I said, "how do you know that? How do you know anything about him? You haven't even met the guy."

Nan's chin went up. "We've been writing each other for over a week now, Bert. I know Derek better than a lot of guys I've dated. You'd be surprised how open you can get, writing to somebody like this. It's really rather wonderful. He always seems to know exactly what to say to put me at ease."

I took a deep breath. "It could be that he knows what to say because he's had a lot of practice."

Nan's mouth tightened. "Bert, you don't understand. Derek actually seems kind of naive. He was married for ten years to a really awful-sounding woman, and he's been divorced for almost a year now. He's just starting to date, and it's really been very difficult for him."

"Hmm," I said. "It's been *very difficult* for a guy who looks like he does? And you don't find that hard to believe?"

Nan gave me another look. "Derek is shy, Bert. He really is. He's sweet and sensitive and shy."

Oh brother. Nan was making the guy sound like Mr. Rogers. "He doesn't walk around singing 'It's a Beautiful Day in the Neighborhood,' by any chance, does he?"

I knew at once I'd gone too far. Nan's eyes looked as if tiny fires had been lit behind each one. She opened her mouth, no doubt to let me know just how much she appreciated my input, but I raised my hand to cut her off. "OK, OK, don't get mad at me. All I'm saying is that I'm worried, Nan, that's all. This is somebody you don't really know. He could just be feeding you a line, and I don't want you getting—"

Nan interrupted me. "Look, would a man feeding me a line sound like this?" She clicked a few keys and then turned her monitor toward me. "Come here and read this."

I remained where I was. "Nan, this is *your* personal mail. I really don't think that I should be—"

"It's addressed to *you*," Nan reminded me.

I couldn't argue with that. And, let's face it, I was more than a little curious. Doing my best, however, to look as if Nan were twisting my arm, I sighed, got up off the sofa, and crossed the room to stand right behind her. Leaning over her shoulder so that I could see clearly what was on the computer screen, I read:

> *Dear Bert, I can certainly understand why you might feel uncomfortable about us meeting this way—hell, I feel uncomfortable, too. And yet, is this meeting any less likely than a chance meeting in a noisy bar? Or being fixed up by friends who are sure they know someone perfect for you but don't have a clue? Why don't we just see where this goes? I'd really like to meet you. In person and soon.*

I read the message twice before I spoke. "He sounds great," I admitted. "He really does. So what do you think is wrong with him?"

Lord. If Nan had been a dog, I think she might've growled at me. "What do you mean?" she said, her voice rising as she turned around to face me. "Why does there have to be anything wrong with him?"

I sighed again. "Nan, the guy is meeting women on the Internet. Why can't he do it the old-fashioned way? I mean, look at that picture of him. He should be beating women off with a stick. So all I'm asking is: What's wrong with him?"

Nan blinked at me a couple of times. She was clearly at a loss—for about a second. "Hell, you could ask the same thing about me—what's wrong with me? Why can't I meet men the old-fashioned way?"

I shook my head. "No, you answered that already. You've got a job that makes meeting the right kind of man a little difficult. I'll give you that. But didn't Derek Stanhope say that he owned his own graphic design business?"

Nan nodded. "I looked it up in the phone book—Derek Stanhope Graphic Design and Marketing, Inc., is located in the Commonwealth Building in downtown Louisville." Her tone said, "See, contrary to popular belief, I *did* do some checking on him."

I wasn't impressed. "It seems to me that his job should allow him to be out meeting women left and right. So I'll ask my question again—what is wrong with him?"

"Maybe he just doesn't like the bar scene! Maybe it's as simple as that!" Nan was actually yelling now. She'd gotten up from her desk chair and was punctuating her every word by jabbing her finger in my face.

I hate that. Someone's finger in my face always makes me want to bite it. I raised my voice to match Nan's. "Maybe that photo on the Internet isn't even his picture! Maybe it's as simple as *that*!"

Nan stopped and just stared at me.

I seemed to have her attention. "Maybe Derek weighs five hundred pounds, and the reason he's meeting women online is that it's too much of an effort for him to waddle outside."

Nan smirked.

I tried again. "Maybe Derek isn't even a he. Maybe he's a she. You've never actually talked to this guy, so how would you know? I saw this show on *Oprah* once featuring a lot of women who made a living by answering those 1-900 phone-sex lines; some of them weren't women at all. Some of them were men."

Nan blinked.

I couldn't tell if I was getting to her or if she just had something in her eye. I hurried on. "Some of the women were housewives who answered the phone and talked filthy while they were ironing."

Nan frowned this time. "I don't think Derek can type an e-mail message and iron at the same time."

I sighed. Nan appeared to be missing my point. "All I'm saying is that sometimes people can appear to be something other than what they really are. And when all you know of a person is just from messages sent over the Internet, you can be easily—"

As I spoke, Nan crossed the room and sank down on her sofa looking glum. "You can be quiet now, Bert," she added, interrupting me. "I get what you're saying," she said. She sounded so depressed suddenly that I felt sort of bad for pointing all this out to her. "You're right, you know," she said. "His photo might not be current."

I nodded. "Could be that picture was taken forty years ago. Maybe he's eighty years old and looking for a live-in nurse."

Nan just stared at me for a moment. From the look on her face, I'd guess that she thought the live-in nurse idea was something of a stretch.

"All I'm trying to tell you is to go slow," I said. "Take it easy. Set up a meeting with this guy in a very public place, and—"

Nan was clearly no longer paying any attention to me. "He does own a graphic design business," she said, interrupting me. "So he's got to have Photoshop. He could doctor his photograph easily. Remember Andrew?"

I did remember Andrew. A few years ago, Nan had gone out briefly with Andrew Whatshisname, a graphic designer with an alcohol problem. On the rare occasions when he was sober, Andrew made a living doing graphics with a computer program called Adobe Photoshop, which could do unbelievable things. The guy had once taken a photo of Nan, scanned it into his computer, and made her a platinum blonde with a few clicks on the mouse. As a graphic designer, Derek could make his photo look exactly like George Clooney, if he wanted.

"Maybe that photo is the way Derek used to look. Maybe that's why he hasn't set up a meeting yet. Maybe he wants to break it to you gently about the unfortunate industrial accident that left him horribly disfigured," I pointed out cheerfully.

Nan barely gave me a glance. She was still thinking it all over. "You know," Nan said, "it would be a good idea to find out what Derek really looks like, before I spend any more time writing him."

"You ought to insist that you two meet right away. Face-to-face. In a large restaurant with a lot of people around."

Nan was obviously not listening to a word I was saying. Tapping on her chin, she said, "I could pop over to the Commonwealth Building and sneak a peek at him before I go on the air tomorrow."

Oh, for God's sake. This was not at all what I'd been after. "Nan, just set up a meeting, OK? And go slow until you two really know each other, that's all I'm—"

Nan had apparently gone stone deaf. "It won't take two seconds to find out whether he's the guy in the picture or not," she said, as if I had not even spoken. "I can just run in, get a good look at him, and run right out."

I shook my head. "Nan, you'll find out what he looks like when you go out with him."

Her hearing problem had apparently cleared up, but now Nan was looking at me as if I had suddenly started speaking a foreign language. "Bert," she said, "do you really think I want to go out with this guy if he doesn't look like his picture?"

I shrugged. "Well, now, Nan, you've not exactly been honest yourself, you know. As I recall, you do happen to be pretending that you're somebody else. So I don't think it would be fair exactly to hold a little fudging on his photo against the guy, do you?"

Nan still just stared at me. "Bert, I'm not talking about being fair. I'm talking about whether or not I want to go out with this guy if he's not good-looking."

For a moment, I just stared at her.

Oh.

Well.

Apparently, I'd been wrong. In movies *and* in real life, good looks continue to be a powerful motivator.

Nan looked defensive. "Life is too short to dance with ugly men."

Words to live by, if I'd ever heard them.

Nan glared at me. "And don't give me that look."

I didn't think I was giving her anything.

She shrugged. "Hey, it's just as easy to fall in love with a good-looking guy as an ugly one. So why shouldn't I make sure that Derek looks every bit as good as he does in his picture on MySoulMate?"

I wasn't about to get into a knock-down-drag-out

fight with her. Besides, there didn't seem to be enough time to change Nan's entire value system. Not to mention, she had that stubborn set to her mouth. I was well aware that I myself look exactly like that when my mind is totally made up.

I sighed again. If I couldn't talk her out of it, I also couldn't possibly let her go see a total stranger alone. What if this Derek person was another Ted Bundy? "OK, Nan, if you feel that you absolutely have to check him out, I'm going, too."

Nan shook her head. "Oh no, you're not."

I nodded mine. "Oh yes, I am." As luck would have it, my next temp job did not start until Monday of next week. I'd intended to spend Wednesday cleaning my apartment and doing my laundry, but I'd force myself to put it off a little longer.

Nan shook her head again. "You are not coming with me. I'm a grown woman. I don't need anybody holding my hand."

I didn't even hesitate. "I have no intention of holding your hand, but I *am* going. Because if I don't, I'm going to phone Derek and introduce myself. Hello, Derek? I'm Bert, the woman you have *not* been writing to all this week."

Nan's eyes narrowed.

Blackmail can be such an ugly thing.

Also, highly effective.

# Chapter Six

## Nan

OK. I admit it, already. I care what a guy looks like.

Puddles are deeper than I am.

So?

Frankly, I don't know why I should even feel bad about wanting the guy I date to be good-looking. Men have been caring what we women look like, oh, I'd say, since the dawn of time. In fact, I have no doubt that the first thing Adam said to God when Adam was being fixed up on the very first blind date was: "What does this Eve look like?"

Actually, now that I think about it, that is probably not what Adam said. What Adam more likely asked Him was, "How much does Eve weigh?"

I guarantee that Adam never once asked if Eve had a nice personality.

Given the way men are—and have always been—regarding a woman's appearance, I don't think it was exactly outrageous of me to want to see Derek Stanhope in the flesh, so to speak, before I consented to a face-to-face meeting with him. I believe just about every man in the world would want to do the same thing if he were in my position. In his last e-mail, Derek had asked for my home telephone number, and I wasn't about to give it to him without knowing exactly what he looked like.

Actually, I do believe I was being very kind. There was no use in Derek and me wasting our time going through the motions of a first date if there was no way I was going to be interested. I was doing Derek a favor, for God's sake. He wasn't going to have to spend any of his hard-earned money going out with somebody who took one look at him and then told herself, *"OK, keep calm, you only have to get through one drink. Then you can complain of stomach pains and get the hell out of here."*

In my opinion, I should be getting extra credit for being so considerate. It was clear, however, from the moment Bert rang my doorbell the next morning that she was not going to be giving me any credit, extra or otherwise. "I don't see why you don't just make a date with this guy," she grumbled, following me out to the driveway to my Neon.

She'd evidently dressed for the occasion. She was wearing her favorite Liz Claiborne navy blue wool blazer, her favorite Liz ivory silk blouse, a short gray Liz skirt, her Liz navy blue heels, and navy blue leather gloves. Her hair had been sprayed so that it stood out a little from her face.

Not to be outdone, I'd also dressed for the occasion. I was wearing black Gap jeans, a black sweater, black down jacket, and black ankle boots. I figured, since I was conducting a surveillance operation, and more or less sneaking around, I ought to look like a cat burglar.

"If you just went out with him once," Bert went on, "you'd find out right away what he looks like, and you wouldn't have to go to all this trouble, trying to sneak a peek at him, in the dead of winter." As she spoke, she rubbed her gloved hands together. You might have thought it was thirty below, instead of thirty above. "You could just go out with the guy one time, get a good look at him, and that would be all there is to it." Bert's tone implied that I did not have enough sense to have figured this out on my own.

I couldn't believe it. Apparently, Bert had not heard a word I'd said the day before. I was going to have to go over it with her all over again. "Look, Bert," I said as I slid into the driver's seat and put my seat belt on. "You haven't dated as much as I have, so maybe you don't realize how truly horrible a date can be with somebody you're not the least bit attracted to."

Bert had gotten in on the passenger side of my Neon, and she managed somehow to shrug and put on her seat belt at the same time. "How bad can it be? A date only lasts a few hours."

"Believe me," I said, starting the engine, "a few hours with somebody you find repugnant can seem like years." Long, dark, tedious years. Years from the Middle Ages. Or, in the case of some of the guys I've gone out with, the Inquisition.

"Nonsense," Bert said. "Besides, it's not as if you'd ever have to go out with the guy again if you don't want to."

I glanced over at her as I pulled out of my driveway. "It's not just the time involved, Bert. At our age, it's pretty much taken for granted that at the end of the evening, you'll—at the very least—kiss the guy good night. If you don't, you have to suffer through this really awkward moment at your front door, trying to keep your lips out of range while scrambling in your purse for your door key."

As usual, Bert was intensely sympathetic. She rolled her eyes.

I went on as if I hadn't noticed. "That's why I made it Rule Number One a long time ago: Never go out with anybody you don't want to kiss."

Once again Bert was intensely sympathetic. After she finished rolling her eyes this time, she said, "I can't believe we're going to all this trouble just to see what Derek Stanhope really looks like. You know, Nan, there *are* more important qualities than looks."

OK, now she was making me mad. "No kidding," I said. "Really? You don't say? Other qualities, huh? I never knew that. Why, thank you so much, Bert, for pointing that out to me."

Bert sniffed. "Sarcasm is so unnecessary."

To my way of thinking, it was very necessary. "Look, Bert," I said, "I'm forty years old this year, a fact which I do believe you already know. I already know yet another fact: Looks aren't the most important thing. I also know that I should not have to apologize for wanting to date somebody good-looking. If men don't apologize for it, I don't think I should."

Bert sniffed again. "All I'm saying, Nan, is that there are plenty of other qualities—"

I couldn't help it. I interrupted her. "Next you'll be telling me that Quasimodo was a terrific catch because he had a great work ethic."

Bert's mouth tightened, a bad sign for sure. "What I'm telling you is that good looks don't necessarily mean anything about a person," she said. "My goodness, Ted Bundy was good-looking. In fact, if he hadn't been so good-looking, he probably would not have been able to lure so many women to their deaths."

"Yeah, well, I'm telling you that every handsome guy is not a Ted Bundy. Any more than every ugly guy is a Quasimodo. Sometimes, you know, ugly men are Ted Bundys down deep, and handsome men really are Quasimodos."

The bad thing about talking in metaphors is that after a while you're not quite sure what the hell you're saying. After that little exchange, Bert just looked at me for a long moment. Then she crossed her arms across her chest, settled back against the seat, and stared out the window. You might've thought Bert had suddenly become totally absorbed in the buildings we were now passing, but in reality, I believe she just couldn't think of what to say back to me. Particularly since she wasn't at all sure what in the world I'd just said.

For the rest of the drive downtown, Bert stared fixedly at all the buildings we were passing. Oh my, yes, all those old offices lining Bardstown Road were just fascinating. Not to mention, the ones lining Broadway, then Second Street, and then Market. Finally, the gray stone facade of the Commonwealth Building loomed ahead.

I'd planned to just pull up, park at the curb, and let Bert keep the motor running while I dashed into the office building to take a quick look at Derek. All the more to make a quick getaway. But, as I pulled the car close to the curb, Bert must've realized my intent. "Oh no, you don't," she said. "I said I was coming with you. I most certainly am *not* sitting in the car."

I finished pulling up to the curb. "But what if he should see you?" I asked. "That could ruin everything."

Bert's eyes narrowed. "Oh really? You mean if he saw the two of us together, he might begin to wonder which twin you really are? He might actually begin to wonder if you are a liar and a cheat?"

Now it was my turn to glare at her. "Noooo," I said, drawing out the word and trying to make my voice as pleasant as possible while gritting my teeth. "I just don't want to confuse him right off the bat."

Bert crossed her arms over her chest again. "Hmmm. You want to wait awhile before confusing him—is that it?" She frowned, adding, "Besides, it's not as if you haven't already warned the guy that you're a twin. Even if he does see me, what's the problem?"

"Seeing us both together can take a little getting used to."

Bert shook her head. "He's a big boy. I think he can handle it. If you can pretend to be me, I am certainly not going to sit in this car twiddling my thumbs while you get a gander at this guy."

I shook my head, too. "You are *not* going in."

"Oh yes, I am. If he does see us, he probably won't even think we're twins. We're not exactly dressed alike."

Good point, but it didn't make any difference. The last thing I needed was Bert clopping after me in her heels. "Bert, I mean it, you're going to sit right here until I get back."

"Nan, I mean it, I most definitely am not."

We glared at each other for a couple of minutes.

Another problem with being twins is that your twin has the same willpower as you do. It occurred to me that Bert and I could sit there, glaring at one another, until the sun went nova. A compromise was clearly in order.

"All right already, come on," I finally said. "But you can *not* let Derek see you. And I don't want you following me any too close. I don't want us attracting any attention whatsoever, OK?"

"Fine," Bert said. "I'll hide behind a post or something."

"Good idea," I said. I tried to remember if the Commonwealth Building had any prominent posts inside, or any large potted plants sitting around, as I got out of the car, fed the parking meter, and headed toward the building with Bert right in back of me.

As it turned out, the question of hiding places became very important as soon as we went through the revolving glass doors of the main entrance. The lobby of the Commonwealth Building looks a lot like many of the older office buildings in downtown Louisville, with gray marble interior walls, gray marble tile floors, and an antique brass mail chute between two elevator doors that face you as you enter. I hurried through the revolving door, intending to head straight for the elevators, and then drew up short.

Oh my God.

If I was not mistaken, Derek Stanhope was standing not ten feet away, in the middle of a small group of people, waiting for one of the elevators. There were two men in business suits, an auburn-haired young woman carrying a briefcase, but to tell you the truth, the only one I really saw was Derek.

Derek was in conversation with Miss Briefcase, but he turned toward me as I came through the revolving door. I would've liked to think that I'd immediately caught his eye, but in truth, he'd probably just heard Bert. As soon as she spotted Derek, Bert gasped. She jerked her head around and sort of leaped out of the revolving doors, off to one side, flattening herself between a wall and a large potted philodendron. From that vantage point, she fluttered her hand at me to go on ahead.

I sighed, staring at her. Mata Hari, she ain't.

Judging from the sound Bert had made, Derek must've thought that somebody had gotten something vital caught in the revolving door. Luckily, by the time Derek looked my way, Bert had already jumped out of his range of vision.

Standing there, trying not to outright gawk at the man, I had to admit it—Derek looked even better in person than in his picture. His brown hair was longer now; it curled a little around his ears, giving him an endearing little-boy look. In the snapshot on the Internet, you couldn't see how broad his shoulders were, or how tall he was. He was wearing a tan overcoat that looked as if it could actually be cashmere, unbuttoned to reveal a white shirt with no collar, and khaki-colored slacks. Did I mention that he was *gorgeous*?

So much for Bert's industrial-accident theory.

Derek was now looking directly at me, his expression questioning but friendly.

Our eyes held for a second or two, and then Derek did something that actually made me go a little weak in the knees. He slowly smiled at me.

Oh my.

He certainly passed my Rule Number One with flying colors. I wouldn't mind planting one on him right this minute.

I returned his smile. And then it occurred to me that maybe he'd recognized me. I had mailed him a photograph—a color copy of a publicity still that the radio station had posted on the WCKI Web site. I'd sent it by regular mail, though, a couple of days ago. Could he have gotten it this quickly?

With him staring straight at me, it seemed rude not to speak to him. I took a deep breath and moved straight toward the group standing in front of the elevators. "Derek?" I asked. "Hi. You asked for my home phone number, so I decided I'd give it to you in person. I'm Bert Tatum."

Behind me, I could almost feel Bert cringing at my lie. I put out my hand to shake his.

Derek, however, made no effort to take my hand. He just looked at me, tilting his dark head to one side as if confused. "Excuse me?"

I thought maybe he hadn't heard what I'd said, so— like an idiot—I repeated the entire thing again.

Derek still looked confused. "I'm sorry, miss," he said, "but I think you have me confused with someone else."

I blinked.

The other people with whom Derek was standing had all turned to look at me by then, their gazes clearly curious. The men in the business suits both saw fit to look me up and down, appraisingly. Miss Briefcase openly stared.

Naturally, being the amazingly cool person under fire that I always am, and totally accustomed to being the center of attention, I began to stammer. "C-c-confused? With someone else? No, no, I don't think so— that is, I don't believe—n-no, I'm not confused—no, not at all—"

As I blathered that amazingly articulate statement, I was studying Stanhope's face. Could I have been wrong? Was it possible that I'd made a mistake? Did this guy have a twin, too?

"You are Derek Stanhope, aren't you?" I asked.

"Yes, I'm Derek Stanhope," he said, his tone polite. Lines, however, were forming between his brows. "I'm sorry, but I have not had the pleasure . . ." His voice trailed off.

"It's me, Bert Tatum," I blurted. With everybody in his little group now looking holes through me, I felt like an idiot. "I can't believe you don't remember— Derek, we've been e-mailing each other for almost a week now."

Derek's handsome face continued to look blank.

I was so astonished by his reaction, I couldn't quite process what was happening. Like an absolute fool, I told him my name again—that is, Bert's name. "BERT TATUM. You know—from MySoulMate.org?" I added weakly, "I'm OfficeTempTwin?"

The two suits exchanged looks at that little tidbit.

"Mr. Stanhope?" asked Miss Briefcase. She actually looked concerned, as if maybe I were some kind of stalker. Implicit in her question seemed to be another: *Should I call security?*

He glanced over at her, smiled, and shook his head. "It's OK, Kelly. She's just made a mistake, that's all. She's confused me with someone else."

The guy was talking about me as if I weren't even standing there. I'd had all the fun I could stand. I turned to go. "I'm sorry to have bothered you," I mumbled.

It was then, as I turned, that I caught sight of Derek's left hand. It was just the very briefest of looks, so at first I thought maybe I'd been wrong. As I moved away, I turned back once to make sure I had really seen what I thought I had.

Well, well, well. What do you know? That certainly explained a lot.

There, gleaming on old Derek's third finger was a wide gold wedding band.

# Chapter Seven

## Bert

Oh dear.

I think I've seen charging bulls on the Discovery Channel in a better mood than Nan.

"That son of a bitch!" she hissed as she rushed past me, pushing through the revolving door of the Commonwealth Building to the sidewalk beyond. The door picked up so much speed with the force of Nan's exit, I was afraid to jump inside. My luck, I'd stumble, and the door would drag my body around and around. That would probably hurt some, but even worse, it would probably do irreparable damage to my very favorite Liz Claiborne navy blue blazer. I'd spent a fortune on this blazer, back when I was still married and could afford it, and I was going to make sure it lasted until I was eighty.

When the door finally slowed down and looked reasonably safe again, I hurried through it, no longer worried in the least about being seen by Stanhope. For one thing, I'd heard the whoosh of elevator doors, so he was no doubt already on his way up to his office. Not to mention, judging from the look on Nan's face, I was pretty sure she would not have cared now if he'd spotted a whole herd of me's.

Nan was standing on the sidewalk just outside, going through her purse and her down jacket, no doubt looking for her car keys.

"What happened?" I said. "What did he say to you?"

From my hiding place between the wall and the rubber plant, I'd watched Nan and Stanhope speak briefly. Whatever he'd said, its effect on Nan had been dramatic. She'd stared at him as if he'd morphed into an alien before her eyes.

"That asshole acted as if he didn't even know me. Or, rather—you."

I wasn't sure how to take that. It sounded, in fact, as if Stanhope had agreed with what I'd been saying from the start. How could you possibly really know somebody you'd only met through e-mail? Wisely, however, I did not say this out loud.

Nan found her keys and stomped off down the sidewalk toward her Neon. Running to keep up, I said—or, rather, gasped, "No kidding!"

"And do you know why he acted like that?" Nan's voice was shaking with anger. "Do you know why he acted as if he didn't know me?"

"Because he *didn't really* know you?" was the answer

that immediately sprang to mind. Once again, however, I wisely kept quiet.

"The asshole is married! He was wearing a wedding band, big as anything!"

That one stopped me in my tracks for a moment.

"Oh, Nan," was all I could say. The guy had, indeed, morphed in front of her eyes. From charm to smarm in a split second. "I'm so sorry."

"I'm sorry, too!" Nan said. "I'm sorry I didn't slap him right in front of all those people he was standing with. The nerve of that guy!" Nan said—OK, yelled—as I caught up with her. "The unmitigated gall! Making me feel like I was the one out of line, when all the while the asshole is playing around on his wife!"

Reaching her car, Nan unlocked the passenger door and flung it open so hard the entire vehicle seemed to jump off the asphalt a little. Nan didn't even seem to notice; she just started moving toward the driver's side of the Neon. It was at that point that I grabbed her car keys.

The way Nan was feeling, she'd probably peel out of here, doing 120. If I didn't want us both to be scraped off the highway with a putty knife—which would, yes, do considerable damage to my blazer—I figured I'd better step in. Drunkenness isn't the only reason for designated drivers—blind rage is an excellent reason, too.

"Let me drive," I said.

Nan didn't even put up an argument. She let me take her keys without missing a beat in her tirade. "That son of a bitch!" she kept saying. "The nerve of that jerk!

Writing all those sweet, oh-so-sensitive e-mails! *'I think you may be my soul mate. You seem so special.'* Oh yeah? Am I as special as your wife, you damn asshole? *'You sound like the woman I've been looking for my whole life.'* Oh? Why don't you look around your house? There's a woman there!" Nan ran her hand through her hair. "I can't believe I fell for all that crap! I actually thought Derek was truly interested in getting to know me, when all along he was just setting me up for the 'Lucky Duck Offer'!"

Nan has explained the Lucky Duck Offer to me before. According to Nan, men make offers to women all the time. To the women they truly care about, they offer marriage and love and a family. To women they don't care about, they simply say, "You lucky duck, I am willing to sleep with *you* tonight." When I first started dating after my divorce, Nan told me more than once that a woman can always get the Lucky Duck Offer from some guy. Since it's something men offer to just about any woman who's breathing, it's not exactly a huge compliment.

Nan was so angry, her voice quavered. "What a sleaze. Then when I show up and there's all these people around, who probably know Stanhope's wife, for God's sake, he's forced to act as if he doesn't even know me!"

"What a horrible man," I said. Although I really didn't need to say anything. Nan was so angry now, I don't think she even heard me.

As I pulled into traffic and headed back toward our duplex, Nan ranted on. "You know, he's probably been doing this for years! I can't believe the gall of the guy.

He's actually cheating on his wife right out in the open!"

"Well, out in the open on the Internet, anyway," I said.

"That's out in the open, Bert!" Nan said.

She was right. It was. Most everybody seemed to be on the Internet these days. Wasn't the guy afraid of getting caught? And if he wasn't, why not? "You know, Nan, maybe Stanhope and his wife have an understanding," I suggested.

"Yeah, right," Nan replied from the passenger side.

"No, what I mean is, maybe his wife knows about his affairs."

"Bert, she doesn't know—believe me."

"You could have misunderstood what he said in his profile," I suggested gently.

"I know what he said." Nan glared at me, but I could tell she was thinking it over. "OK, Bert, you've got a point. I *have* noticed a few married men on the MySoul-Mate Web site trying to make dates. They've been very open about it. And some do say that they are doing it to add some excitement to their lives, and that it's with the blessing of their wives. Hell, some of them want to make it a threesome, you, them, and their wives."

Good Lord. There were actual people out there who did such things? On purpose?

I didn't even want to think about it. I returned to the subject at hand. "So see? Maybe Derek Stanhope's not a jerk, after all. Maybe he's just a, you know, a free love sort of guy."

I could hear Nan sigh her I'm-so-exasperated-I-could-scream sigh. After forty years of knowing a woman with the same face and body as yours, you can easily tell one sigh from the other. I braced myself. "Bert," Nan said through her teeth, "free love is not what they call it anymore. Not since the sixties, anyway. In this decade, everybody calls it *swinging*."

"Hmm," I said. I hate it when Nan does this. Acting as if perhaps I'd spent most of my life in a cave somewhere. I had heard the term *swinging* before, thank you so much. It just had always sounded so ridiculous to me. I mean, swapping partners and going to bed with just about anybody who showed up sure didn't sound like something that should be called swinging. Swinging made me think of children and seesaws and park playgrounds. Or maybe Tarzan going from vine to vine. It certainly did not make me think of Tarzan passing Jane around to all the natives.

I thought about explaining all this to Nan, but she did look pretty upset. It might not be the best time to discuss just how inappropriate I thought the term *swinging* was. She was liable to start swinging herself— swinging something heavy at my head. "Swinging. Sure, that's what I meant," I said. "For all we know, the Stanhopes could be swingers."

"Hmm," Nan said. I wasn't sure if that meant she agreed with me, or that she thought I was so far off base, it was no use talking to me.

Personally, the entire concept seemed pretty off base to me. I couldn't imagine any sane wife actually deciding one day to swing. Can you imagine coming up with *that* little idea over the dinner table? "Gee, dear, I'm bored. *What say we spend the night with the neighbors?*" I mean, why not just be honest and say, "Hon, I'm really tired of you in bed, and I want to be unfaithful without feeling like that's what I'm doing. *So howzabout it?*"

Jake, I know, would've leaped at the opportunity, even if buried in the proposition somewhere was a clear indictment of his performance in bed.

"Maybe Stanhope's wife is swinging on the Internet, just like her husband," I said. "And neither one of them particularly cares what the other one is doing."

"Right," Nan said, looking thoughtful. "Then again, maybe his wife is not the least bit computer literate."

What could I say to that? Nan clearly had a point. We'd apparently said all there was to say, because we drove home in silence after that. Nan rode the entire way with her arms folded across her chest, frowning as she stared into space.

I, on the other hand, couldn't stop thinking about the expression on Stanhope's face when he first saw Nan. How had he looked? Surprised? Confused? What? For sure, he'd looked uncomfortable. Even a little uneasy. It was a look I'd seen before—on Jake's face. Yes, that was it. Stanhope had looked a lot like my ex-husband had always looked when he was afraid that he'd just been caught.

By the time we pulled up to our duplex, I was leaning toward agreeing with Nan. No matter what they called it these days, most people were not swingers. More likely than not, Derek Stanhope was cheating all by himself— and Mrs. Stanhope knew absolutely nothing about it.

Nan was still silent as we both got out of the car. Not

a good sign. I gave her a quick smile as we walked up the sidewalk to her front door. "Well," I said cheerily, "that wasn't much fun. But, at least, it's over."

Nan glanced over at me as she unlocked her front door and stepped inside. Just a quick little glance, but I can't say I liked the look on her face. She looked too still, too coldly determined. I liked it a lot better when she was ranting and raving and throwing her arms around. That seemed, oddly enough, less ominous.

"So," I said brightly, taking off my coat and sitting down on Nan's sofa, "do you want to get together after you get off work? We could order a pizza—heavy on the mushrooms, double cheese." I had a date with Hank, but I knew he'd understand if I took a rain check.

Nan didn't answer. She walked straight to her computer and turned the thing on.

Uh-oh.

"Nan? What are you doing?"

Once again she didn't answer. I wasn't sure she'd even heard me, she was so intent on typing whatever she was typing. The screen soon began to fill with the MySoulMate.org home page.

"Nan?" I said as I moved to stand behind her.

"Look, Bert," Nan said. "I knew I wasn't wrong." She stood and pointed at the screen. She looked, for all the world, like an attorney pointing out the accused to the jury.

I looked at the screen. Sure enough, there it was in black and white, just like I remembered it when I'd read it the first time: Derek Stanhope's MySoulMate.org profile. He had even listed his marital status in all capitals:

*SINGLE, unfortunately.* He'd also stated that he was looking for "a long-term relationship."

"It's that word *unfortunately* that really steams me," Nan said, pointing at the screen. "It sounds so sincere. I'd bet real money that asshole's wife doesn't know a damn thing about this listing. She has no idea what a smarmy creep she's living with." Nan looked very pale. "What really irks me is that men like him always count on women like me to keep our mouths shut. These philandering jerks never expect the women they hit on to tell their wives."

I really didn't like where this was heading. "Yep, that's a darn shame, Nan, but that's the way the world is. No use kicking against the bricks, and—"

Nan interrupted me. "It's as if these guys are making us a part of their deception. As if, right from the start, all we women have actually agreed to help these jerks sneak around on their wives!"

Nan almost never cried, but I could see tears now sparkling in her eyes My throat tightened up. She must've really had her hopes up with this Derek guy.

I reached over and touched her arm. "You know, Nan, it's lucky you found out now," I said. "Before you ever went out with him. Or got really involved."

Nan nodded. Two bright spots had appeared on each of her cheeks. "Men like Derek Stanhope—and that jerk I used to date—should have to walk around with a bell. Like lepers used to, during biblical times. Only instead of these guys yelling 'Unclean!' like the lepers, they should have to yell 'Unsafe! Unreliable! Unfaithful! Women Beware!'"

That seemed like an awful lot to yell, particularly if you're ringing a bell, but Nan was clearly on a roll. It has long been my theory that if there really is such a thing as spontaneous human combustion—and there really might be, considering how often it's written up in astonishing detail in supermarket tabloids—the phenomenon is, no doubt, caused by suppressing anger. Never, ever just letting go. Holding everything in until one day: *kaboom!* Nan, I'm happy to say, will probably never spontaneously combust.

"Well, you know what, I'm not going to let Derek Stanhope get away with it this time!" Nan said. "I'm not going to let that man make me a party to deceiving his wife. I am NOT!"

From the look on her face, I believed her. Which, of course, scared me quite a bit. "Now, Nan—" I began, but once again she went right on as if I'd said nothing.

"I'm going to go tell Derek Stanhope's wife exactly what he's doing behind her back," she said. "I'm going to give that poor woman a little tour of MySoulMate."

I shook my head. "Now, Nan, I really don't think that's such a good idea. Maybe she already knows, or maybe she doesn't want to—"

Nan was opening her desk drawer and getting out the Louisville phone book. "You know, I believe I saw Stanhope's home listing next to his business listing." She started flipping through the pages.

"Nan, some women don't want to know what's going on," I said. "Because if somebody brings it all out in the open, they'd have to do something. To save face. Maybe Mrs. Stanhope likes the way things are now. That old saying could be right, you know: Ignorance is bliss."

Nan was already shaking her head. "Nope, ignorance is just ignorance. The only bliss here is Derek Stanhope's. He's perfectly blissful deceiving his wife. Well, that's about to change." She got a piece of paper and a ballpoint from her middle desk drawer, and scribbled down the address. Glancing at her watch, she added, "I don't think I have time to drop in on Mrs. Stanhope before I have to be at the station, so I guess I'll pay her a little visit after I get off the air."

Nan started to brush by me, but I grabbed her arm. "Nan, I really think you ought to think this over. You don't know what a can of worms you could be opening."

She shook off my hand, grabbed up her purse, and headed for the front door, without giving me so much as a glance. "I most certainly do know what a can of worms I'm opening. I'm opening a can containing just one worm, as a matter of fact. Derek Stanhope. That worm is going to wish he'd never heard of"—she paused then, apparently recalling just exactly who it was that Derek Stanhope had heard of—"you."

I stood there, watching the door close behind my furious sister, and all I could think of was just two words.

Oh dear.

# Chapter Eight

## Nan

If I'd been thinking more clearly, I would have never gone over to Derek Stanhope's house to see his wife. I would have listened to Bert and done what most single women do when a married guy hits on them—simply pretend it never happened.

The one thing you never do is tell the wife. It's practically an unwritten law. Not to mention, ninety-nine times out of a hundred the wife won't believe you, anyway. She'll just insist that you must've done something that tempted her darling true-blue hubby past the point of human endurance and enticed him to make a pass. You Jezebel, you. You homewrecker.

Yeah, right.

All of this should've occurred to me. It wasn't as if I didn't have any time to think about it. I had my entire

time on the air—from 10 to 3—and then another hour
or so in the studio while I taped some commercials to
be aired the next week. In my defense, I must point out
that it's a bit difficult to think about how much you
truly loathe the latest man in your life when you're
speaking in thirty-second segments about a Louisville
auto dealership in tones that suggest that buying an au-
tomobile could possibly be an orgasmic experience.

Even so, let's face it, I had plenty of time to think.
Not to mention, when I returned home late that afternoon, Bert immediately appeared on my doorstep.
"You're not really going over to the Stanhopes', are
you?" she said. "You've thought it over and decided that
it is a very bad idea. Right?" Evidently, Bert had been
watching for me, and had rushed over, still intent on
getting me to change my mind.

"Wrong," I said, "I just came home to print out a
copy of Derek's listing on the SoulMate Web site. Just in
case his wife doesn't have a computer. He could've just
been using the computer in his office, you know."

"Oh dear," Bert said. In fact, in the next few minutes,
while I connected to the Internet and finished printing
out a hard copy of The Case Against Mr. Derek Stanhope, Bert must've said, "Oh dear" about a hundred
times. Or maybe it just seemed like it. She went on and
on about how dangerous this whole thing was.

And, like the stubborn, pigheaded, foolhardy person
that I always insist that I am not, I didn't listen.

A few minutes later, while Bert watched me pull out
of my driveway with much the same sort of look on her
face that she would've had if she'd been watching

Thelma and Louise pull away, I headed straight for the Stanhopes' without so much as a backward glance.

The address I'd read in the phone book turned out to be in a new subdivision called Eastridge Pointe, off Shelbyville Road. I knew, as soon as I saw the subdivision's name on the creekstone and cedar sign at the entrance, that the homes in there had to be pretty expensive. Around Louisville, putting an *e* on Point is worth at least $50,000 more per lot.

Of course, even without the prestigious *e*, the huge homes sitting on tiny, well-manicured lots and the predominance of late-model BMWs parked in the driveways would've told me that this was a neighborhood that did not often see ugly scenes. It was obviously a neighborhood of neat, tidy lives.

Like I said, I wasn't thinking clearly, or the second I'd spotted the *e* on *Pointe*, I would've turned around and headed right back where I came from.

Mostly, I guess, I was thinking angry—angry at the idea of some married slimeball playing hooky on his wife and tricking me into believing that he was a nice guy looking for a nice relationship.

I'd heard it said that when people are angry, mostly they are angry at themselves. And I admit it, I *was* angry at myself—for being such a love-hungry fool as not to see through this guy. I was angry for beginning to let myself daydream about this jerk, to go over and over in my mind what he'd said to me in his e-mails, to look at that photo of him in his MySoulMate profile and actually begin to imagine that maybe, just maybe, I'd finally found a truly wonderful man.

Hell, I'd even defended him to *Bert*. And Stanhope must've been giving off major clues that I should've picked up on because even Bert knew to be wary. Bert, for God's sake, the woman who would've insisted that Genghis Khan was simply misunderstood.

Oh yeah, I'd been a first-class idiot. I guess that was what got to me the most. Derek Stanhope had made a fool of me.

Well, I was not about to let him get away with it. His wife had a right to know what he was doing behind her back, and I was just the person to enlighten her.

All this was going through my head as I turned in at Eastridge Pointe. I spotted the home of Mr. and Mrs. Derek Stanhope, near the end of Pointe Ridge Trace, an imposing two-story brick house with dark green shutters. Even in bleak February, the house had a warm, welcoming air, with its perky herb wreath on the door and its fluffy white Priscillas at all the front windows. Looking at that house, I got even angrier. Derek Stanhope had this absolutely lovely home—what was the matter with the guy?

I didn't really take note of the car sitting in the driveway until I'd already pulled up in front of the house. The car was a shiny silver Mustang, parked right in front of the closed garage door. It was only after I'd put my own car into PARK that I noticed something else: Wouldn't you know it, *someone was sitting* inside the Mustang, in the driver's seat.

Even from where I was sitting, there was no mistaking who it was.

Derek Stanhope.

My mouth went dry.

Derek was just sitting there, making no move to go inside. Of course, it was true that he must've just come through Louisville's rush hour traffic, so maybe he needed a moment to catch his breath.

More likely, however, what had happened was that he'd spotted me the second I'd pulled up. Derek was probably just sitting there, watching me in his side-view mirror, waiting to see what I was going to do.

Well, if he thought that he could intimidate me and keep me from talking to his wife, he could think again. It was just as well that he was here. I'd like to hear him try to talk his way out of this one.

I took a long, deep breath and got out of my Neon. Once I was already out, I realized that, to walk up to the front door, I was going to have to pass right by Derek.

Well, I'd just dare him to try to stop me.

I slung my purse over my shoulder, lifted my chin, and marched up the driveway, passing the Mustang with my head held high.

Once I was past him, though, and Derek hadn't said so much as a word to me, I couldn't resist glancing back at him. I half expected to see him bounding out of his car, running toward me, intent on trying to prevent me from getting to his front door.

That one quick glance told me that the whole bounding-after-me scenario was going to be a pretty difficult one for old Derek.

Impossible, actually.

He was staring straight ahead. And there was a large dark red splotch of something that looked like ketchup spreading down the front of his tan cashmere coat.

Oh God.

Not really wanting to, but unable to stop myself, I turned to take a closer look. Derek's dark red ketchup had an even darker hole in its center.

He didn't look at all handsome anymore. His head lolled slightly to one side, eyes half open, and his mouth was an open grimace. His body was slumped toward the door, held up only by the seat belt that was still around his waist and shoulder.

Oh God, oh God, OH GOD.

I think I screamed. I'm not absolutely sure, but I think I did. What I am sure about is that everything seemed suddenly to have been turned up to high speed for the next several minutes or so. I started breathing—more like gasping—through my mouth, my own huffing and puffing sounding to me like a woman attending a Lamaze class. It seemed as if I stared at Derek for several long minutes. Good Lord, could he really be dead?

After some time—I'm not quite sure how long, it might've just been seconds—it finally seeped through my stunned consciousness that the window on the driver's side was down, and as long as I was there, I really ought to check to see if Derek was still alive.

Maybe he'd managed to survive all that. I mean, it was possible, wasn't it? People had terrible things happen to them, and they lived through it. Sure, they did.

I think I had to believe that Derek might be OK. Because, if he wasn't, I really didn't think I could bear the idea of touching a dead guy. I gritted my teeth and reached inside the car, taking Derek's wrist to feel for a pulse. I didn't feel any heartbeat at all, and, worst of all, his skin felt clammy and cold. I was instantly reminded of raw oysters.

I've never really liked raw oysters.

I'm ashamed to admit it, but I really did scream then—just a quick little shriek as I dropped his hand. Of course, it was the middle of winter—that could easily be why he felt so cold. It occurred to me then that I really needed to get someone out here—a doctor, an ambulance, the police—hey, I wasn't picky. I'd take just about anybody besides me, somebody who actually knew what they were doing would be a plus.

I ran up the sidewalk to Derek's front door and rang the doorbell. No answer. I banged on the brass knocker, then knocked on the door, then finally started yelling. "Mrs. Stanhope! MRS. STANHOPE!"

No one answered.

It looked as if maybe Derek's wife hadn't arrived home from work yet. Or, was it possible that she, too, had been shot? I peered through the front windows, but nothing seemed to be out of order. No pools of blood. No overturned furniture. And, even more important, no Mrs. Stanhope.

I then ran to the Stanhopes' next-door neighbor and did the ringing, knocking, banging, and screaming thing all over again. There wasn't anyone home there, either. I tried the neighbor on the other side, and still nobody answered. Where was everyone?

I glanced at my trusty Timex. It was a little after 5:00 P.M. It occurred to me then that this neighborhood was, no doubt, made up of upwardly mobile, two-income households. DINKs (Double Income No Kids). In other words, most everybody around here—including Mrs. Stanhope—was at that moment on their way home from work.

But, surely, there had to be somebody around here who didn't work. Someone *had* to be home somewhere.

I started knocking on doors then—eventually going around the corner and then up the street on the opposite block. About midway down the block, I finally found someone home—an elderly woman in a chenille bathrobe with her unnaturally red hair in tiny pin curls all over her head. The woman gave me a steely look and absolutely refused to let me inside to use her black rotary telephone. I could see the damn thing just inside the door on one of those old telephone stands, too, but the woman absolutely would not let me come in.

To give her the benefit of the doubt, I probably did look a little wild at that point—she probably thought she was risking her life just to let me stand on her porch outside the locked glass door while she dialed 911 and gave the dispatcher my name and Derek Stanhope's address. I told her to tell them that it was a matter of life and death. Which, of course, it was. It mainly leaned toward the latter, but it didn't seem like that great an idea to spell all that out to Old Lady Chenille. She seemed rattled enough as it was. As soon as I turned to go, I heard her double-lock her inside door. Hey, I didn't blame her. I knew for sure that there was a killer in her neighborhood.

I was not all that eager to return to the Stanhope house to wait for the cops. The idea of spending any more time with Derek Stanhope in his present condition—or, in fact, any condition—did not exactly appeal to me.

I walked as slowly as I could. When I turned the corner onto Pointe Ridge Trace, I noticed right away that something was odd. It took me a moment, though, to realize what it was.

And then it hit me.

All the driveways on this street were empty.

*Including Derek Stanhope's driveway.*

My heart started to pound. Breaking into a run, I made it to Stanhope's house in about a half minute, hardly daring to believe my eyes.

The Mustang and Derek and the ketchup were *gone.*

Like an idiot, I stood in the middle of the Stanhope driveway, in front of the neat brick garage where there should've been a silver Mustang with a dead guy in it, and turned around and around, as if somehow the car with its dead driver would suddenly reappear.

What the hell had happened?

I could've sworn that Derek Stanhope was dead. And, the last time I checked, dead men generally do not drive cars.

After a moment of just standing there, feeling stunned, I went up to the garage, shaded my eyes, and peered through one of the small rectangular windows into the darkened garage. As if I actually thought it was possible that Derek, in his last few seconds of life, had decided to pull the car inside. Even in the dim light, it was clear the garage was empty.

I heard the hum of a car motor pulling up behind me, and I turned around. The crazy thought that dead Derek had somehow returned to life to go motoring and was coming home now skittered for a second through my brain. When I saw who it really was, I thought I really might prefer to visit with the recently deceased Derek.

Hank Goetzmann and his partner, Barry Krahzinksy, were slowly climbing out of an unmarked brown Cavalier. Unfortunately, I have a history with these two cops—not just because Hank once dated me and now dates Bert, either. Nope, even worse. These two are the cops that seem to show up whenever I least want them to. I don't know why it is, but these two seem to come to all my murders.

"Nan?" Hank said, nodding at me. Hank is an attractive guy, if you like the oaf type. When I was dating him, I thought he looked like the actor Brian Dennehy, big and muscular, and a little overweight—the huggable-teddy-bear type. Now I think he looks more like the Pillsbury doughboy, only with more hair and less smiles. Hank's eyes swept our surroundings, and apparently, he saw nothing that kept his glance from returning to me. As usual, Hank looked pissed off.

Barry, on the other hand, just looked puzzled. Although he's only a few years younger than me, Barry always looks to me like a teenage boy playing cops and robbers. Maybe that's because the poor guy still has acne and a pretty bad cowlick. "Yo, Nan, got your squeal. So, not to be pushy here," Barry said, "but where's the body?"

Barry always tries to talk cool. I think he believes that one day *Miami Vice* is going to be revived and they'll want him to play the Don Johnson role.

I was tempted to say "Yo, Bare" right back to him. But there was really no reason to start things off by making everybody mad at me. Instead, I gave them a brief rundown on what had happened since I'd arrived at the house. About halfway through my story, Hank was frowning big time and shaking his huge head in undisguised annoyance. When I finished, he was every bit as warm and considerate as I'd expected.

"Did you think maybe it really might've been ketchup?" Hank said. I couldn't help remembering just how unspeakably annoying he had been when we were dating. Hank continued, his tone implying that he was just trying to be helpful, "You didn't happen to notice any McDonald's or Burger King bags in the car, did you?"

I glared at him. "Why are you asking? Do you think Ronald McDonald might be your murderer? Or maybe the Hamburglar?"

Barry smirked.

Hank shot him a look.

"For your information, ketchup doesn't make your eyes roll up in your head or your mouth hang open," I said. "This guy was dead. I think I know a dead person when I see one."

"I guess you do," Hank said. "The way you've been going, I'm surprised you're not seeing bodies in your sleep."

Barry openly grinned at that one. "By the way," he put in, his tone indicating that he'd only just thought of this, "you're not planning to mention this on WCKI anytime soon, are you?"

I just looked at him, unable to trust myself to respond. Could this yo-yo actually be thinking that this might be a *publicity stunt* for the radio station? Was he kidding? I've been falsely accused of such a thing before, and it was just as irritating this time as it had been in the past.

OK, it was true that WCKI had made me do some unbelievable things to try to increase our ratings. I've rid-
den an elephant down the middle of Louisville's Main
Street with a sign draped across the large smelly beast
proclaiming: WCKI NEVER FORGETS ITS LISTENERS. I've sat
on a flagpole for three long and occasionally rainy days
until our ratings rose sufficiently that the program director would let me come down. And I've walked
around the Mall in St. Matthews with a monkey on a
leash. That time I carried a hoop that the small smelly
beast jumped through. Yes, you guessed it, I also wore a
sign on my back: WCKI JUMPS THROUGH HOOPS FOR ITS
LISTENERS.

In spite of all this, I do believe the radio station
would not go so far as to actually murder somebody to
raise its ratings.

I was pretty sure, anyway.

Swallowing my anger, I said slowly, "Now, boys, you
know very well that WCKI could never be this creative.
The station has done some idiotic things in the past,
but none of them involved playing hide-and-seek with a
dead—"

I was interrupted by a little red Mercedes zipping
into the driveway and coming to a stop behind Hank's
brown Cavalier. Hank, Barry, and I all turned to watch
the woman who got out of the Mercedes. She was
blond, petite, and dressed in a navy trench coat that
showed the plaid Burberry lining and a flash of long
legs as she got out of the car. She wasn't really pretty, so
evidently, she'd decided a long time ago that she'd go
for expensive-looking. "Hello?" she asked, making the

greeting seem more like a question. "May I help you?" Her eyes traveled to each of us as she went around to the other side of her car and reached in. She emerged carrying a little blond girl who looked to be about two, and was nearly asleep on her mom's shoulder.

I gaped at the kid. OK, sure the moppet was cute— but, if this was who I thought it was, here was one more little detail that the late Derek Stanhope had left out of his MySoulMate profile. If he wasn't dead, I'd want to kill him myself.

Hank and Barry introduced themselves—I noticed they left me out of the picture completely—and the woman said, "I'm Lauren Stanhope—Mrs. Derek Stanhope. Is there a problem?"

Before Barry could answer, Hank jumped in, "No, no, not that we know of. Mrs. Stanhope, do you know where your husband is?"

Lauren's lips tightened for a second, and she glanced at her daughter. For a moment there, I actually thought she was going to say she'd just found her hubby dead in the driveway and called an ambulance. Instead, Lauren merely sighed. She glanced again at her sleeping daughter before whispering, "My husband moved out last night. He's supposed to contact me where to send the divorce papers. So, if you're waiting to talk to Derek, you'll be waiting a long time."

*I'll say,* I thought.

"So what's this about? Is Derek in some kind of trouble?" Lauren asked.

*"Not anymore,"* was the obvious answer to that one. Barry, however, answered, smiling, "Oh no, not at all.

This is just routine. We just needed to talk to him about an inquiry we're working on—false reporting of a crime." He glanced over at me.

I looked away.

"Well, Derek can probably be reached at his office; he generally works late. That was one of our many problems," Lauren went on. "Or I guess he could be at his girlfriend's."

Hank's eyes widened.

Barry tried unsuccessfully to suppress a smirk.

What went through my mind, however, was this: *I came here for nothing.* Mrs. Stanhope already knew that her husband was cheating on her.

What she didn't know I was not about to tell her: He's very dead.

"Do you by any chance have the name and address of the girlfriend?" Hank asked.

"Well, there are more than one, I can tell you that," Lauren said. "I found e-mails from a woman named Genevieve Carson that were pretty explicit. Another woman Derek had been e-mailing just recently, though, had a man's name." She looked down at the pavement as she thought about it. "Wait a sec—I've got it." She snapped her fingers. "Bert. Can you imagine? A woman named Bert. Bert Tatum."

Hank must've had a lot of practice in not revealing what he was thinking. He just stood there and blinked a couple of times. Other than an odd stillness in his face, you'd never have known that he'd even recognized the name.

Barry seemed far more shocked. He immediately

coughed and then, like the little twerp he was, asked Lauren to repeat the name.

So she said it again. A little louder. "Bert Tatum."

"Yes?"

At the sound, we all turned, and there was Bert. She was picking her way up the driveway on her navy blue Liz heels, still wearing the power Liz suit that she'd been wearing earlier when we'd gone to get a peek at an about-to-be-dead man.

I'd been so engrossed in Lauren's spilling the beans, I hadn't even heard Bert's car pull up. As Bert walked toward us, her expression was one big question mark, her eyes going from Lauren, to me, to Barry, and then to Hank.

Hank's neck had turned a dark beet red under his collar, and he didn't say a word to Bert. He just stood there, staring at Mrs. Stanhope, and looking as if the top of his head were about to come off.

I swallowed. Like Lucy of the *I Love Lucy* show, I had a lot of *'splainin'* to do.

# Chapter Nine

## Bert

Two seconds after I parked my Camry in front of the Stanhope residence, I wished I'd stayed home.

Of course, if I had, I would have still been pacing the floor, worrying about Nan and what was happening with her and Derek Stanhope. Nan had looked as angry as I'd ever seen her when she left, and I'd been afraid that Derek might get angry right back.

The longer I'd thought about it, the more worried I'd gotten. In the mood Nan was in, there was no telling what could happen. I kept imagining truly ugly scenes. Pretty much all of them involved hitting and punching. In some of the ugliest scenes, it was *Nan* doing the hitting and punching.

None of the awful scenes I imagined, however, quite measured up to the real thing.

My first thought as I walked up to the group standing in the driveway was: *My goodness, what're Hank and Barry doing here?*

I didn't get a chance to ask, though, because everybody started talking at once.

"Bert, I need to talk to you—" Nan began.

"You're Bert Tatum?" the blond lady with the little girl in her arms interrupted. Her blue eyes looked as if fires had been set just behind them. "Look, lady, you've got some nerve—"

"Bert, you really don't need to be here right now—" Hank interrupted.

"—coming here," the blonde continued, "after sneaking around with my husband!"

Well, that pretty much explained who she was. For a woman whose husband was running around on her, Mrs. Stanhope looked pretty good. A little taller than Nan and me, and quite a bit thinner, she had shoulder-length blond hair, big blue eyes, and cheekbones like Loni Anderson's. Of course, I suppose if a woman had to choose something of hers that she'd want to be like Loni Anderson's, it would not be Loni's cheekbones.

"Look, Mrs. Stanhope, it wasn't Bert," Nan said. "It was me." She turned back to me. "Bert, we really need to talk."

Hank stared at Nan. My goodness, his neck was awfully red. It looked as if he'd scribbled on it with a red Magic Marker. "What do you mean, it was you?"

The blonde's eyes started doing what Nan and I call the Twin Bounce. First, her eyes bounced over to Nan. Then they bounced back to me. "You're twins? Oh my Lord, have you *both* been sleeping with my husband?"

"Oh man, this is great! Even better than *Jerry Springer*!" Barry said. He appeared to be the only one who looked like he was having a good time.

Nan turned back to the woman. "Mrs. Stanhope, your husband told me that he was single! And I have never slept with the man. I barely knew him!" Then back to me. "Bert, I need to talk to you—in private—"

"Bert, go back to your car," Hank interrupted. "I'll speak with you in a moment."

I stared back at him. Was he ordering me around in his professional capacity as a cop? In which case, I certainly understood. Hank was just doing his job.

Or was he ordering me around as my boyfriend? In which case, I didn't understand at all. Who did he think he was, talking to me in that tone of voice?

More importantly, who did *I* think he was? I couldn't decide which Hank was ordering me around—the one who had a right to, or the one who didn't—so I just stood there, motionless, trying to make up my mind whether I should obey or not.

"Well, I don't believe that for a minute. You're both whores! That's what you are! WHORES!" Mrs. Stanhope said, tightening her hold on her daughter and raising her voice even louder. "Don't you two have even a shred of decency?"

Speaking of which, I could not believe that she would say such words right in front of her little girl. Having her mother yell in front of her must not have been all that unusual an occurrence because the child didn't look startled or anything. She just stirred a little, leaning against her mother's shoulder.

Nan glared at Mrs. Stanhope. "Look, ma'am, I'm

sorry to say this, but your husband was a liar. If I'd had any idea that he was married, I would never have started e-mailing him."

"Bert, I told you to go to your car," Hank said. Even his ears were red now.

"Oh, you expect me to believe *you?*" Mrs. Stanhope said. "I'm supposed to take the word of somebody like you. Hell, you and your trashy sister are just sluts, that's all. You're—"

By this time, my head was starting to throb, and I hadn't even opened my mouth yet. So I did something I really try never to do. I raised my voice.

"EVERYBODY, PLEASE SHUT UP!" I said.

Everybody did shut up, too. For about five seconds.

Stanhope's wife, however, apparently didn't like my tone any more than I liked Hank's. "I AM CERTAINLY NOT GOING TO SHUT UP!" she shouted. "NOT IN MY OWN DRIVEWAY!"

At this last bellow, the little girl in Mrs. Stanhope's arms jerked awake and began to cry.

Loudly.

Very loudly.

All around us, neighbors just arriving home stopped whatever they were doing and stared in our direction. The couple right next door had just pulled into their driveway, but instead of getting out of their Mercedes and going inside, they just sat there. The windows on both sides of the Mercedes went smoothly down. Lord. We must've been better than the radio.

Pleased with her ready-made audience, Mrs. Stanhope roared, "YOU'RE NOTHING BUT WHORES!

GET OUT OF HERE, YOU—YOU TWIN TRAMPS, AND STAY AWAY FROM MY HUSBAND!"

The little girl began to shriek.

Oh, for Pete's sake. I couldn't believe what that awful woman was saying. It was bad enough to say all that out loud in front of the neighbors, but in front of her own daughter? There seemed to be only one thing to do to get her to hush. I abruptly turned and started hurrying back to my car.

"THAT'S RIGHT!" Mrs. Stanhope yelled after me. "YOU'D BETTER RUN! YOU'D BETTER NEVER LET ME SEE YOU AGAIN!"

I could hear Hank behind me telling Mrs. Stanhope to calm down and to have her husband phone him or Barry if she heard from him. "This is just a routine matter," he finished, then started after me.

What was he talking about—*what routine matter?* I would've liked to have known the answer to that one, but I wasn't about to go back and ask.

To her credit, I could also hear Nan telling Hank as fast as she could, while running alongside him in my direction, that she'd been using my name on the Internet and that it was she, not me, who'd signed up with the MySoulMate dating service. I don't know, when somebody starts talking very fast, they just don't sound like they're telling the truth. Even if they are.

The entire time Nan was talking, Hank just kept right on walking. You could easily have gotten the idea that he wasn't even listening.

Mrs. Stanhope had already gone inside by the time Hank, Barry, and Nan had caught up with me. A quick backward glance, however, was all it took to see that the frilly white window curtains in the left front window were moving. No doubt, just on the other side of those curtains, that crazy blond woman was still getting an eyeful. And an earful, if possible.

"I mean it, Hank," Nan said, "It was me. All me. Bert had absolutely nothing to do with this."

Hank glanced briefly over at me, but his eyes didn't hold mine. "Well, then," he said flatly, "that explains it."

I looked at him, my hand now on the door handle of my Camry. Hank sounded matter-of-fact, and yet, something in his voice sounded odd. Could he actually believe that I was trying to find another man? Did he really think that I was truly matchmaking on the Internet? *Me?* Was he kidding? I had trouble trusting an ATM. And Hank might actually be entertaining the notion that I'd give cyberdating a whirl? The idea was laughable.

Nan apparently wasn't convinced by Hank's statement, either. "*I* signed us both up, Hank," Nan repeated. "I did it. Bert wasn't involved at all. And I answered the responses for both of us. *Really.*"

Hank's neck, I noticed, was still showing signs of a Magic Marker attack. "I heard you the first time." Although he was speaking to Nan, Hank's eyes met mine. I couldn't tell if he was angry or just embarrassed. His partner, Barry, was standing right there, silent as an eavesdropper on a party line, taking in every word.

I could feel myself doing a slow burn, and this time I wasn't even sure whom I was mad at: Nan for getting us into this mess, Hank for acting so suspicious, or even Barry for being so tickled pink with the drama of it all.

I coolly stared back at Hank before opening the door to my car. "This is ridiculous," I said. "I'm certainly not having a relationship with Derek Stanhope."

"Especially since he's dead," Nan said.

That one spun my head around. "What did you say?"

So then Nan finally started telling me about what had happened before I'd gotten to the house. It would've been nice if she'd spoken up a little sooner.

Hank interrupted when Nan got to the part about the body disappearing. "This was where we came in," he said. "We'll nose around—see what we can find out about Stanhope's whereabouts." Then he nodded at me—a very curt little nod, like something you'd give your butcher if you thought he'd shorted you on the pork chops—and turned to go.

Barry, however, took hold of Nan's arm. "If Stanhope turns up kicking, we're going to want to talk to you again about a certain false report."

Nan shrugged off his arm. "If Stanhope turns up kicking, you've got more problems than just false reports," she said.

Barry just grinned at her and shook his head, as if the whole thing were one big joke. After that, he and Hank climbed into their unmarked brown Chevy and drove off.

Nan and I stood there, looking after the car. "I really don't like *not* being believed," Nan said.

"Tell me about it," I said.

"Of course, on the positive side," Nan added, "the man that Hank thinks you're playing around with is probably stone-cold dead."

I stared at her. "Nan, if Derek Stanhope is dead, he

cannot tell Hank that he's never met me, can he?" I took a deep breath, trying to control my anger. I knew Nan had never intended all this to happen, but hadn't I told her right from the start that switching would be a bad idea? "You know," I finally said, "it really would be nice if Derek would show up and inform Hank that the rumors of my being his e-mail girlfriend are greatly exaggerated."

Nan frowned. "I wouldn't hold your breath on that one."

"Nan," I said, trying to keep from gritting my teeth as I spoke, "dead men don't generally wake up and drive away. Which kind of makes me think that Derek could be alive."

Nan was shaking her head before I'd even finished what I was saying. "I'm telling you, Bert, the guy is dead. Deceased. Met his maker. Gone to his reward. He is stone—"

I held up my hand. No telling how many ways she could say *dead*. We could be here all night. This was one of the occasions that I'd mentioned earlier, when I really wanted to push Nan's OFF button. "OK, then we both have a good reason to find out for sure."

Nan just looked at me.

"You need to find out if he really is dead. I need him to be alive so he can talk to Hank. Either way, we need to find him."

"So where do you suggest? Start hanging out at Cave Hill Cemetery?"

I sighed. "Why don't we try something a little less *Night of the Living Dead*, OK?" I suggested. "Maybe Stanhope was just playing some kind of sick joke on you."

Nan gave me another look. "You really think that he faked his own death to avoid confronting me? He saw me coming up the driveway, and so he quickly squirted himself with ketchup—which he always carried around with him for just such an occasion—and then he played dead?"

I sighed again. "Why don't we just see if Stanhope shows up for work tomorrow?"

Nan shrugged.

I wasn't sure what she meant by shrugging, but I decided to take it as *good idea.*

"So we go to his office tomorrow morning before you go on the air, right?"

Nan nodded this time.

Nan started to walk back to her Neon, but then she stopped, turned around, and looked at me. "You think Hank is OK with all this?" she asked.

"Well, it would help if Stanhope could explain things to him," I said. "But Hank's coming to my place for dinner tonight—I'll explain it to him myself then. Once we're cozy in front of the fireplace and he's got a brandy and a nice steak-and-potatoes meal in him, it'll be fine."

"If I had to feed a guy to get him to believe me," Nan said, "we'd both starve."

I noticed the curtains in the Stanhope house moved again as Nan pulled her Neon out onto the road and I followed her home.

My telephone was ringing when I walked in. I tossed my coat and purse on the sofa and grabbed the phone.

"Bert?" It was Hank. I was surprised to find that the one word could be delivered with such an edge to it.

"Yes?"

"Is that you?"

I felt a flash of irritation and couldn't help but answer with an edge in my own voice. "Who else would it be?"

"Well, with Nan playing you all the time, I thought I'd better check."

I took a deep breath. OK, so he was a bit miffed. "Now, Hank," I said, "don't you think you're exaggerating a little—"

He cut me off. "Listen, Bert, I can't come over tonight, after all—I've got to work." He started to leave it at that but apparently thought better. "I'll call you."

I was stunned. "But, Hank, I was going to—"

But that was that. Hank didn't give me the chance to say anything more. The line went dead.

For a moment, I just stood there, staring at the receiver in my hand, the hum of the dial tone sounding loud and plaintive in my silent apartment.

Oh dear.

# Chapter Ten

## Nan

I was not in my best mood.

The very idea that Bert and I would be running over to Derek Stanhope's office for the second time in as many days was annoying enough. But to run over there for the sole purpose of proving that I was telling the truth about his being one of the recently departed went way beyond annoying.

Excuse me, but it is not exactly out of line to expect dead people to have the good grace to stay put.

Not to mention, I really didn't want to spend any more time even thinking about the guy. I'd already wasted far too much time and energy exchanging e-mail with him. And now, hey, I was very sorry he'd gotten dead and all, but for the short time I'd known him, he hadn't made all that great an impression. I don't exactly have a warm spot in my heart for people who don't tell me the truth. As far as I was concerned, if Derek's headstone began, *"Here lies . . . ,"* well, it would pretty much say it all.

I can't say I'd support whoever killed him—that seemed to be taking everything a bit too far—but I certainly didn't relish spending any more minutes of my own life thinking about the man.

I'd already checked the morning paper's obits. Apparently, Stanhope had still not made it to the official dead list yet. I'd also made a quick call to Barry right before I left my apartment, too. Barry confirmed that he and his fellow cops were still sans body. He also didn't miss the chance to make a not-so-veiled threat about the legal consequences of falsely reporting a crime. "People who make false reports think they're so smart, but they can end up spending some time in jail," Barry said cheerily.

Thanks so much, Barry, for that little news flash.

As we'd agreed, Bert appeared on my front porch around 9:00 A.M., wearing yet another power suit—this one a gray flannel Jones New York. I usually don't pay attention to what label something is, but Bert had told me more than once that this suit was a "Jones" and that she'd gotten it on clearance at the Galleria downtown for 50 percent off.

I half expected her to tell me again, but Bert was strangely silent as we headed downtown. To be precise, Bert was not silent the entire time; she kind of snorted when she first saw me. After which she turned on her heel and followed me to my Neon. I was pretty sure that

Bert's snort could be interpreted as "Here's another fine mess you've gotten us into, Stanley."

Apparently, visiting the office of a potentially dead person wasn't high on Bert's list of fun projects, either.

I watched her as she got in the front seat and put her seat belt on. She didn't look as if she'd been crying or anything. Nope, she just looked angry.

My mind somewhat relieved, I started the car.

Bert glanced over at me. "Hank didn't come to dinner last night," she said. "He said he had to work." Then she just stared straight ahead.

"Oh." It was pretty much all I could think of saying. Bert being mad at me wasn't exactly earth-shattering. However, her being upset because she and Hank were on the fritz—mostly because of me—well, that pretty much made me feel guilty beyond belief.

For once, I got a good parking space—right in front of the main entrance at the curb. Once again Bert and I pushed through the revolving doors of the Commonwealth Building and stood facing the bank of elevators. I smacked the red UP button as Bert took a quick glance around. I knew, even without her saying it, that she was half expecting to see Stanhope standing there with a group of people, just like he'd been yesterday. I, on the other hand, was most assuredly *not* expecting to see Stanhope standing around anywhere, not unless he was decked out in a white robe and carrying a harp.

In truth, I didn't blame Bert for wondering if I might've made a mistake, though. I was actually beginning to wonder myself. With the dawn of a brand-new day, the sight of Stanhope's body, ketchup and all, seemed more and more like a horrible dream.

According to the building directory hanging on the wall to the right of the elevators, the office of Derek Stanhope, Graphic Design, was located on the fourth floor. Bert and I took a quick, stomach-lurching ride, and when the elevator doors opened, the deep mahogany double doors of the Stanhope office were facing us. You would've had to be blind to have missed it. Stanhope's name was written in gleaming brass letters no less than a foot high.

Oh no, this guy had not had an ego problem. None at all.

Apparently, Stanhope had been doing all right for himself, too—before his unfortunate demise, that is. His offices were professional-looking, stylish, and if I were not mistaken, they occupied the entire fourth floor. Of course, in the mood I was in, the curved brass door handles against the mahogany of the wood door looked a lot like the handles on a coffin to me.

Inside, the office was thickly carpeted in a dark maroon plush and furnished in the same dark mahogany furniture—very much like, you guessed it, what they make caskets out of.

At the far side of the room, a young woman was standing behind a desk, literally wringing her hands. She was probably very pretty when she wasn't so overwrought. She only stopped wringing both hands in order to run one of them through her tousled auburn hair and flip through a desk calendar with the other. Behind her, the computer screen was filled with flying windows, but it was giving off a funny grinding noise. It was pretty hard to concentrate on any one thing because in the midst of all this activity, the phone on her desk was ringing off the hook. Auburn Hair seemed to be ignoring everything. She didn't even seem to notice Bert and me as we opened the door and walked across the thick carpeting.

"Miss?" I said.

The girl jumped at least a foot as she looked up, practically yelling, "WHAT?" Brushing an auburn strand out of her eyes, she squinted at us. It was then that I recognized her. She was the young woman with the briefcase who'd been standing with Stanhope and his group at the elevators yesterday.

"Hello," I said. "We don't have an appointment, but we want to—" I stopped there, momentarily at a loss. We wanted to—what? Make sure Derek Stanhope was dead? I couldn't exactly say that. Attend the viewing? Offer condolences? See if he was still breathing?

"We'd like to see Derek Stanhope," Bert finished for me.

I nodded. Did we ever.

The redhead's eyes had started doing the Twin Bounce, going back and forth between Bert and me. Her eyes flicked over to me and widened. "Oh my God. There's two of you." She stumbled back a step and sat down hard on her office chair, her eyes continuing to flit back and forth, forth and back, between Bert and me. We have that effect on some people. I can't explain it. It's as if they have to keep checking and rechecking their initial impression.

"Yep, there's two of us," I said. I introduced myself and Bert, and Auburn Hair struggled out of her chair, extending her hand.

"I'm Kelly Putnam," she said, "Derek Stanhope's ex-

ecutive assistant." She said the job title with a proud little toss of her auburn head. Personally, she looked too
young to be an executive anything.

I nodded.

She smiled.

The phone rang. Again.

"About your boss—"

"Oh, he's not here," Kelly said quickly, looking down
at her paper-strewn desk. "He hasn't been in all day.
Hasn't called, hasn't e-mailed, hasn't anything."

I glanced over at Bert, hoping she could read my
mind. *Did this sound like a living person to you?*

Kelly's voice was almost a whine now. "I called his
home about eighty-thirty this morning—Mr. Stanhope
is always here by  seven. His wife wasn't there. It's not
like him to just take off work without calling me and letting me know in advance. I don't know what to do, I really don't."

I had to keep myself from elbowing Bert. It was beginning to look more and more like I'd been correct in
what I'd seen.

Bert didn't even look my way. She just kept right on
looking straight at Kelly. "Has Mr. Stanhope ever done
this before?"

OK, it was a good question.

Kelly cocked her head to one side and thought about
it. "Nope, don't think so. I thought maybe he had the
flu or something. His wife told me, though, that she
hasn't seen him since he left for work yesterday morning." She lowered her voice, even though it was just the
three of us in the room. "Although, to tell you the
truth, she didn't seem all that concerned, one way or

the other. I think the two of them might have finally split up."

*The hard way,* I thought.

"Why do you say that?" Bert asked.

Kelly shrugged. "Just the way the two of them have been acting these last few months. You know, really cold to each other. And her manner on the phone. Like she was just trying to get rid of me. You can just tell. Anyway, I had to cancel all his appointments for today. Now I've got to figure out what to do about tomorrow if he doesn't come in then. You know, some of his clients were not very nice to me about his not being here today. And I've got all this work for Mr. Stanhope to go over, waiting for his signature, but I can't do anything until he approves it. I just don't know what I'm going to do."

Certainly, not answer the phone. The telephone continued to ring without her even making a move to pick it up. Kelly noticed my glance toward it. "Listen, I've been screamed at so much today, I've decided I am not taking another call. They can just rot, as far as I'm concerned." I think she would have stamped her foot, if she'd have thought of it.

"But what if it's Mr. Stanhope phoning in?" Bert asked.

Kelly shrugged. "Oh, I've got everything going to voice mail—I just check it every half hour or so." The girl sighed and looked back at us. "Look, I'm sorry; but I really can't help you, and I've got all this work—"

She stopped midsentence and squinted at Bert, asking what she'd probably been dying to ask since we came in the door. "Say, didn't I see you here yesterday?

Weren't you at the elevator?" She didn't wait for an answer but immediately glanced over at me. "Or maybe it was you."

I nodded. "Right. It was me."

Kelly's eyes narrowed. "So he did know you, after all. I knew it. I just knew it. I can always tell when Mr. Stanhope is not being completely—" She broke off as something else occurred to her. "So why are you asking me where he is? Don't you know? I mean, maybe I should be asking you instead of the other way around—"

Something in her prickly tone made me irritated. "Look, if I knew where he was, I wouldn't be here. And you're wrong, I didn't even know the guy," I said.

Even as she nodded her head, Kelly looked doubtful. "Yeah, sure," she said.

I tried not to get angry, but I lost. "Listen, I had no idea that Derek Stanhope was married. We just exchanged a few e-mail messages, that's all, and he never once said anything about having a wife." I heard myself saying this, and I could feel my cheeks growing warm. Was I actually getting defensive in front of this near-teenager? Even Bert was looking at me, as if to say, "Why bother explaining?"

"Of course," Kelly said. "I see." Her tone was cool now. "Well, like I said, I don't know where he is. Now, if you'll excuse me, I really don't have time to—" She turned back to her desk, picked up a stack of paper, and tried to look busy by glancing through it.

Bert must not have been impressed. She interrupted. "Do you know anyone who might know of Mr. Stanhope's whereabouts?"

Kelly started to shake her head no.

"Because I really did want to apologize to him," I put in.

Bert turned to stare at me, her eyes wide with surprise.

Kelly looked surprised, too. "Apologize?" she repeated.

I nodded. "Yeah, I wanted to apologize for the misunderstanding yesterday at the elevator," I went on.

Kelly let that sink in for a while as she continued to glance through the stack of paper.

"You know," Bert said, turning to me, "maybe he really is with a girlfriend." I couldn't tell whether Bert was serious or if she was just baiting Kelly.

Regardless, Kelly seemed to be taking the bait. She was now frowning big time.

"Has there been any particular woman calling Derek lately?" Bert went on. "Someone that you wondered about?"

Kelly finally stopped straightening her paper and looked up, her eyes angry now. "No, there certainly was NOT. Mr. Stanhope did not have any other women in his life other than his wife—he wasn't that kind of man."

I stared at her. *Wow.* You just can't buy that kind of employee loyalty these days. Maybe these days it's not the wife, it's the *secretary* who's the last to know.

"Does he receive personal e-mails here at the office?" Bert went on.

"Ye-e-s," Kelly answered hesitantly. "Of course, he did. He was here all the time."

"Can you retrieve and look at his e-mail?" Bert continued.

Kelly looked as if we'd insulted her. "Of course not! I don't know his password. Besides, even if I could, I wouldn't. That's his private mail."

Good grief, where did he find this girl? I didn't think they made clerical help like her anymore.

Kelly really looked steamed now. "I really don't like what you're insinuating. It's not my place to read my employer's mail."

She apparently thought we were accusing her of going through his mail. "Oh, I wasn't talking about you specifically," I jumped in. "We just wanted to know if you knew any women Mr. Stanhope was seeing. Names, addresses, anything, would be a—"

Kelly's chin went up. "That's what I was talking about. I don't like what you're insinuating about Mr. Stanhope. He's really a decent man. Just because his marriage is a little rocky, it certainly wasn't his . . ." She apparently had said more than she meant to; she let her voice trail off.

"Are there any family members that we could talk to?" Bert asked.

"There's *his wife*," she said pointedly.

I sighed. "Other than his wife." It was my opinion that anything Mrs. Stanhope had to say, she'd already yelled at Bert and me.

Kelly thought for a moment. "Mr. Stanhope's parents live in the south end of town in the Auburndale area, but I don't think he sees them much. He never mentions them, and I don't even have them on my Rolodex."

Oh. Well. No Rolodex listing—that certainly said it all.

Kelly went on. "He does have an older brother. He's a plumber or something. Benjamin lives out in the Westport area." Kelly's tone had gone from cool to icy.

"Do you have an address for Benjamin?" Bert prodded.

"Is he on your Rolodex?" I couldn't resist asking.

Kelly sighed. "Will you two leave and let me get some work done if I give you Benjamin's address?"

"With pleasure," Bert said with a smile.

Kelly scribbled out a name and address on the back of a green While You Were Out notepad, snatched off the piece of paper, and thrust it at me. Bert grabbed the paper instead, and we headed for the door.

"If you don't believe me," Kelly called after us, "you can ask his brother about what a fine family man Derek Stanhope is."

Sounded like a great eulogy to me.

# Chapter Eleven

## Bert

I knew what Nan was going to say before she said it. It wasn't because she was giving off twin vibes, either. Mainly, it was the smug, self-satisfied look on her face as she climbed into the car next to me and put her seat belt on.

"Well, I guess that proves it," Nan said. She started the car and pulled away from the curb.

"Proves what?" I said.

Nan gave a little gasp of annoyance. I thought for a second it was Louisville's slowpoke downtown traffic bothering her until she looked over at *me*. "That proves Derek Stanhope really is dead."

I picked some nonexistent lint off my Jones New York skirt. "No, all that proves is that he didn't come to work today."

"Don't be ridiculous, Bert. I mean, where else could he be?"

I could not believe she'd push this. "He doesn't have to be in the great beyond. He could be anywhere—with a girlfriend, for all we know. Or he's finding a new place to stay since he and the little woman are on the skids. He could be out shopping for furniture for his new bachelor pad—"

Nan interrupted me. "Without calling his office?"

I shrugged. "OK, that does seem odd. But it certainly doesn't prove that he's dead. It just proves that he's absentminded. Which, I believe, we already knew. The man did sign up for Internet dating, apparently totally forgetting that he was married."

Nan ran her hand through her hair. "For God's sake, Bert, he's dead and I know it. What's it going to take to prove it to you?"

I was pretty sure she already knew the answer to that one, but I answered her, anyway. "A body, Nan. An honest-to-God dead body. One that doesn't wake up and drive away."

Nan looked annoyed but she didn't argue anymore. Instead, we made a plan to visit this Benjamin person, Derek's brother, as soon as Nan got off the air. Then she let me out next to my Camry and pulled away, looking pretty glum.

I sat behind my own steering wheel, staring straight ahead for a while. What exactly was I going to do for five hours while Nan was doing her thing on the radio from ten to three?

As I mentioned earlier, I was between work assignments right now—that being one of the great things about being a permanent temporary. The agency where I worked liked to let you get a little breathing room in between putting up with the maniacs they sent you to work for. They sometimes even worked your assignments around your personal life.

When my daughter, Ellie, had her brief brush with the law, my agency had encouraged me to take some mental health time to, as they put it, "get over the personal trauma." Probably, they just didn't want to have a basket case working for their clients; but I was pleased to have the time off. Now, I was quite pleased that my next assignment didn't start until next week.

I looked at myself in my rearview mirror. Going back to my apartment to clean and do the laundry made me exhausted already. I'd have to get dressed all over again to meet Nan.

If I waited downtown for Nan to get off work, I'd probably just shop at the Galleria and spend money that I didn't have. If I were being efficient, I could get my car's oil changed and the tires rotated. Or I could take some clothes to the dry cleaner. I could even balance my checkbook.

Or—and I think I knew that this was the option that was in the back of my mind from the get go—I could go see Benjamin Stanhope by myself.

Why shouldn't I? I was a big girl. I certainly didn't have to wait for Nan. Maybe Benjamin would know where Derek was. After all, they were family. I could locate Derek, have him say a few choice words to Hank about the twin he met wearing scruffy jeans and a

jacket, and I'd be back home before Nan had signed off
for the day.

With that decision quickly made, it only took me two
hours and ten minutes to drive out to Westport and locate Benjamin Stanhope's house at the address Kelly
had written down for Nan. This, for a forty-five-minute
drive, mind you. As luck would have it, the I-64 express-
way in downtown Louisville afforded me the not-at-all-
rare opportunity to sit dumbstruck, several cars back,
behind a three-car traffic accident, waiting for the necessary tow truck and the appropriate traffic cops while
three drivers stood in the middle of the highway, yelling
at each other so loudly that my car windows seemed to
shake from the noise. Unfortunately, I'd been between
exit ramps with no way to get away from the human
drama unfolding in front of me.

I was beginning to consider making it a four-car accident when a policeman finally flagged me through.
The wait had given me time to think, though—which
wasn't good. I could feel the first flickering of real annoyance at Hank beginning to stir. After all, I was sitting
in this stupid traffic jam because of him. Because I was
running around trying to get someone to tell Hank that
I was telling the truth. When he should have believed
me in the first place.

All this was running through my mind as I pulled up
in front of the house in Westport. Benjamin's house
with its gigantic yard was one of those 1960s brick
ranch-style houses—the ones with the huge picture window, the attached double garage. This one had one of
those white plastic rail fences in front that never re-
quires painting, and looks exactly like white plastic.

A small sign in front of what looked like a detached workshop advertised carpentry and repairs—not exactly plumbing, as Kelly had said, but still in the general building trades. Apparently, if Benjamin did carpentry for a living, he didn't want to spend his free time building a wood fence for his own yard. An even smaller sign to the left of the doorbell told me to RING BELL FOR SERVICE.

I'd have known that the man who answered my ring was Derek Stanhope's brother, even if I'd met him on the street. Although I'd only seen Derek briefly, Derek's face had been one that a woman remembers. Vividly. With heart palpitations.

This man certainly had all of Derek's features—the square jaw, the dark hair, the wide forehead, the almost-black eyes. Only this man's features were just a little off—just enough to keep him from being actually good-looking. His dark eyebrows were a little too bushy, his square jaw jutted forward a bit too much, his mouth was a little too small, and his straight, even nose a little too long. He also outweighed his brother by about fifty pounds.

I was so struck by the differences when he opened the door that I just stared at him for a second. He made me suddenly wonder about the brothers of really handsome men—like George Clooney's or Richard Gere's brothers, if they had them. What would it be like to grow up in that kind of shadow? This guy had to go through life feeling like one of God's little jokes.

I was still staring, when he spoke. "Can I help you, miss?" That's when I noticed that, like his brother, he also had the same straightforward, direct gaze.

"Are you Benjamin Stanhope?" I asked, although I already knew that he was.

"Yep, that's me," he said with a grin. His left front tooth was chipped. Oh dear.

"I'm looking for your brother," I blurted. "Derek Stanhope? Have you seen him recently?"

Benjamin grinned again, even wider. Make that two chipped teeth. "Sure haven't. 'Course, I should've known a pretty little lady like yourself wasn't coming looking for me. Won't you come in?"

I had a sudden flash of this big guy getting me alone inside his workshop with all his saws, hammers, and blades, and before I could stop myself, I was shaking my head no. There was certainly nothing the least bit menacing about Benjamin Stanhope, but then again . . . if murderers looked like murderers, nobody would be murdered, would they?

Besides, this guy's brother had possibly been killed— shot to death, if Nan was right about what she saw. So how did I know who had killed him? Maybe a man who, over the years, had grown to resent his good-looking sibling.

"No thanks, Mr. Stanhope," I said. "I'm fine right here. I, uh, like the outdoors." We both glanced at the sky then. Gray and overcast, it threatened rain. Or, maybe, considering the icy chill that seemed to blow right through my coat, snow.

Benjamin Stanhope was looking at me uncertainly now, but I smiled at him as if I didn't notice. Jamming my hands into my pockets, I introduced myself and then asked again, "Have you spoken to your brother lately?"

"Nope. Sure haven't. Sorry." Benjamin gestured toward a wooden bench to the side of the door. "Well, if you won't come inside, at least have a seat. It'll get you out of the wind, anyways."

I took him up on that offer. Benjamin grabbed a fur-lined leather coat from a coat rack next to the door, and he came out, settling himself in a nearby lawn chair and folding his arms across his ample belly. "So I'm guessing you've tried Derek's house," he said.

I nodded. "His wife doesn't know where he is, either."

"And his work?"

I nodded again. "His secretary doesn't have a clue."

"So what's this all about?"

For a moment I just stared at him. I hadn't thought what I was going to answer if he asked me why I was so interested. I blinked a couple of times, and then I remembered what Nan had told Kelly at Derek's office. "My sister met Derek on the Internet and they had a misunderstanding when they met. She wants to apologize. Face-to-face."

"No kidding," he said, his direct look a little too direct now. "So you're helping your *sister.*" He didn't sound like he believed me. Probably in his life, Benjamin had dealt with a lot of women trying to contact his brother. His direct look made me feel a little uneasy. Unfortunately, when I feel uneasy, I tend to babble.

Without really intending to, somehow in my babblings, I managed to fill Benjamin in on what Kelly and Lauren had said about Derek's disappearance. I left out the parts where his brother had been sighted dead in his own driveway and had apparently driven away shortly after that, and then his wife had called both myself and my twin sister whores. All that seemed like extraneous information that Benjamin Stanhope really didn't need to know.

Benjamin nodded when I finished. "Funny you should mention the Internet, because, while it's true I haven't talked to Derek on the phone for a while, I got me an e-mail from him just last night. Around seven o'clock."

My heart did a little jump. "At seven, you say?" That would have been long after the time Nan had seen Derek's body.

Benjamin nodded again. "Yep, we pretty much stay in touch over the Internet these days. Hard to find Derek home and I'm out here in the workshop so much, I miss a lot of phone calls."

"Are you sure about the time?"

"Yep, it was right before my programs come on," Benjamin said. Glancing over at me, he added, "I know because I'm a single man—"

No surprise there, I thought.

"—and I generally get on the computer up until my TV programs come on at eight. Anyways, I guess I can tell you what Derek told me in his e-mail, because I don't think it's any big secret. Fact is, I guess you probably already know that Derek's been having marital problems. He said in his e-mail he was going off to think what to do."

"Oh," I said. Nan had to have been mistaken in what she'd seen. She had to. Or Benjamin here was lying.

I studied him. Could he be making all this up, to give

himself an alibi? I cleared my throat. "Did your brother say if he was going alone?"

Benjamin glanced over at me and frowned. "Well, sure. Of course, he was going alone. A man can't do much thinking unless he's alone."

"What I mean is, was Derek with his girlfriend?"

Benjamin raised a bushy eyebrow. "Derek doesn't have a girlfriend. I understood that it was Derek's wife who was playing around on *him.* Not the other way around. Derek has been complaining for a long time about not trusting Lauren. He had to work late so much, and he didn't trust leaving her alone."

I stared at him. "Lauren was having an affair?"

He shrugged. "That's what Derek told me. Started about six months ago, Derek said. I know for a fact that my brother would never be unfaithful—Derek was a deacon in our church, you know. He strongly believed in the sanctity of the marriage vows. He'd never think of breaking them."

Unless his wife was breaking them, too. I wondered what Benjamin would've thought had he seen his brother's listing on MySoulMate.org. I guess the Web site did have a nice biblical ring to it.

Benjamin went on. "Derek even taught Bible classes at our church for married couples, cautioning the young folks about the evil of infidelity. When Derek himself started having trouble keeping his own wife in line, it sure made me think twice about ever getting married myself, I can tell you that."

*That is not going to be a concern,* I thought.

As soon as the thought crossed my mind, I was mad at myself for thinking it. Lord, I was as bad as Nan.

Benjamin seemed to be a very nice man. He was just not good-looking, that's all. That fact alone did not necessarily eliminate the poor guy as marriage material.

Benjamin was warming to his topic now. "Derek didn't believe in divorce, either. Nosirree." He paused here and gave me another pointed look. "He thought marriage should be just like God made it—let no man put the bond asunder, and all that."

"Till death do you part," I added.

Benjamin nodded. "Exactly. So even if he isn't living at home anymore, I'd bet Derek still won't be getting himself a divorce. Even if his wife wants one." He gave me one of those direct looks again. "Derek thinks marriage is forever."

I stared back at him. And then it hit me. What all these direct looks had been getting at.

Benjamin actually thought that I was chasing after his brother.

Like, no doubt, a lot of women before me.

Good Lord. I could feel my neck growing warm under this man's direct stare. Which no doubt made me look even more like I was intending to break up his brother's marriage. "Well," I said, "that's good. Divorce is a terrible thing."

Benjamin now seemed to be looking at me with pity in his eyes. "I know, Miz Tatum, that you're not telling me everything, but that's OK. I guess you have your reasons."

I tried to look shocked that he'd think such a thing, but I'm really bad in situations like this. If somebody thinks I'm not telling all I know, I start acting guilty

whether I am or not. It didn't help that I did know that
Derek was on the Internet soliciting dates, and I wasn't
exactly forthcoming with the information.

I eagerly changed the subject. "Do you think that
Derek would go to your parents' house?"

Benjamin looked a little shocked at the very idea.
"Oh no," he said quickly. "He and our folks had a kind
of falling-out a few years back. Left some real hard feelings on both sides. I doubt Derek would ever go to
them—he hardly even speaks to them. Just at Christmas
and Thanksgiving, you know."

I stared at him. Boy, I bet the holidays were a real fun
time at the folks' house.

"What was the problem between them?" I asked. "If
you don't mind my asking." Actually, I didn't particularly care whether he minded me asking or not, but it
seemed like the polite thing to say.

Benjamin looked at the sidewalk, the sign on his
building, the brown weeds in his yard, anything except
me. "Well, I really don't like to say," he said.

No kidding. I already picked up on that nuance.

"It was personal—family stuff," Benjamin explained.
"I heard both sides of the story and I still don't know
who to believe. So I just stay out of it." He gave me a direct look now. "Easier for me," he added. "I get along
with both sides."

I could understand his position. Neutrality had certainly worked both for individuals and nations in
heated conflicts—at least, up to a point. Still, I wondered what the uproar had been about and how angry
his parents really were at Derek. After all, Derek wasn't

all that he appeared to be. The thought reminded me of something else.

"Do you know a woman by the name of Genevieve Carson?"

Benjamin grinned. "Oh sure. We went to high school with her. Both Derek and I have known Genevieve for ages. Nice girl," he said. "I even thought about dating her back then. She's kind of homely, though. Too bad."

I stared at him, thinking about pots and kettles and black. "Derek's been e-mailing Genevieve a lot, according to Lauren."

Benjamin scratched his big stomach. "Well, so do I. It doesn't mean anything. Genevieve's kind of busy, so it's the only way we can stay in touch. She's a pal. A buddy. You know, one of the guys."

"Do you think Derek would go to stay at her house?"

Benjamin laughed. "I doubt it. Not if he wanted to get any sleep at all. But you can try over there, if you want. Ginny lives not too far from here. I'll give you her address and phone." He paused, then added, "If you want."

It was the second time he'd said, *"If you want."* I was getting the idea he really didn't think I should want.

I nodded. "Would you mind giving me your parents' name and address, too, while you're at it?"

"Sure thing, but I'm telling you, they won't know anything." Benjamin went inside and came back out in a minute or so with the information written on the back of one of his blank invoices. "Here you go," he said, handing me the paper.

I reached out to take it, but he held on to the slip of paper for a second too long, making me glance up at him. "You seem like a nice person, Miz Tatum. You might want to think about whether or not you really want to find Derek," he said. "Because I'm telling you. Derek is not ever going to divorce his wife. Not for *anybody*."

Oh, for goodness' sake.

Now I knew what Hester Prynne felt like. All I needed was a scarlet *A* sewn on the pocket of my gray Jones New York blazer. Like an idiot, I could feel my neck getting warm all over again.

It did seem unlikely that Benjamin would go to the trouble of trying to warn me about the dangers of pursuing a relationship with his brother, if he already knew that Derek was dead. Unless he was actively trying to make himself look innocent of the crime.

For all his size, this guy didn't look like he could kill a roach. I could be wrong, but it sure looked like the rumor Nan was spreading about Derek's death was greatly exaggerated.

With Benjamin standing right there, looking at me with pity in his eyes, I thought about just denying outright what he was thinking. However, I was pretty sure he wouldn't believe me. So I just nodded as I took the piece of paper out of his hand. Thanking him, I left as quickly as I could.

The big guy was probably going to pray for me tonight.

Oh well, I guess I could use a few prayers.

I'd definitely need them when I had to tell Nan that her dead guy was still sending e-mail messages.

# Chapter Twelve

---

## Nan

The lobby of WCKI offers about as much privacy as Grand Central Station. Come to think of it, the radio station even has a public-address system much like Grand Central, in the person of our beloved receptionist, Bambi.

With her having a name like that, you'd expect Bambi to be doe-eyed, petite, and charmingly shy. In actuality, Bambi weighs close to two hundred pounds, is given to wearing sweatshirts and sweatpants to work, burps in public, and smokes like a house afire. Repeating anything in front of Bambi is like publishing it on the front page of the *Courier-Journal*.

I mention all this because it was in the lobby of WCKI that Bert saw fit to tell me her latest news the second I appeared. "Derek Stanhope sent an e-mail message last night!"

I'd known, of course, that behind her receptionist's desk, Bambi had actually leaned forward the moment Bert spoke, and yet, I couldn't help myself. "What do you mean," I blurted, "Derek sent an e-mail message?"

All right, all right, I knew I sounded a lot like President Clinton asking what his interrogator meant by the word *is*. But this didn't make any sense. How could a dead guy send messages? Was it really possible that I'd been mistaken all along?

Bert sighed. "Nan, Stanhope did send an e-mail message. Around seven last night. His brother told me so."

I blinked. "His brother? You already talked to Benjamin Stanhope? I thought we'd decided to talk to him together."

Bert shrugged. "It seemed more efficient just to go while you were at work." She hurried to change the subject. "Anyway, it sure sounds like Derek isn't dead, after all."

I immediately flashed once again on Derek. In the car. Staring straight ahead, seeing nothing. That was a dead guy. If not, Derek was a sure winner in any breath-holding contest.

"Come on, Bert," I said. "I saw him with my own eyes. Derek Stanhope is extremely dead. Bullets do that to a person." From the corner of my eye, I could see Bambi's eyes increase in size by about three hundred times. I swear I could also see her brain clicking into RECORD mode. I lowered my voice. "Unless it's postmarked *Pearly Gates*, Stanhope is not sending e-mail to anybody, let alone his brother."

Bert shrugged. "His brother sure seemed to be telling the truth," she conceded, giving me one of her I'm-just-telling-you-what-he-said looks. She did, of course, leave out what was obvious. That somehow what I'd thought I'd seen must've been all wrong. Derek Stanhope was alive and well, and corresponding in cyberspace.

Bert had the good sense to move a few steps away from Bambi before she went on, telling me in great detail all about her little visit to Derek Stanhope's homely brother, Benjamin.

I tried to pay attention, but to tell you the truth, I was running another tape in my mind the entire time Bert was talking. Could I have been wrong? Could Derek still be alive, after looking the way he did? I'd gotten a pretty close look at the guy. If that wasn't dead, I didn't know what dead was. Then again, I wasn't a doctor. Or a coroner. Maybe I really didn't know what dead was.

When Bert got to the part about Derek's fight with his parents and his friendship with Genevieve Carson, one of Stanhope's other e-mail buddies, I started getting interested again. "You know," I said, "we ought to pay visits to Mr. and Mrs. Stanhope and Genevieve—just to make sure."

I didn't spell out what we needed to make sure, but I didn't have to. Bert nodded. We needed to make sure that Mr. and Mrs. Stanhope weren't murderously angry at their son, and we definitely needed to make sure that Genevieve did not have a dead man hiding out at her house.

The slip of paper that Benjamin gave to Bert indicated that a Mr. and Mrs. Melvin R. Stanhope lived in

Unit 102 of the Auburndale Plaza Apartments in Louisville's south end. While I drove the twenty minutes to get there, down Third Street to Southside Boulevard, then over to Old Third Street Road, Bert went over again her entire conversation with Benjamin Stanhope, including his repeated assurances regarding Derek's fidelity. Obviously, Big Ben hadn't checked out the Internet dating sites lately. Of course, if Bert's description of the man was accurate, I could certainly understand why not.

"You know, I really think Benjamin thought I was chasing after his married brother," Bert said.

"Maybe it's happened before," I said, turning right at the large barn-wood sign that read: AUBURNDALE PLAZA APARTMENTS—IF YOU LIVED HERE, YOU'D BE HOME BY NOW. I drove for about a quarter mile into a neat, well-kept apartment complex, and pulled into one of the empty slots in the spacious parking lot in front of one of the brick four-plexes.

According to a sign in front of their four-plex, which also announced that there was a vacancy, Mr. and Mrs. Stanhope had landed one of the development's garden apartments. Which apparently meant that they had a yard allotted to them slightly larger than the postage stamp everyone else seemed to have. This time of year, their garden consisted of a couple of withered brown mums in terra-cotta planters on each side of their front door.

Bert rang the doorbell. A woman opened the door almost before the sound of the bell had stopped. She must've been spring-loaded, or she'd been sitting within inches of the front door.

"Yes?" she asked. This woman was in her sixties, but right away, I could see the family resemblance to Derek Stanhope. She was attractive, with streaks of gray throughout thick dark hair; a straight nose; and the same direct gaze in her dark brown eyes. She was wearing the standard uniform of elderly women in Kentucky: tan polyester slacks, silky polyester pullover in an eye-popping floral design, and Dr. Scholl's slip-ons. Reading glasses hung from a silver chain around her neck.

"Mrs. Stanhope?" I asked.

"Yes, I'm Thelma Stanhope. What is it?" Her manner gave me the impression that we had interrupted something vitally important, an affectation she'd no doubt cultivated to discourage door-to-door salesmen. Or maybe I was leaping to conclusions. Maybe this elderly woman really was right in the middle of something. Who knew? Maybe she'd left the next Salk vaccine bubbling on the stove.

"Who is it, Mother?" The man who appeared over her shoulder looked at least ten years older than Thelma. Balding with a gray fringe of hair worn in the style made popular by Friar Tuck, he had a skimpy gray mustache and deep lines between his eyebrows.

In spite of what he'd called her, I assumed that this was not Thelma's son but Mr. Stanhope himself. He was, no doubt, using the old Southern custom of referring to his wife as "Mother." Bert's and my mom does not much care for this custom. In fact, if our dad ever called her "Mother," she'd probably try to give him up for adoption.

From the portly look of Mr. Stanhope, combined

with Bert's description of the Stanhopes' other son, I'd assume Benjamin took after this guy. Mr. Stanhope, no doubt to match his wife, was wearing the standard uniform for elderly men in Kentucky: white long-sleeved knit golf shirt buttoned to the neck with a crocodile embroidered on the pocket, black polyester slacks hanging low over a very large paunch, and yes, the ubiquitous pair of Dr. Scholl's slip-ons. To his ensemble, Mr. Stanhope had added a trace of individuality by wearing both a belt and suspenders—the better-safe-than-sorry look.

"I don't know who it is, Melvin, they haven't said yet," Thelma answered her husband. She sounded as if he, too, had interrupted her in the middle of doing something terribly important. I was beginning to suspect that this was her standard speaking tone.

"We're Bert and Nan Tatum, and we were wondering if you had—" Bert began, but the woman cut her off.

"Why, you're twins, aren't you?" Thelma asked, her eyes widening as she looked us both up and down. "Oh my. Would you look at that." Marveling at the freaks of nature that had appeared on her doorstep, she turned around to her husband.

"Look here, Melvin. They're twins." She gestured at us as if he might possibly miss the two women filling the doorway.

"They're not dressed alike," Melvin grumbled.

I gave them my best PR smile. "My sister and I are twins, yes, and we're—"

Thelma interrupted me. "See, Melvin, twins don't dress alike all the time, especially not when they're *this* old." She pointed at me. "Look, this one's hair parts on the opposite side."

"I think that one's right eye is bigger—see that?" Melvin asked. "That other one's face is more made up, too." He was indicating Bert.

It was getting more and more difficult to smile at these two. "Look, you all," I said, cutting to the chase, "we were wondering if you've seen your son lately."

Thelma looked up from examining the differences in our hands. "Oh? Do you know Benjamin? Such a nice boy. We haven't seen him recently, but he phoned us just this morning. Checking on us, you know. Such a wonderful son. Listen, why don't you two come on in? Would you like some coffee?"

Melvin stared at her in alarm. "Mother, we don't even know these ladies."

"Oh, pshaw," she said, turning back to us. "Pay no attention to him. Come on inside, you two." She stepped aside, allowing us to slip past her into the living room.

Once inside the apartment, I could see why Thelma had been so quick to answer the doorbell. She had indeed been sitting next to the door. In fact, if you were sitting anywhere in that tiny room, you were sitting next to the door. The room contained only a sofa with an Early American print, two matching burnt orange wing chairs, and a television, but the room was packed. Beside one of the chairs was a basket of needlework; the other chair had a stack of paperbacks next to it.

Although we declined the coffee, Thelma totally ignored us, going back to pour us cups of coffee in the kitchen area that was visible from the living room. The apartment was apparently based on the concept of the great room, because there were no walls separating the kitchen area from the dining room area. From the size of these areas, though, the term *great room* was a gross exaggeration. The entire place smelled of lemon Pledge, mothballs, and something in the oven that had a lot of onions in it.

Bert and I took our places on the sofa, the seating obviously reserved for guests. We exchanged uncomfortable smiles with Melvin, our hands folded in our laps. Old Melvin had immediately lowered his ample self into the orange chair on our right, which groaned at the added weight.

While we all waited for Thelma to quit bustling around, I flashed to visits to our own grandmother when Bert and I were small, the uncomfortable silences as I tried to think of something to say that would not reflect badly on my childish self while I earnestly tried not to spill anything on the furniture. Just like I'd been taught back then, I smiled and said thank you when Thelma handed Bert and me the steaming cups on their saucers. She then sat down on the other orange chair on our left, picking up her crochet needles and a doily she'd been working on.

"Actually," I said, turning to Thelma, "we were wondering about your son, Derek. We'd like to speak to him." *And see if he can actually speak back.*

The mention of Derek's name had an almost electric effect on Melvin. I think if his bulk would have allowed it, he'd have jumped to his feet—that is, if he could have done so without bursting something vital. Instead, Melvin sort of lurched forward. "Show them out, Mother!" he bellowed, pointing to the door. Just as if we couldn't find our own way out. Hell, it was only right in front of us.

Thelma acted as if he hadn't even said a thing. "Just ignore him," she said to us, waving her crochet hook. "Melvin and Derek don't get along very well."

"I don't get along with thieves!" Melvin bellowed again. His face was turning a dark red, and the cords in his neck were beginning to stand out.

Thelma looked at him. "Melvin, Derek isn't a thief," she said firmly. She looked back at us. "What did you want Derek for?"

I drew a blank at that one, but luckily, Bert had a ready answer. "We just had a little misunderstanding with Derek, and we wanted to apologize to him. In person."

Thelma stared at us for a second. I don't think she believed us, but she smiled knowingly and nodded. It looked to me as if she was accustomed to women chasing after her good-looking son—just like Benjamin was. "I suppose you've tried his home and business?" she asked. We nodded.

"Why would you want to apologize to a thief?" Melvin roared. His face looked even redder now. I was starting to worry. How excited did an old man have to get before he had a stroke? Or a heart attack?

Thelma was apparently used to her husband's tirades. "Oh, Melvin, how you do go on. Derek is not either a thief. He just hasn't paid you back the loan, that's all."

Bert and I both perked up at that one.

Thelma went on, punctuating what she had to say by waving her crochet hook in the air. "Melvin loaned Derek a little money—" Thelma began, but Melvin again interrupted her.

"A little money? A *little* money?" Melvin roared.

Thelma again ignored him. "It was just to start Derek's

graphic design business, you know, and, well, Derek just hasn't paid it back yet."

Melvin was working himself up into a real snit. "You work thirty years selling life insurance so you can retire in comfort, and what happens?" he bellowed. "Your own son, your own flesh and blood, up and steals you blind!"

Thelma hooked her crochet hook in the doily and didn't even look up while her husband yelled. "Derek did *not* steal from us," she said firmly. "He's going to pay it back. I really think that it's that wife of his who keeps him from doing it, too. Every time Derek tells us that he's going to write us a check, why, Lauren—that's his wife—comes up with a new reason why it's just not a good time."

"It's never a good time for a thief!" Melvin yelled.

Thelma didn't even blink. "First, they'd just gotten a new house," she went on, "then it was the birth of their daughter, Cissy. And then—oh, I can't remember all the excuses she's given. She's really got poor Derek wrapped right around her little finger." Thelma shook her head sadly and continued to crochet.

"Poor Derek? Poor *Derek*?" Melvin yelled. "How about poor Melvin? And poor Thelma?"

This guy was giving me a headache. I looked around to see where I could put my coffee cup down and realized there was no coffee table. Also no end tables. I was stuck with the thing.

Bert, on the other hand, was taking a polite little sip before she asked, "How long ago was this loan, Mrs. Stanhope?"

Thelma looked off into space. "Oh my. Let me see—"

"Over ten years ago, ten long years!" Melvin screamed.

"And I know Derek's business is successful, but does he pay me back? No! Now all I can do is just read books about other countries rather than getting to travel to them!" He gestured toward the stack of paperbacks on the floor next to his chair.

Thelma's eyes remained on her crocheting. "Now, Melvin, don't get yourself all worked up. Derek is doing real well. It makes me feel real proud. Except, well, I honestly don't know what Lauren and Derek do with their money."

Bert and I exchanged looks. What, indeed?

Melvin had a bit more to say on the subject. "Woe to him with an ungrateful son! Woe to him and pity him!" he lamented. It sounded as if it could've been a quote from the Bible, but I was pretty sure it was really from the "Book of Melvin." "We took Derek and Benjamin to church every Sunday, morning and night, and what do we get? A sinful, thieving, poor excuse for a son, that's—"

Thelma had apparently heard enough. She fixed Melvin with a look. "Hush now," she said. "I mean it." Her voice was very quiet, but it had an amazing effect. Melvin actually hushed. After which Thelma turned back to us, with a little smile. "Well, you know what they say: A son is a son until he takes him a wife. Luckily, our other son Benjamin hasn't married yet."

I nodded. From Bert's description, it looked like Benjamin might be a son forever.

The mention of Benjamin started Melvin up again. "I gave Bennie a loan to start his business, too—not as much as Derek, but then he wasn't starting such an elaborate setup as Derek's. Bennie paid it back in a

year! With interest! But Derek? Nosirreebob! Not a
NICKEL!"

OK, I was tired of listening to the old man yell. I
started to get to my feet, my coffee cup still in hand.
Bert, on the other hand, took yet another polite sip. "So
I guess neither of you has seen Derek lately?" she asked.

"We have not!" Melvin said.

"Or heard from him?" I asked.

"We have not!" Melvin said.

"Or gotten e-mail from him?" Bert asked.

Thelma looked up, her eyes big and blank. "What's
e-mail, dear?"

OK, that settled that.

Bert and I said our good-byes soon after. Thelma said
good-bye to us at the door, taking our saucers and coffee cups away from us then, thank God. I was afraid I
was going to have to take the darn thing home with me.

Melvin, who now seemed to want to act like a gentleman, insisted on walking us to the car.

As we stood at our car door, he leaned toward us,
pulling at his suspenders in a self-important way. "If you
do see Derek, be sure to tell him I've finally had
enough," he said. At least, the old guy wasn't yelling. I
was grateful for that. "You tell him I've been downtown,"
Melvin went on, "and now I've got ways of making him
pay me what he owes me. Tell Derek's money-grasping
wife for me that she'd better start counting their pen-
nies, because I want my money. I'm gonna have to have
me some knee surgery soon, and I ain't going under
the knife worrying about my bills."

"How much does Derek owe you, Mr. Stanhope?" I
asked.

"Never you mind that," he said. "You just tell Derek what I said. And you be sure and tell his wife." He snapped his suspenders. "I may be old, but I ain't an old fool." And then he ambled away.

Bert and I stood there and watched him go. I certainly hoped the old guy had something in writing, just in case I did happen to be right, and Derek was in no condition to confirm that he did indeed owe his parents quite a bit of money.

# Chapter Thirteen

## Bert

Nan turned to me just as soon as she pulled away from the Stanhopes' apartment complex. "What do you think old Melvin meant by saying he'd been downtown and now he had ways of making Derek pay?"

"Probably not what you think he meant." I glanced at her, wondering if she was really keeping her eyes on the road. Southside Drive was stop-and-go traffic all the way, and people had a very bad tendency to pull out on the road from the various grocery stores, tanning booths, and video-rental stores along the way without ever once checking for oncoming traffic.

"Well," Nan said, "I think Melvin could have hired someone to bump Derek off. There was certainly no love lost between them."

I stared at Nan. She always seemed to jump to the

most outlandish, not to mention most violent, scenarios possible. "Nan, if Melvin had Derek killed, how exactly would Melvin get paid?"

Nan smiled, clearly anticipating my question. "Didn't you hear him? Melvin sold life insurance. I'll bet he has a nice fat policy on his son. In fact, if I was Thelma, I'd start wondering how much of a policy he had on me."

"Oh, for goodness' sake," I said. "Did you ever think Melvin merely went downtown to file a lawsuit against his son? There are quite a few law firms in downtown Louisville, you know. Maybe he met with a lawyer and decided to take his son to court."

Nan cocked her head to one side, giving that one some thought. "Well, there's one way to find out." The tires on her Neon screeched as she whipped into a nearby parking lot and then turned the car around.

I glanced at my watch. Drat, there was still time to make it to the courthouse before it closed for the day.

No surprise, Nan made it back downtown to the Circuit Court Clerk's Office at Sixth and Jefferson with about twenty minutes to spare.

The young woman at the counter was obviously very ready for the day to be over. In fact, from the bored look on her face, she looked as if she'd been ready for the day to be over when she'd walked in this morning. With a tube of Revlon in one hand, and a small hand mirror in the other, she was dabbing at her lips, no doubt in preparation for tonight's hot date. The concept immediately made me think of Hank, but I willed the image of him right out of my mind.

Miss Revlon did stop, her lipstick tube in midair, the

very second we walked in the door. "Come back tomorrow," she said. She lifted the hand mirror and peered at her reflection with the concentration of a quality-control inspector. Frowning, she apparently decided more lipstick was called for. This time she layered it on as if she were coloring with a crayon.

"This will only take a second," Nan said.

"That's what they all say," she snapped, putting the lipstick down and pulling a brush through brittle hair so stiff, the electricity sparked like a halo. "I said, come back tomorrow."

Nan began to bristle. "All we need to do is to look at just one case."

"*Tomorrow.*"

Before Nan took the hairbrush away from the woman and showed her how to really use it, I stepped up to the counter. "Jerry asked us to check on this case for a friend of his."

The young woman was applying blush now, without even looking up at me. "Oh yeah? Jerry who?"

"Jerry Abramson?" I would have used the name of Louisville's current mayor, but I was afraid that she might actually check with that office. My luck, and she'd have the mayor's office on her speed dial. The name of Louisville's former mayor, however, still had a powerful effect.

The young woman's head snapped up. Her eyes widened as she took in my power suit and heels. I watched her inward struggle, wondering whether my story really could be true or not. And also wondering if Jerry Abramson could possibly have any contact with her own boss. Her frown deepened. "OK. What's the case?"

"*Melvin Stanhope* versus *Derek Stanhope,* probably filed within the last few days or so. I don't think Derek Stanhope has been served any papers yet." Wow, temporary work at a couple of law firms actually made me sound like I knew what I was talking about. Even Nan turned to look at me in wonder.

"No case number?" Miss Revlon asked. She was already clicking on the keyboard of the computer in front of her.

I shrugged. "Sorry."

"No matter, here it is," she said, her voice radiating a total lack of warmth and good humor. "Filed Monday. Serving the defendant by mail." She sighed heavily. "I'll get you the folder." She disappeared into a side door to the left of the counter.

What could I say? Our tax dollars at work.

"Way to go, Bert," Nan whispered to me. "Though I personally would've liked to hit her with that brush a couple of times."

Miss Revlon reappeared within minutes, slapping a legal-size manila folder on the top of the counter.

"We close in six minutes," she said, picking up her blush and the hand mirror again. "Copier-is-over-there." She said this last as if it were all one word, pointing with her mirror at the ancient Xerox against the far wall.

Nan didn't even give the Xerox machine a glance. She quickly opened the folder, and we both bent to study the documents inside. Apparently, dear old

Melvin was suing his son, all right. Nan and I both gave a quick intake of breath when we got to the amount he was suing Derek for.

Fifty thousand dollars.

Oh my.

"Wow," said Nan. "The big bucks."

I thought of that tiny, tiny apartment and the little man—all right, big man—sitting in his armchair reading about countries he wanted to visit. Unfortunately, his son had taken his retirement money and wouldn't repay the loan. No wonder the old guy was so mad.

I glanced at Nan, realizing that she was thinking the same thought: *Was Derek's father mad enough to kill his own son?*

As we left the clerk's office—I heard Miss Revlon lock the door as we walked down the hallway—Nan said, "Why on earth hasn't he paid back the money? I mean, from what I understand, his business looks like it's pretty well established. And, my God, his offices look pretty posh."

"Thelma said it was Lauren who had all the excuses," I pointed out.

"Yeah, but Derek's the one who's avoiding his parents," Nan said. She tapped her chin as she thought it over. "Maybe old Derek had a gambling habit. Maybe he spent it all on the casino boat lodged on the Ohio. Maybe it's one of the organized-crime families who killed him."

Like I said, Nan has a wild imagination. I was just opening my mouth to answer her, when I saw something that drove everything else right out of my head.

Make that, someone.

Make that, two someones.

Nan and I had just left the courthouse and were descending the steep concrete steps. There at the bottom of the steps stood Hank. Standing in front of him—a little too close if you ask me—was a very attractive policewoman who couldn't have been much more than thirty. Dressed in the standard uniform that on a lot of women looks manly and austere, she looked fantastic. Maybe because she looked as if she'd been poured into it. She had a tiny heart-shaped face, a pouty red mouth, and Julia Roberts hair. Not the hair Julia has these days, the hair she had in *Pretty Woman*—wild, and curly, and tumbling into her face.

Pretty Policewoman had her hands behind her back, and she was leaning back to look up earnestly at Hank as he spoke, the pose making her look very shapely in her navy blue shirt. In fact, if she leaned back any farther, she was no doubt going to lose a couple of buttons in front.

I couldn't hear what Hank was saying, but whatever it was, it must've been hilarious, because the young policewoman suddenly threw back her head and laughed. As she laughed, Hank laughed, too, reaching out and touching her arm.

Their laughter drew Nan's attention, naturally. She took one look and quickly glanced over at me.

"Now, Bert, don't jump to—" she began, but I was already skipping down the steps toward Hank and his little friend.

Hank stopped laughing and looked in my direction only seconds before I reached him. "Bert! Nan!" he said, immediately taking his hand away from his companion's arm.

"Hi, Hank," said Nan.

I found myself searching his face, just like I had done not so long ago with Jake, looking for telltale signs of guilt and discomfort. Hank did not have a trace of either on his face. He only looked a little angry. So was he still angry over the MySoulMate mess? Or was he angry that I'd interrupted his earnest conversation with Pretty Policewoman?

"Hello, Bert," Hank said again, his tone formal. He nodded at the young woman officer. "This is Officer Turnley; she's in Traffic but hoping to move into the Homicide Unit some day. Officer Turnley, this is Bert Tatum and her sister, Nan."

The young woman turned to me. "Oh, hi! I've heard so much about you from Hank and Barry."

Nan spoke up first. "No kidding? We haven't heard a thing about you," she said easily. She turned to look directly at Hank.

When I finally found my voice, I said, "Hank, may I please speak to you for a second?"

Hank glanced at the young woman. "Officer Turnley, Nan, will you please excuse us for a moment?"

Behind his back, Nan was rolling her eyes. I could almost hear what was going through her mind: *Oh, for God's sake, could he be any more formal?*

Hank took my elbow, and we moved over to the edge of the steps. As we moved away, I heard the young officer saying to Nan, "I listen to your show on WCKI all the time. I just love it. I really do."

Great, a fan.

"What is it, Bert?"

I stared at him. My goodness. His tone was definitely angry. In fact, I didn't think I'd ever seen him so furious. I could feel tears smarting behind my lids. I now wished I'd never even tried to talk to him. And yet, I had to say something. He was standing there, staring at me, with a stupid frown on his face. "Hank, I know you're mad, but we really do need to talk about what happened at the Stanhope house."

He held up a hand. "Not here we don't."

Excuse me? Was he telling me when I could and couldn't speak?

"Hank, this is just a misunderstanding," I continued.

"Bert, this is my workplace." Can you believe, he indicated the city around us with a broad sweep of his hand. "I know it looks like a city street to you, but I'm still on duty. You know I don't like to do personal business when I'm at work."

Oh, for the love of Pete. Now he was making *me* angry.

For a second, I couldn't speak. He was being absolutely ridiculous. This whole mess was probably just pre-engagement jitters. Sure, that was it.

Now all I had to do was figure out which one of us had them. I was beginning to think I was just as jittery about becoming engaged to him as he was to me. After all, what had really been going through my head when I saw Hank with that pretty young officer? I really did not want to think about it right now. Not when I might tear up right in front of Hank. When, for God's sake, the man was at *work*.

I opened my mouth to say something, and then

whatever it was just evaporated. I finally just turned around to walk back to Nan without another word.

Hank must have seen the change in my face, because he ran to catch up with me, snagging my arm. "Bert, I don't mean that I don't want to talk about it *ever*," he said. His eyes had softened as he looked at me. I could even feel the warmth of his fingers through the sleeves of my suit coat. "Just not this minute, OK? Listen, I'll call you."

I shrugged him off. Hank really needed to learn that he wasn't the only one who could decide when we talked and when we didn't.

As Nan left her adoring fan and came up to me, I didn't even glance at Hank as I said, "Let's go see Genevieve Carson and see if she's got a houseguest."

With that, I left Hank standing there with his coworker on the street corner of his work.

# Chapter Fourteen

---

## Nan

I kept glancing over at Bert as we walked back to my car. Wordlessly, she climbed into the passenger seat, locked the seat belt around her, and then stared straight ahead.

I got in the driver's seat. In the rearview mirror, I could see Hank standing in front of the courthouse, looking after us. Although he annoyed the hell out of me, he did look a little forlorn. Plus, a little pissed off.

Bert looked over at me. "Drive, OK?"

I stared at her. "You've got the address, remember?"

Bert sighed, then dug the address out of her Dooney & Bourke shoulder purse. "Genevieve Carson lives out in Westport. In fact, not very far from Benjamin's," Bert added. She read the address to me as I grabbed a

Louisville map from my glove compartment, handed it to her, and took off.

I will not dwell on how long it took to get out to Westport, nor the two near-misses I had with eighty-mile-an-hour semis hurtling toward certain death on the fifty-five-mile-an-hour portion of I-65. Suffice it to say, we found the address and continued somehow to be alive to tell about it.

Genevieve Carson's ranch-style home would have been pretty, had it not been for its exterior. And its interior. And, oh yes, its yard.

The entire place looked as if the term *maintenance* was an unknown word in the owner's vocabulary. Gutters drooped, paint flaked off trim, and the front porch sagged. The patchy grass was winter brown, and every square foot of the front yard was littered with children's toys—balls, plastic Nerf bats, Big Wheel plastic bikes, wagons, skates, parts of bicycles. The Carson lawn looked like the place where toys that had been bad were sent. Hell, if Stanhope were hiding here, he could stay out in the front yard in broad daylight, and nobody would notice him.

Bert and I glanced at each other, and together we checked the address again. Yep, this was the place. As we picked our way around toys up the sidewalk to the front door, I was aware of a gradual increase of noise. It pretty much sounded like a low rumble, and—what do you know—it was coming from the house.

The woman who came to the door at our knock—make that loud banging, which I had to do several times to make myself heard—was wearing no makeup and a shapeless flowered housedress that still didn't hide the fact that she was about fifty pounds overweight. Her limp brown hair had been pulled into a ponytail, but that didn't disguise the fact that it badly needed a shampoo. She carried on one hip a baby dressed only in a diaper, while another toddler wearing blue-footed pajamas clung to her skirt. Behind her, what looked to me like a swarm of children of assorted ages tumbled around the room, while the television went full blast. Did I mention that all the children seemed to be yelling? At the top of their young lungs?

I think, if she had not been so stunned by the blur of activity behind the woman, Bert would have turned tail and run. The woman at the door, however, didn't even seem to notice the noise. She squinted at us, frowned, and then mouthed something unintelligible that looked like it was probably "Yes?"

I tried to introduce us. I say *tried*, because the noise level in the house was so high that it was impossible to be heard. After a couple of attempts at trying to hear me, the woman finally yelled, "Shut up!"

For a second there, I thought the woman was talking to me. The decibel level in the house dropped almost imperceptibly.

"Mrs. Carson?" I asked uncertainly.

The woman rolled her eyes and tried again, this time at the top of her lungs, "I SAID, SHADDUP!"

This time, I couldn't tell any change at all.

The woman turned to face the swarm this time, giving us a really good look at the kid on her hip—he had some kind of brown sticky goo all over his face—and shrieked, "SHADDUP OR NO TV FOR A WEEK!"

The room fell silent as pairs of shocked little eyes turned toward her.

The woman turned back to us with a self-satisfied air. "You were saying?"

The television was still blaring, but at least I could make myself heard. "Are you Genevieve Carson?"

"Sure am. Who might you be? I do have to warn you, I'm not buying anything you're selling, unless it's baby clothes." She laughed.

I introduced Bert and myself, but before I could go on, Genevieve interrupted. "Hey, are you all twins?" As she spoke, her eyes were doing the Twin Bounce.

I have found over the years that there are usually only two possible reactions when a person first realizes that Bert and I are twins. Either the person is a little annoyed, as if he or she believes we're doing this whole twin thing just to make his life more difficult, or the person is delighted, like the Stanhopes had been, as if being in the presence of natural clones is akin to finding a four-leaf clover or some other lucky oddity of nature. Genevieve obviously fell in the latter category, too. Her eyes actually seemed to light up as she studied both of us. Back and forth, back and forth. Grinning.

"Oh yeah, you're twins all right," Genevieve went on. "Wow. This is so great. Twins. Wow. I've always wanted twins."

Bert's eyes widened. I tried not to, but I couldn't help sort of staring at the brood in back of her. This woman needed twins like the desert needed sand. One of her precious little boys appeared to be trying to paste a picture in a scrapbook and was spreading every bit as much glue on the carpeting as he was on the picture. Another was chewing on the buttons of a throw pillow. Yet another was keeping time to the music of the Toyota commercial now playing on the television by kicking the wall. In my estimation, the kid had talent.

Genevieve, who had to be blind, as well as deaf, continued, "In fact, I'm still hoping I'll have a set of twins myself someday."

The question "Why on earth?" leaped to mind, but I didn't ask it. Mainly because her saying such a thing pretty much left me temporarily speechless. Around us, the noise level was slowly beginning to rise again.

Bert recovered first. "Genevieve, do you know Derek Stanhope?"

"Oh sure, I know Derek. Went to Westport High with him." She cocked her head at us. "Are you friends of his? Did he send you all over here for me? Kind of like a care package?"

"Excuse me?" I asked.

She was grinning even bigger. "He did, didn't he? He knew I needed some company. And twins, to boot. Listen, ya'll come on in. You want a Coke? It is so nice to have some human contact."

I looked at the tumble of children behind her and wondered what exactly these creatures were.

Genevieve stepped into the room, apparently expecting us to follow her, and as she glanced back at us, she saw my look. "I mean *adult* human contact. I sometimes think all I can do is talk baby talk. My goodness, I even started cutting up my husband's food at dinner last night." She laughed, a delighted little giggle.

Genevieve tousled one of her boys' blond locks—or

was it a girl; its hair was kind of long—as she passed
through the living room into the kitchen. The little
urchin that was hanging on her skirt tagged along like a
caboose.

"This is so like Derek—I was just telling him a few
days ago I needed someone to visit with. I was getting so
lonely. Isn't he a sweetheart?" Genevieve went on.

I stared at her. Maybe she and Derek had been having an affair. I certainly wouldn't blame her. If anyone
needed an affair, this woman did. Of course, I couldn't
quite picture this woman having the strength for an affair.

The big eat-in kitchen that Genevieve led us into was
bright, sunny—and an absolute mess. I am not the best
housekeeper in the world myself, but I had to hand it to
Genevieve. If trashing a house were a sport, she'd
turned pro. The sink was stacked with dishes that were
not just dirty; they were filthy. The counter held half-
eaten sandwiches, crumbled cookies, and opened jars
of grape and raspberry jelly. In the middle of one
counter were a shredded bag of Fritos, a spilled package of frozen Tater Tots, and a handful of chocolate
chip cookies. And everywhere you looked, there were
toys. Legos, Tinkertoys, and miniature Furbys. The entire kitchen was a food-and-toy collage.

Genevieve stepped over a Tonka truck to get to the
refrigerator, but once she made it over there, she
stopped and frowned. "Abel!" she shrieked. "Cain! I
told you guys to clean up after you made sandwiches!"

"Cain and Abel?" Bert asked.

Genevieve laughed again, getting cans of Coca-Cola
out of the refrigerator, and kicking the Tonka truck out

of the way. "Cute, huh? My husband wanted to do biblical names. We've got Mark, Matthew, and John. This is
Gideon." She hugged the little one at her skirt. "And
here's Luke." She rubbed the baby's bald little head.
He'd fallen asleep on her shoulder and was snoring tiny
little baby snores. Genevieve's face actually softened as
she looked at his sticky little face. Genevieve glanced
back at us. "Anyway, don't worry—Cain and Abel get
along just fine."

Genevieve opened the refrigerator, pointed at the
kitchen table chairs, said "Sit," and handed us each a
Coke. I had a feeling that was what she did to her brood
at dinnertime, too. Genevieve sat down at the table,
popped the top of her Coke, and took a long sip. "As
you can see, I haven't had any girls yet, darn it," she
continued. "But we're still hoping." She patted her
tummy wistfully. "Aren't we, Rachel or Abraham?" she
cooed to her stomach.

I stared at her. This woman wasn't fat. She was pregnant. Again. Lord, she was a human copy machine.

"About Derek Stanhope," Bert prodded.

"Um. What about him?" Genevieve asked, taking a
long sip.

"Have you seen him lately?" I asked.

"Heavens no," she said. "It's been ages. He doesn't
like to come over here, what with all the boys running
around and everything. Says they make him nervous."

No kidding. The noise level in the other room had
resumed its eardrum-exploding proportions.

"But Derek and I talk all the time. He and Benjamin
both." She looked up at us. "Do you know Benjamin,
too? Those Stanhope brothers are the nicest guys. Of

course, Derek is the gorgeous one. He used to make all the girls in school absolutely foam at the mouth." She laughed and took another sip of soda, rearranging the snoring baby on her shoulder like a rag doll.

"So you dated Derek?" I asked.

"Me?" She hooted with laughter. "Derek would never have looked at me twice. Benjamin either. But, God, we are such good friends. Maybe because we never had to worry about that whole dating scene. We could just be ourselves. These days I guess I talk to them both at least once a day." She giggled. "Pity calls, I guess they are. They can't imagine me living the life I do."

It struck me that this woman was actually happy. She was delighted with her destroyed home, and her rambunctious brood, and what to me would be a lifestyle from Hell.

"Have you talked to Derek today?" Bert asked.

"Not yet. And I guess I should have said, *write*. Not talk. It's e-mail, really. You know." She gestured toward a computer on a little table in the corner of the room. I hadn't noticed it before with all the clutter. It was the one thing I'd seen in the house that looked neat. "The kids know they had better not touch Mommy's computer. God, if I didn't have my computer, I'd go insane." She laughed again, as if that had to be a joke.

I tried to smile, but as far as I was concerned, she wasn't joking. If I had a house full of screaming kiddos, I'd already be insane. Hell, I'd had to make a big adjustment when I started living with a cat.

"So when did you last hear from Derek?" Bert asked.

Genevieve looked at us then, her eyes doing the

Twin Bounce again, but there was a question in them now. "Derek didn't send you guys over to cheer me up, did he?"

I decided not to share with this friend of Derek's the news of his possible demise. No use upsetting a pregnant woman until I was sure. "No, actually we're just looking for him," I said. I also left out the part where we really didn't know him all that well. "No one seems to know where Derek is."

Except the Grim Reaper, that is.

She frowned. "Hmm. Well, I got an e-mail from him last night—I think he said he was going out of town."

Bert and I exchanged glances. "You got an e-mail from Derek last night?" Bert repeated. "What time?"

"Oh, about ten, I think." She went over to the computer, and, with one hand on her sleeping child and the other on the keyboard, tapped a few keys. The computer hummed and something nearby whirred to life. I looked down to see the printer on the bottom shelf of her computer stand spitting out a piece of paper.

Genevieve handed it over. It was a copy of the e-mail he had sent to her last night. "See?" Genevieve said. "It was about ten. He sounded kinda upset about his so-called wife. Isn't Lauren the absolute pits? I really hope he decides to leave her, don't you?"

Bert nodded, trying to act as if Derek and she were best buds, but I wasn't paying much attention. I was staring at the e-mail note. It was short and to the point.

*Hey, Ginny. I'm at home now but I'm about to take off. I'm going to be away from a computer for a while.*

*I've got to get away by myself and think about Lauren
and my marriage. I'll write when I get the chance. Later,
Derek*

The time was listed as last night at 10:06:57 P.M. I noticed at the bottom of the printout, there was something called Return-Path and a bunch of letters and
numbers and words. It all looked like gobbledygook to
me.

"What's all this?" I asked, pointing to it.

Genevieve looked at the bottom of the page. "I don't
know. I don't really know anything about computers,
except I know if they don't work. I've never noticed all
that language there before—I guess it's printed there
by the Internet service."

The only words I could actually understand in the
gobbledygook were *AOL.com* and *Prodigy.net*. Both of
those companies provided e-mail services for computers. "Which Internet service do you use?" I asked.

"AOL, America Online—you know, just like in that
movie, *You've Got Mail*. Benjamin and Derek both use
AOL, too."

I glanced at Bert, wondering if she'd noticed the
same thing I had. If Derek Stanhope and Genevieve
both used AOL, what was the word *Prodigy*—the name
of another Internet provider—doing on the e-mail he
sent?

# Chapter Fifteen

## Bert

"Nan, Derek Stanhope is still sending e-mails to people," I said for, oh, about the one hundredth time. I was opening my refrigerator door, trying to figure out what we were going to have for supper. I hadn't expected to have company, so the pickings in my Amana were pretty slim. "Call me crazy, but e-mail sounds pretty undead to me."

We'd been over and over this while driving from Genevieve Carson's house to the radio station to pick up my car. It had been a little difficult to get away from Genevieve. The poor woman kept coming up with things to entice us to stay. She'd offered us cookies. Peanut butter sandwiches. Another Coke. Before she offered one of the kids, we'd insisted that we really, really had to go. A pressing engagement. Dinner plans.

Scheduled heart surgery. Any excuse to get out of there.

Finally we made it to the dilapidated front porch, where Genevieve told us, "Well, now, you two, don't be strangers, you hear? I'd sure love to have you all come back and visit. Anytime. Really."

"Sure thing," Nan had said, smiling. Me, I'd just smiled.

Once we were in the car, I had to ask. "Do you really intend to come back here and visit?"

"Not in this lifetime," Nan said.

"Or in Derek's?" I asked.

I probably should not have said that last. Nan immediately got all huffy. "Derek's lifetime is over, Bert."

That's when the whole dead-men-don't-send-e-mail discussion had started. Actually, I hadn't minded having something else to think about besides Hank and Pretty Policewoman. Arguing with Nan occupied my mind with something else besides seeing Hank and that pretty little cop laughing together.

By the time Nan and I had gotten back to WCKI, gotten into our separate cars, and driven home, though, wouldn't you have thought that the whole discussion would have, no pun intended, died down?

"I just think it's awfully fishy that he'd be sending e-mail through Prodigy *and* AOL," Nan said. Again. She was standing right behind me, looking over my shoulder into the yawning abyss that was my refrigerator. "You have to admit it looks odd to have both services mentioned on an e-mail that should only be coming through AOL." Nan was carrying her cat Gemini in her arms, stroking his silky ears, his purr humming loud and deep like a living motor. The two of them apparently were going to be my dinner guests, Nan having beelined over here with Gemini almost the second we got back.

I opened the freezer door and glanced back at her. "Nan," I said, "I don't know anything about e-mail services—maybe they route messages back and forth through each other, just like airlines do with people. I don't know," I repeated. "And I don't think you do, either. All I know for sure is that, on average, it's mostly living people who use them." I rooted through the cellophane-wrapped packages in my freezer. Nothing looked remotely edible.

Nan was frowning, but it wasn't because of the contents of my freezer. "Don't you see?" she said. "It might mean that someone else could be sending e-mails for Stanhope. Someone who uses Prodigy to get onto the Internet."

I rummaged in the freezer some more. Let me see. Chicken breasts that looked as if they'd been in there since the Ice Age. Or a lasagna Popsicle. I glanced at Nan. "Stanhope could have been using someone else's computer that one time to send his e-mail to Genevieve."

"He said he was at home," Nan reminded me. "So don't you think we ought to at least take a look at Stanhope's home computer and check his e-mail files? Just to see if Prodigy actually shows up?"

I turned to stare at her, a frozen package of hamburger in one hand. "How exactly do you plan to do that, without breaking any laws?"

Nan shrugged, still petting her cat. "Well, except for

that last part about lawbreaking, we could run over to Stanhope's house early tomorrow morning, after Mrs. Stanhope leaves for work. Then we could—"

"Excuse me. What do you mean: *we?*"

Nan opened her mouth, but fortunately, the phone rang. I really didn't want to hear her answer, anyway. I snatched up the receiver that hung on the wall next to the fridge, the frozen hamburger patty in one hand. "Hello?"

"Bert?"

"Hank?"

There was a long silence after that one word. If he was doing that Is-it-Bert-or-is-it-Memorex? act again, I was really in no mood. However, I somehow willed my voice to be kinder and gentler. "How's it going, Hank?" I wanted to add, "Have any more tête-a-têtes with your lovely coworker?" But I didn't.

"Fine. I just wanted to check in, since we didn't get to talk at the courthouse. And we missed our date last night. I thought maybe we ought to talk for a minute or so." The words sounded nice, but the tone was all wrong. I frowned, trying to hear what wasn't being said. Of course, I could just be projecting my own irritation at the whole situation. I decided to give him the benefit of the doubt.

"OK," I said, feeling a little wary for some reason. "What do you want to talk about, Hank?" Yes, I was a little abrupt, but I'd had a hard day. "Have you found out anything more about—"

I was going to ask about the Stanhope investigation, but Hank cut me off. "I didn't get to tell you at the courthouse that I went to see Benjamin Stanhope. You know, Derek's brother?"

Uh-oh.

"Oh, really?" I said, keeping my tone light.

Hank went on, that tight note in his voice growing more apparent. "It turns out that I was just following in your footsteps. Can you believe it? What a coincidence. Mr. Stanhope told me you'd been there, too. By yourself. I'm assuming it really was you, since Nan was on the air at the time."

I decided to let that one go. "Yes, Hank, I did go to see Benjamin Stanhope today."

Next to me, Nan's eyes grew larger. "What? What?" she mouthed, but I shook my head.

Hank continued, "Well, I have to admit that I was a little surprised at what Stanhope said."

There was another pause. Why did I feel as if Hank was using his interrogation techniques on me—leaving long pauses for me to jump in and fill with incriminating information? Obviously, he didn't realize just how long I could wait him out in any silly game. I was the mother of two, after all.

So I waited.

And waited.

Hank finally cleared his throat. "I'm not saying I believe Stanhope or anything. But, apparently, he has the same crazy idea as Mrs. Stanhope that you have a romantic interest in his brother."

There was another long pause.

I waited some more.

Hank took a deep breath. "What surprised me,

though, was he indicated that you didn't even bother to deny it to him. Just left without even telling him that it wasn't true."

This certainly explained Hank's grim behavior at the courthouse earlier. I had a sudden image of Hank asking Benjamin Stanhope to repeat everything I had said in nauseating detail. It was not a pretty picture. In fact, the more I thought about it, the angrier I got.

I had had enough.

"You know, Hank, I think I have already explained myself once," I said. "But I do need to tell you something. I want to confess that I've made a terrible mistake."

"You have?"

I let the silence build between us before I continued, just like he'd done with me. Let him imagine the worst. I swear I could actually hear him hyperventilating over the phone line. I finally went on.

"Yes, I made the mistake of not realizing my significant other—other *what*, I don't care to say—would be grilling Benjamin Stanhope about me. If I had realized that, I certainly could have told Mr. Stanhope exactly what to tell you." I was so furious by then, my voice was shaking.

Hank must've realized how angry I was. "Now, Bert," he put in, his tone a lot more conciliatory, "I was only—"

"I know what you were doing, Hank," I said.

Hank took a deep breath, apparently deciding to change tactics. "Bert," he said, "I was really only thinking of your safety. Derek Stanhope is no doubt hiding from his wife, but we don't know that for sure. Until he turns up, your nosing around in this business could be dangerous. You should stay away from—"

"Good night, Hank," I said, and hung up on him.

I turned to see Nan, eyebrows raised. I ignored the obvious question in her eyes, trying to get the fury out of my voice when I spoke. "OK," I said, "what exactly was it that you and I will be doing at the Stanhope house tomorrow morning?"

The next morning I had the unenviable task of figuring out what to wear to a break-in. I went with an outfit similar to Nan's when we'd gone downtown to see Derek Stanhope—black slacks, black laced-up hightops, black turtleneck, black jacket. Even black leather gloves. When I met Nan in our mutual driveway, she was wearing exactly the same thing. It was the first time we'd dressed alike since grade school. It was either the Twin Mind Meld, or we'd both watched way too many episodes of *MacGyver*. I personally went with the latter.

Naturally, I began to get cold feet as soon as we pulled up in front of Stanhope's house on Point Ridge Trace. What on earth was I doing?

Nan, of course, hopped out of the car and was heading toward the front door like a cow that has sighted the barn. I, on the other hand, opened the passenger door slowly, looking all around as I got out. Luckily, there was no one to be seen in either direction. The entire street looked deserted, with everyone no doubt at work trying to earn enough money to continue living in this upscale neighborhood.

I ran to catch up with Nan and snagged her arm. "Nan, maybe we ought to tell Hank and Barry about the e-mail message to Genevieve, and let them follow up on it."

Nan gave me a look as she rang the front doorbell. "Do you enjoy being laughed at?" she hissed.

"Do you enjoy being arrested?" I hissed right back, praying that Mrs. Stanhope was sick with the flu and didn't go to work today.

Neither Mrs. Stanhope nor anyone else came to the door.

Nan knocked again. There was no answer.

As Nan was trying the doorknob, I put my hand on her arm. "Nan, I think that we should let someone else do this."

Nan turned the doorknob, anyway.

Naturally, the door was locked.

I continued, "Maybe Benjamin Stanhope could ask his sister-in-law to check his brother's computer. I'm sure you'll agree that this house-breaking thing is a pretty stupid stunt—"

Of course, I was saying all this while Nan busied herself, trotting around to the back of the house and trying each screen and window that she came to. Unfortunately, the fourth one she tried slid open easily. I couldn't have been more disgusted. You'd think people in as nice a neighborhood as this would check to make sure all their windows were locked.

On second thought, it was probably a good thing that Nan found a window unlocked. I'd hate to think what she might've done, had she not been able to get inside. Nan gave me a triumphant smile as she hefted one leg over the sill and disappeared inside.

Once Nan was gone, I just stood there, frozen, staring at the open window.

Nan reappeared in the window in a second. "Are you coming? Because you standing there, outside an open window, looking guilty, is kind of attention-getting."

I heaved a big sigh, threw one leg over the sill, and hauled my guilty self inside. Then I closed the window and turned around.

Luckily, the large windows in the room provided enough light for looking around, so we didn't have to switch on any lamps or overhead lights. The room we'd entered appeared to be the master bedroom. A four-poster bed, a long dresser, a chest, and a chifforobe were all beautiful golden oak. A multicolored braided rug lay next to the bed.

Mrs. Stanhope had not bothered to make her bed this morning. Her navy flowered comforter, electric blanket, and matching sheets lay in a tangle on the king-size bed. I recognized the floral pattern on the bedding as one of Ralph Lauren's.

Nan nodded, indicating the bed. "Does that look like both sides of the bed were slept in?" she asked.

I looked at the identical indentations in the king-size pillows. "Maybe Stanhope came back."

"Hardly," Nan said. "I checked with Barry again before I left my house. Stanhope is still among the missing."

She strode out of the room. I stared after her. I really, really wanted to go home.

From down the hall I could hear doors opening and closing. I caught up with her in what appeared to be Stanhope's study. Everything in this room was heavy walnut, from the desk to the credenza to the closed armoire behind the desk. I looked around. "So where's the computer?" I asked.

When Nan opened the armoire's doors, I could see it wasn't an armoire at all, but a complete computer outfit—monitor, speakers, printer, hard drive—the whole shebang housed on shelves at different levels behind the doors. I thought of my beat-up desk at home. Stanhope had merely to swivel in his desk chair to be seated directly in front of the computer behind his desk.

A maneuver that Nan executed perfectly.

She gave a satisfied little sigh as she flipped on the computer. It hummed in response, and the black screen of the monitor filled with letters and numbers as it powered up. I truly believe that Nan loves to be where she shouldn't. When the computer stopped humming, she clicked keys on the computer and maneuvered the mouse, grinning as she did so.

Me, I was shaking in my shoes.

"Here's his e-mail program," Nan finally said, and made a few more clicks. "It *is* AOL, just like Genevieve said." She clicked some more. "We're in luck—his password has been saved by the computer."

I actually knew what that meant. People who use e-mail at home often have the computer save their password so they don't have to reenter it everytime they log on to get their e-mail messages. What it meant to us was we wouldn't have to know Stanhope's password to link onto his e-mail messages on the Internet.

After a few more clicks, Nan frowned. "They aren't here," she said.

"What do you mean?"

"The letters he sent me—they aren't here."

I stared at her. "Maybe you're looking in the wrong place."

I sat down next to her, fitting about half my butt on the chair. I reached for the mouse and clicked on the little picture of a file folder labeled, SENT ITEMS. The screen immediately filled with a list of letters that Stanhope had recently sent. The latest dates of the letters were for Wednesday morning—the day Nan said she saw his body.

"See?" Nan said. "He hasn't sent a letter since he died."

I ignored her, scanning the list. All of the letters seemed to relate to Stanhope's work as a graphic designer. The list did not include any letters to Office-TempTwin, nor were there any letters to Genevieve or his brother, Benjamin. I clicked on the folder marked OUT BOX and I even opened IN BOX. Nothing.

"Maybe Stanhope deleted the letters he sent to me," Nan said, "so his wife couldn't read them."

It made sense. I couldn't imagine a philandering husband leaving incriminating letters on his computer for his wife to read at her leisure. Especially without the security of a password.

Nan reached for the mouse and clicked on the little picture of a trash can. Many people don't know that just clicking on the delete button doesn't actually remove the documents from the computer's hard drive, but my son, Brian, had explained this to Nan and me. In the Windows operating system, you actually have to open the recycle bin—that's the little wastebasket— and delete it yourself to really get rid of the items for good.

The screen again filled with a list—this time with so-called deleted files and letters. Together Nan and I scanned the list. There were some deleted letters, even from months before, but there were no letters to—or from—OfficeTempTwin. In the list, there were also some letters from Benjamin and even Genevieve, but not the letters that they said they'd just received.

This was really puzzling. Where were the letters? I hated to consider it, but could someone else really have sent them?

I turned to look at Nan. She had stopped looking in virtual folders and was busy looking in real ones. She opened each of the front drawers in the walnut desk and rooted through its contents. Nan lifted out a set of three keys on a brass key ring, each key labeled in a chicken scratching that was hard to read. They all looked like door keys. Nan slipped them into her jacket pocket.

"Nan! Put those back!"

She gave me a look. "Believe me," she said, "he won't miss them. Besides, we might want to get inside the house again." She clicked on the keyboard to close the Internet connection and then turned off the computer.

I saw a ray of hope. "Does that mean we're leaving?"

Nan didn't respond, but she did leave the room. I

followed her out and back down the hallway as she continued to open doors and glance inside. One door revealed a pretty little room all done in lace, ruffles, and pink rosebuds. "Has to be the little girl's room," Nan said. Another door opened to a small guest bedroom.

I was just beginning to believe that we were really and truly about to get out of there, when Nan opened the door to what appeared to be another office, this one with a distinctly feminine feel.

The desk and credenza were similar in style to Stanhope's but made of an antiqued white pine, accented with stenciled flowers on the desk drawers and the front doors of the closed armoire. A rose-colored blotter and matching pen set were in the center of the desk, a vase of dried flowers to one side. The office would've been pretty, had there not been the letters, bills, receipts, and opened envelopes stacked in piles everywhere.

"Something makes me think Lauren Stanhope doesn't like to file," Nan said. She opened the doors to the armoire behind the desk to reveal another computer outfit. And more pieces of discarded mail, some even in tiny wads. I glanced at the overflowing paper in the garbage can at our feet.

"Lauren Stanhope doesn't like to empty her garbage, either," I said.

Nan went through the same process as she had with Derek's computer—turning it on and starting up the e-mail program. She glanced at me as she clicked the keyboard. "Her password is saved, too, but the program she's using is Prodigy," Nan said. She said it with a tiny expectant trill to her voice.

I glance over her shoulder as Nan looked in the IN BOX, the OUT BOX, and finally in SENT LETTERS on the computer screen.

Nothing was there.

"OK, that does it," I said. "Let's go."

Nan ignored me and clicked on the little picture of a wastebasket. Her sudden intake of breath made me turn back to look.

There on the screen was the list of files and letters that Lauren Stanhope had meant to delete.

"Look. They're all here," Nan said.

"How can that be?"

"I don't know, but they're there. In *Lauren's* computer." Nan looked like the Cheshire cat.

She got up and moved in back of me so I could sit down at the desk and get a better look. Sure enough, there were the letters Derek had written to OfficeTemp-Twin. I searched the list of letters. Derek's e-mail messages to Benjamin and Genevieve were still among the missing.

"Lauren Stanhope's computer even has the letters that were routed through MySoulMate.org," I said. "The ones that you sent to Derek."

"You mean that *you* sent," Nan added.

I stooped to read the list of letters from Office-TempTwin. Was it possible that Mrs. Stanhope had been sending e-mails and signing them from her husband, just like Nan had been sending them from me? And yet, why would Lauren do such a thing? What would be the point? "What does it mean?" I asked.

Nan didn't answer.

I scanned the list. "Do you really think that Mrs.

Stanhope has been sending e-mails, pretending they're from her husband? She was getting him dates? Why, that's just crazy." Of course, maybe Lauren Stanhope was a swinger, just like Nan and I had talked about earlier.

Nan still didn't respond.

"Nan?"

When I turned around, I could see why Nan wasn't saying anything. It probably had a lot to do with that really big man's hand across her mouth.

# Chapter Sixteen

---

## Nan

You'd think that being unable to speak would be a deejay's worst nightmare.

However, I'd have to say that being grabbed from behind by a huge, muscle-bound oaf who puts his sweaty hand over your mouth to keep you from screaming is the epitome of worst nightmares. Now I knew what Fay Wray had felt like. And, believe me, I'd never wanted to know.

I was probably being unfair to make comparisons to King Kong, however. That is, I was probably being unfair to King Kong. That big gorilla was, no doubt, a lot more civilized than the big gorilla who'd grabbed me.

I'd never have believed that anybody as big as this guy could have moved so quietly that I wouldn't have heard him. And yet, his massive hand was tightly clamped across my mouth before I'd even been aware that Bert and I were not alone.

I felt myself being lifted off my feet as Bert turned around, her eyes widening at the sight of whoever it was who had me. My own fear was mirrored in Bert's eyes as the big ape's other arm tightened around my waist.

When Bert and I were little, and some kid put his hand over my mouth, I'd always stick out my tongue and give his palm what Bert and I used to call a "Wet Willie." The wetter the Willie, the better, as a matter of fact. Back when I was six, nobody ever put his hand over my mouth for long. Now, though, the prospect of licking this guy's palm made my stomach churn.

I did it, though. I stuck my tongue out and gave his palm a Wet Willie that at the age of six, I would've been proud of.

Instead of taking his hand away, though, the ape tightened his grip. "ARRGGH!" he said, giving my head a little shake, as if maybe he thought he could rattle my tongue back inside.

What can I say? He thought right. I pulled my tongue back in only a little faster than a snake's. That didn't get Kong to loosen his grip, however. His fingers seemed to be digging holes in my cheeks.

If he ever removed his smelly, sweaty hand, I was going to look like one of those elderly ladies you see every once in a while, who dab on rouge in small red circles in the middle of each cheek. How attractive. Thanks so much, Ape Man.

From behind us, standing near the open door, a woman spoke. "Nigel, for God's sake, stop playing around and bring them both into the living room."

I recognized the voice, even if she wasn't calling us whores at the top of her lungs. Lauren Stanhope the Not-So-Merry Widow.

"Don't scream," the gorilla named Nigel said to me—or was it to Bert? I couldn't tell since I couldn't see which of us he was looking at. "And don't make any noise. Or we'll make your sister really sorry you did."

"Oh, let them scream—no one is home for blocks around here," Lauren said.

I could certainly attest to that, remembering my search on Wednesday for someone to help me call the police after I'd found Derek's body. However, unless Ape Man took his hand away, screaming was not going to be on my list of things to do in the next minute or so. Bert was going to have to do the honors alone.

I glanced over at Bert hopefully as Nigel put me back down on the floor. *Hard.* Hard enough that I was glad I'd pulled my tongue back inside or I would've bitten down on it.

Nope, screaming was not on Bert's list, either. More's the pity. Bert's lips were clamped together so tight, you'd have thought she'd used epoxy. Apparently, my beloved sister was trying very, very hard to follow Nigel's instructions to the letter.

OK, so I was touched that she wanted to make sure that nothing happened to me. That was very nice. But to hell with doing what Ape Man told us. Maybe somebody was home nearby, after all.

I opened my mouth to let out a bloodcurdling shriek, pulling back my foot at the same time, preparing to kick Nigel where you're never, ever supposed to kick a guy, when Bert caught my eye. With a very pale face, she nodded toward the door. I looked in that direction. Lauren Stanhope was standing in the doorway. More importantly, she had a small but very nasty-looking handgun pointed in our direction.

"You two don't take instructions very well, do you?"

If she was talking about her tirade yesterday morning, when she demanded that we stay away from here, I'd say she had a point. If she was talking about the last minute or so, I'd say she was badly mistaken. At the sight of her gun, I clamped my mouth shut even tighter than Bert's.

Lauren gestured with the gun toward King Kong, who immediately grabbed Bert and me by the arms. I couldn't help but stare. The ape's meaty hand seemed to swallow my upper arm.

"Allow me to introduce Nigel Hampstead," Lauren said, smiling, as he hustled Bert and me into the living room after her. I turned to look at him. He was over six feet tall, probably 250 pounds, and all as solid as a boulder.

I realized, too, that the guy really didn't look all that much like an ape. No, I'd say he looked more like Big Foot. In fact, he looked exactly how Big Foot might look with a haircut and shave, if Big Foot happened to be wearing a green Polo turtleneck shirt, Gap jeans, and Nike running shoes. Nigel's upper arms were the size of my thighs, and his thighs looked like concrete pillars.

"Niger's my personal trainer," Lauren explained.

If you were training for the World Wrestling Federation, old Nigel would be the man for the job.

Nigel hustled Bert and me into the living room and

all but flung us onto the sofa. I looked around for something I could use as a weapon. Wouldn't you know this room would be tidy? There was an oversize sofa, matching chairs on either end, end tables with lamps, a coffee table, all facing a large closed entertainment center. A large multicolored braided rug lay on the floor between the sofa and entertainment center. A combination cordless phone and answering machine sat on top of the coffee table.

That was it. There were no knickknacks with sharp edges, no fireplace with a handy poker, no knives or swords in sight.

"All right, Lauren, now what?" Nigel asked. His voice was soft and amazingly high for a man whose testosterone level had to be off the charts.

"Going home now would be nice," Bert suggested.

"Oh, we can't just let you go home." Lauren's upper lip sort of curled as she said this. Not a good look for her.

"Sure you can," I said. "Or, how about sending us to jail?"

Beside me, Bert frowned.

I hurried on. "You could report us to the police for breaking in. You could charge us with trespassing."

"Or you could let us go home," Bert added.

"You could even charge us with loitering," I suggested.

"Forget that, sweetie. One of you saw Derek." To Nigel, Lauren added, "For God's sake, Nigel, don't just stand there. Get some rope from the garage and tie them up while we decide what to do."

While Nigel lumbered out of the room, I glanced

over at Bert to see if she was processing what that little statement about Derek signified. *Lauren knew that I'd seen Derek dead.* That probably meant that she was the one who'd put a bullet in him. Or she'd had her personal trainer Nigel of Big Foot fame do it.

Bert just stared back at me. I wasn't sure if she got it or not.

Nigel had disappeared out a side door, and now he returned with a short length of rope. He looked kind of sheepish. "I could only find this little piece. You really ought to clean out your garage sometime, Lauren."

Lauren gave an exasperated snort. "Excuse me? *Derek* should've cleaned out my garage—that's who should have cleaned out my garage."

I hated to remind her that killing your husband pretty much prevented his fulfilling any major household duties.

Lauren stared at the rope for a long moment. "OK," she finally said. "Just tie them up back-to-back—that rope should be long enough for that."

Bert gave me a quick sideways look, and I knew the moment our eyes met that she was thinking the same thing I was. Back when Bert and I were in the fifth grade, one of our favorite movies had been *Houdini* starring Tony Curtis. Again and again in the film, Tony had escaped from ropes. Bert and I had been intrigued by how easily Tony had made his escapes, so naturally, we'd decided that we wanted to figure out how to do it, too. Mostly, that meant our best friend, Marilyn, tied us up, back-to-back, and then laughed hysterically as Bert and I struggled to free ourselves. Eventually, we'd gotten pretty good at it, so Marilyn started timing us. Five minutes and a few seconds, as I recall, had been our best time. Not exactly speedy. In fact, under the circumstances, it seemed we really ought to try to break our record.

Lauren kept the gun on us, while Nigel positioned us back-to-back on the floor in front of the sofa. He handled us pretty much the way the real Big Foot would've handled us—like two large sacks of potatoes.

I felt for Bert's hands and held on to them. They felt cold. Which, of course, made me feel sick. I was the one who'd done this. I was the one who'd gotten us into this mess.

Her fingers clinging to mine, I could feel Bert trying to position our hands like we'd done years ago for Marilyn, fingers spread a little, but not so much that Nigel would notice as he wound the length of rope around our wrists. He went around, about three times, and then tied a knot.

"OK. So now what?" Nigel asked, grunting, as he got to his feet.

"I don't see that we have a choice. You're going to have to put them where we put Derek," she said.

I turned to stare at her, feeling cold. Putting us with Derek didn't sound like something Bert and I would be able to walk away from. Particularly since it looked as if nobody had seen Derek walking around lately.

Together Bert and I moved our hands closer to the sofa so that they would be hidden in the shadows.

Nigel looked at the floor. "In the *river*? Gee, Lauren, I don't know—"

"Nigel, listen to me. One of them saw Derek's body in the car. I don't know which one it was, but I saw her from behind the curtains. Because of her, you almost didn't get here in time to get his body out of here. All because of *her*. She's the one who called the police, you know. And she hasn't given up. The two of them have been poking around ever since."

Apparently, Lauren held a grudge.

Behind our backs, Bert and I released each other's hands and straightened out our fingers within the confines of the rope, allowing more room for our fingers to move.

"But the other one doesn't know anything—" Nigel began.

"What? Are you stupid?" Lauren asked.

A rhetorical question, if I ever heard one. I could feel Bert's busy fingers behind me, working at the knot.

Lauren went on. "They're *twins*. What one knows, the other knows. They've got, like, ESP or something."

The woman had apparently been seeing way too many science fiction movies.

"Besides," Lauren said, "they were both looking in my computer. I'm pretty sure they know I sent the e-mail messages for Derek. Otherwise, they wouldn't be so willing to get the police out here. Sure, they want me to charge them with trespassing so they can show the police what they've found out."

I stared at her, the realization of what she was saying finally hitting me.

Oh, for God's sake! It was really true. The Derek Stanhope I'd been corresponding with was a *woman*. His very own wife, no less. No wonder she'd known the exact right thing to say to me. We women know precisely what a woman wants to hear.

My pen pal turned back to us, the gun waving in the breeze as she punctuated her words with gestures. "It was such a good idea, you know. All I wanted to do was make it look like Derek was seeing other people, too. That's all. He was threatening to divorce me and take my daughter away. He was going to try to smear me in court, make me out to be an unfit mother."

And everybody knows that women who kill people make the very best moms. Of course they do. Sure. "Hey, I understand," I said out loud. "Listen, Lauren, we're on your side. We wouldn't tell a soul about anything. We promise."

Behind me, I could feel Bert nodding her head vigorously in agreement, while her fingers continued to work at the ropes.

"Well, it wasn't just your going out with me," Nigel interrupted. "I mean, that wasn't the only thing Derek was mad about." Apparently, old Nigel didn't want us to get the wrong idea. He may be a murderer, but apparently, he did not want anybody to think of him as a homewrecker. "Derek was pretty upset about the drugs, too," Nigel reminded her.

Lauren threw him an exasperated look. "As if a little recreational coke now and again was a problem. Everyone has tried it, but Derek had to make a federal case out of it and start threatening divorce. He was actually talking about sole custody."

Lauren seemed to be whipping herself up into a frenzy. This is not something you like to see in a person holding a gun.

"What an asshole," I put in.

Lauren turned to look at me. "You said it, sister," she said. "I wasn't about to lose my daughter."

"Good for you," I said. "About time women started standing up for themselves." I would've given her a victory sign, but under the circumstances, that was out of the question.

Amazingly enough, Lauren actually smiled at me. "I really didn't want to do any of this, you know. I just didn't have a choice. If Derek hadn't been so high and mighty, none of this—this ugliness would've been necessary. But the man wouldn't listen to reason."

"The shit," I said.

Lauren just looked at me for a long moment. Then, shrugging, she turned back to Nigel. "Anyway, you're going to have to do something about them. Just like you did before."

So much for women sticking together. And, hell, I'd thought we'd bonded.

Nigel stared back at her for a long moment. "*I'm* supposed to do something about them? And *you're* going to do what?" he asked. I could feel Bert tugging at the rope again and again. Did it feel a little looser, or was I just deceiving myself?

"Well, I'll help, of course. Just like I did with Derek." Lauren's tone implied that Nigel should have known this without her having to tell him.

Nigel blinked. "Do you really think that's necessary?"

Lauren drew an exasperated breath. "Of course it's necessary! If they leave here, they're going straight to the police! The police, Nigel! Do you know what that means?"

Nigel just stared back at her, his eyes blank.

I had a pretty good idea of what our going straight to the police could possibly mean, but it didn't seem my place to help old Nigel figure it out.

Lauren looked as if she could cheerfully put a few bullets into Nigel before she got around to us. "PRISON, Nigel! *That's* what it means. PRISON FOR YOU AND ME!"

I don't think you could say it any clearer. Even Nigel seemed to have gotten the message. "Gosh," he said.

I wasn't sure what he meant by that, but it sounded pretty ominous to me.

"Enough whining about what has to be done, Nigel," Lauren said. "We really don't have any choice here. So, come on, let's get on with it."

Behind me, I could feel Bert stiffen. The tugs her fingers were making seemed to pick up speed.

"I need a cigarette," Nigel said. He pulled a pack of cigarettes from his front shirt pocket. Inside the cellophane of the pack was a Bic lighter. He shook out a cigarette and lit up, drawing in several lungs' worth of smoke and then exhaling with satisfaction. And this guy was supposed to be a personal trainer? Was he kidding?

Lauren seemed pretty unimpressed by him right now, too. "Come on, Nigel, stop stalling. You have to do it. We'll put them in the river, and by the time anybody finds them, they'll be fish food."

What a nice way to put that. The woman was a delicate flower.

Behind my back, Bert's fingers worked frantically.

"I don't have to do nothing," Nigel grumbled.

"You did it before," Lauren coaxed.

"Derek was *dead* then," Nigel reminded her.

"Exactly," Lauren said. The woman actually smiled, an expression of complete satisfaction on her face.

Nigel did not smile back. "So why don't you just— you know—"

A look of irritation now flashed across Lauren's face. "Why should I? They're as much your problem as they are mine! For God's sake, Nigel, just do it and get it over—"

We all jumped as the telephone on the coffee table rang.

# Chapter Seventeen

---

## Bert

If I didn't get these ropes loose soon, I was going to go stark raving mad. Behind my back, Nan kept moving her hands, trying to make the knot more accessible to me; but, let's face it, the last time we did this, we were ten. Our hands were a whole lot smaller then. And, of course, our very lives didn't depend on our getting loose. There's a big difference between having your best friend, Marilyn, standing in front of you with a timer, and having Lauren standing in front of you with a gun. I mean, it's just a subtle nuance of difference, but sensitive soul that I am, I picked up on it.

I really don't do well under pressure. I'd thought I was actually making progress with the rope, when that dumb phone rang. At the sound, Nan and I both jumped in unison. Which was poor planning, let me tell you. Our startled movement pulled the rope between us taut and once again tightened the knot.

Lauren and Nigel made no move whatsoever to answer the phone. They just stood there and stared at each other, listening to the stupid thing ring off the hook.

"You know, Lauren, we could just pretend we're not home," Nigel suggested.

Lauren frowned. "Idiot! We can't do that!"

I could not believe the way she talked to a man who was so much bigger than she was. Of course, she did have a gun. If that didn't give you courage, I suppose nothing would.

"We can't possibly act like we're not here," Lauren went on. "The car's in the driveway. In plain sight." She ran her hand through her blond hair. "I knew I should've pulled it into the garage after we took Cissy to day care."

Nigel must've been accustomed to Lauren calling him names, because he didn't even act as if he'd heard it. He just nodded his huge head. "You're right. Someone might've driven by and noticed the car. So they'll know you're here."

Lauren handed him the gun. "OK. Watch the Doublemint girls while I get rid of whoever the hell it is." She snatched up the receiver. "Hello?"

Wow. It was amazing how normal she sounded. All traces of anger were instantly gone from her voice. She sounded suddenly subdued, and maybe a little sad, exactly the way anybody facing a painful divorce ought to sound.

I had loosened the rope to just about where it had

been before, and now I started digging at the knot while Lauren listened to her caller. As she listened, she slowly raised her eyebrows, and her big blue eyes got even bigger. "You have?"

She listened some more as Nigel shifted from one foot to another, clearly impatient to hear what was going on. For a guy holding a gun on us, he didn't seem all that mean a person. When I met his eyes once, he looked almost apologetic that he was having to do what he was doing. In his huge hand, the gun looked more like a toy than the real thing.

"Oh God. Are you sure?" Tears welled in Lauren's eyes. Real tears. They pooled up and actually ran in two rivulets down her cheeks. I was just amazed. I had no idea what had gotten such a response out of the woman, but I wouldn't have thought it was possible. Up to now, Lauren Stanhope had seemed to be a woman capable of running the gamut of emotion from *A* to *A*. Angry to Angry. That she should be so touched by something that she would cry—why, my goodness, it made her seem almost human.

"Oh my dear Lord. I see. All right—yes—OK—" Lauren's voice broke as tears continued to run down her cheeks. She sobbed loudly, turning her back to us. "I—I'll be right there," she seemed to struggle to say.

I couldn't help but stare. My goodness, what could possibly have happened to make a woman like Lauren cry? Nigel had moved closer, and with his free hand, he was now rubbing Lauren's shoulder, apparently trying to comfort her.

"Yes. Thank you. Good—good-bye," Lauren choked out and hung up the phone. Or rather, she tried to. In her distraction, she missed it once and then finally rattled it home with what looked like some difficulty. At least, it looked like that until she turned back to Nigel. The tears had miraculously disappeared. She shrugged off Nigel's hand and took a deep breath. "Damn it!" Lauren said. "The cops found Derek!"

Nigel looked as if she'd given him an electric shock. "They did? How?"

Lauren gave him an exasperated look. "What does it matter how? Some snot-nosed kid playing fisherman sighted the car in the river. Really, Nigel, didn't I tell you that the river was not a good idea? *Didn't I?*"

Nigel hung his head, looking for all the world like a little boy being chastised. "Yes, Lauren, you did say that."

As he spoke, the gun wavered a little in his hand. It was no longer pointed directly at Nan and me, but aimed slightly toward the floor. Having the gun no longer pointed in our direction made me breathe a little easier.

Lauren was tapping her foot in exasperation. "We should have buried Derek in Iroquois Park, the way I wanted to. But, no, you had to put him in the river!"

Nigel shrugged, the gun bouncing a little with the movement. "OK, OK, Lauren, I made a mistake. But what's done is done," he said. "What do we do now?"

"I don't know," Lauren said. "I just don't know. Let me think."

By now, I'd actually loosened the knot enough for Nan to move one hand. I felt her give a terrific tug, the rope tightening painfully around my wrist. I hardly even felt the pain, though, because I could tell that Nan had yanked one hand free. *Free!*

Unfortunately, from what I could feel, Nigel had wound the rope in and out, between our wrists, so that both my hands and one of Nan's were still bound.

Nigel must have sensed movement in our direction. He glanced at us briefly, apparently saw nothing amiss, and then turned back to Lauren.

Lauren had gone from foot tapping to striding around the room, her hands on her hips. "The cops want me to come downtown and identify the body. Can you imagine? Ick." She looked over at Nigel. "Can you imagine what Derek looks like now? After floating in that dirty river for this long? Ick. Ick. Ick."

I stared at her. What kind of a person was she? This was the father of her child she was talking about. Lord. And I thought sometimes *I* was being pretty awful, talking badly about Jake, when, after all, he'd given me two wonderful children. Lauren, though, was a lot more than awful. I watched her in total amazement. Wow. There are those who insist that alien beings walk among us, and now I could confirm it. Lauren was an altogether foreign life-form.

I felt movement behind me and glanced back over my shoulder, trying to see what in the world Nan was up to. What I saw made my breath catch in my throat. Nan was very slowly reaching for the cordless phone that Lauren had put on the coffee table. I looked over at Nigel and Lauren. Neither one was looking this way.

Nan snagged the phone and dropped it quickly into her lap, into the dark shadow in the space between the coffee table and sofa.

I looked back at Nigel and Lauren, trying to look as if nothing had happened. I waited, my eyes fixed on the two of them, knowing that Nan was, no doubt, at this very moment, clicking the phone on. I prayed that Lauren's cordless telephone did not make the little ding that mine did at home whenever it was clicked on. I held my breath. I heard absolutely nothing.

"Well, you don't really have to go identify his body, do you?" Nigel asked, following Lauren around the room like an obedient puppy. "I mean, they've got to be sure it's him, or they wouldn't have called you."

I prayed Nan had already dialed 911. Right now. Please, please, God.

Lauren turned to face Nigel. "Of course, I have to go. Are you a total idiot?"

Once again I was amazed. Nigel had the gun now, and still Lauren talked to him this way. The woman had guts galore, or else, it just never crossed her mind that Nigel might react badly to what she had to say. Poor Nigel probably really was a nice guy. A guy who'd fallen for the wrong woman and just possibly committed murder for her. He was, no doubt, a much nicer person than I was, because just listening to Lauren ranting on and on made *me* want to shoot her.

"If I don't identify the body, they're going to suspect me, you moron! It's my husband, after all. I'm the grieving widow."

"Oh." Nigel looked back at us. Nan and I both stiffened in response. "But, what about them?"

Lauren turned to look at us, too. Her face twisted into a frown.

I tried to meet her look head-on, but to tell you the truth, all I was thinking about was that Nan had surely dialed 911 by now. Surely, she had.

"Well, you have to get rid of them," Lauren said.

Nigel's eyes widened. "Me?"

"You've got the gun," Lauren reminded him.

Nigel's eyes dropped to the gun he was holding. He held it out to her. "Well, here. I don't want it."

Lauren threw him a look of exasperation and then looked back to us. "Well, I'm not doing it, Nigel. What's the matter with you? You do it!"

Nigel just stared back at her. "Lauren, for God's sake." That's all he said. I couldn't tell if that meant he was not going to do what she asked, or if he was, but he wanted to go on the record that he wasn't going to enjoy it.

*Nan, have you phoned 911? If you haven't, now would be a good time.*

Lauren glanced back over at Nan and me, her eyes flashing. "You twins are a real problem, you know that?"

"Mom told us that, too," Nan said.

Lauren smirked. "You're not going to be acting so cute when Nigel gets through with—" As she spoke, Lauren's eyes dropped to the coffee table and then grew about three times their normal size. "Where's the phone, Nigel?" she all but shrieked. "Where is the god-damn phone?"

Nigel looked as if Lauren had slapped him. "I didn't do anything with it."

"Well, I certainly didn't," Lauren snapped.

It was at this point that Nan held the receiver up in her one free hand and waggled it at the two of them. "Lauren Stanhope? The nine-one-one operator wants to talk to you," she said loud enough to make herself heard not only to Lauren and Nigel but to anybody on the other side of the line. "The operator already has your address, but she wants to know why you're holding two women at gunpoint."

Lauren turned white. Then both she and Nigel began running around the room, bumping into each other, the two of them looking for all the world like a scene from a Keystone Cops movie. "Oh my God, oh my God, oh my God," Lauren kept saying. Once again she amazed me. Apparently, people really do wring their hands when they're in major distress.

Nigel finally grabbed Lauren by the shoulders. I was really hoping he'd have to slap her to get her calmed down. Unfortunately, all he had to do was give Lauren a little shake. "We've got to get out of here, Lauren!" he yelled. "No telling how long that phone's been live. The police could be here any minute!"

Lauren stopped running around. She turned and stared at us, her eyes flashing. "You bitches!" she shrieked at us. She turned then and ran out of the room. Nigel didn't give us a second glance—he just lumbered after Lauren, the gun hanging loose from one hand.

In the distance, a door slammed. Then there was the sound of a car starting in the driveway, burning rubber as it raced away.

I let out a shaky breath. The silence in the house was wonderful.

"Oh my God, Nan," I said. "I can't believe it. Thank you so much." I turned around as well as I could to look at her.

At the sight of Nan, my heart actually constricted in my chest. "Oh no. Don't tell me," I whispered.

Nan had the cordless phone in her hand, and she

was carefully punching three numbers on the telephone with her free hand.

When she finished making the call to the 911 operator, she glanced back at me. "Oh, get a grip. It worked, didn't it? Besides, the phone was in the shadow, and I couldn't see the keys. One-handed dialing is not anywhere near as easy as you might think."

Oh my God. It was a good thing my hands were still tied, or I might've hit her.

# Chapter Eighteen

## Nan

The bad thing about being a twin is that you can tell, by just a glance, exactly what your twin is thinking. Like, for example, right now it only took one quick look over my shoulder, and I knew that Bert was seriously thinking about doing me bodily harm.

Can you imagine? OK, so I'd bluffed a little about calling 911, and yes, I suppose I had taken a wee bit of a chance when I lied about having dialed the number already. But the ruse had worked, hadn't it? Lauren and Nigel had run out of here as if the entire Louisville police force were hot on their trail. A fact that I sincerely hoped was true, I might add.

Bert should be continuing to thank me, instead of looking at me over her shoulder, her eyes like saucers. With that look on her face, it crossed my mind that it might not be the worst idea in the world if the police took their time getting here. Maybe Bert's hands should stay tied for a while longer, at least until her violent impulses subsided.

Bert did not seem to think that staying tied up held any great appeal, however. She was working at the ropes again, tugging at the knot behind my back.

"You know," I said, "you can stop fooling with that now. The police will come and untie us any minute now."

"Hmm," Bert replied.

If we had any kind of luck at all, the police officers who showed up to untie Bert and me would be absolute strangers. Officers who had no idea who Bert and I were, and who would never, ever tell Hank and Barry about this little fiasco.

Bert's pulling on the rope didn't seem to be helping the situation. If anything, it was tightening the rope around my wrist. I twisted around, trying to get a better look so that I could help with my free left hand, but all that seemed to do was cut off the blood circulation to my right hand, which was still tied.

OK, so where were the police when you needed them? After a minute or so of Bert twisting the rope painfully around my wrist, I was beginning not to care if the first thing Bert did when she got free was belt me one. I just wanted to get loose, that's all. Old Nigel might be a quart low in the smarts department, but he could sure tie one mean knot. The man should consider a naval career. Once he got out of prison, of course.

I guess it wasn't much more than ten minutes that Bert and I sat there, waiting for help to arrive and trying to get the damn ropes undone, but it seemed like a lot longer. Finally we heard a police siren in the distance, growing louder, and then, at last, a car pulling up in the driveway.

Evidently, Lauren and Nigel had left so quickly, she'd failed to lock her front door. Bert and I looked up from working on the ropes to see Hank and Barry standing in the doorway, their hands on their hips. Neither one of them looked particularly happy to see us.

The feeling, let me tell you, was mutual.

OK, so maybe our luck had run out. Considering, however, how very lucky we'd been to get out of our earlier situation still breathing, I didn't think I had any right to complain.

"Hi, Hank," Bert said cheerily.

I waggled the fingers of my free hand at the two of them.

Neither of the men said a word.

That's right. There was no "Thank God you two are all right." No "Is there anything we can do?" Nothing. Not a peep from Superjerk and his sidekick, Wonder Boy.

Hank's sole reaction was pretty much limited to his face. It seemed to implode into one massive frown. After which he stomped over to us, pushed the coffee table aside as if it were made of cardboard, and started working on our ropes.

I heard the click of a pocketknife open as Hank apparently started sawing on the stupid things.

At least, I hoped that was what he was doing with that knife.

Wonder Boy just stood there, smirking. Apparently, seeing twins tied up had made his day.

"What are you smirking at?" I asked.

Barry's answer was a shrug and another smirk.

For the first few minutes, while Hank sliced and diced our ropes, he didn't make a sound other than to grunt occasionally.

Finally Hank muttered, "Are you all right?" His voice was husky.

He was probably talking to Bert, but I thought I'd give him a quick answer. "We're both peachy, OK? This is our idea of togetherness."

Behind me, Bert sighed. "We're fine, Hank—just a little shaky over all this."

Hank made a really unpleasant noise in the back of his throat. Sort of a cross between a sigh and a growl. "So. You want to tell us what happened?"

"We got tied up," I said.

Barry smirked again and reached inside his coat pocket for his notebook. "You want to, like, add a little detail to that?" Barry asked.

I told him the truth. "No," I said.

So Bert filled them in on our adventures. I jumped in briefly only once when she got to the part about how we'd gotten into the Stanhope house. In my version, the front door was unlocked just as it had been when Hank and Barry came in, and we'd entered only because we'd thought that Mrs. Stanhope had called to us from inside. In fact, we were sure we'd heard her. It had been a shock to go inside and find the place empty. My goodness, what a shock it had been.

It would've helped if Bert had not just stared at me, wide-eyed, the entire time I was fabricating my tiny tall tale. When I turned to her for corroboration, she sort of jumped. "Oh yes," she said vaguely, "yes, that's right. We were, um, surprised nobody was home. Really. Surprised."

What could I say? Bert was clearly not cut out for a career in espionage, or law, or—this last, especially—politics.

I could tell, of course, that Hank and Barry didn't believe either one of us for even a second, but who cared? The way I saw it, Bert and I might as well avoid being arrested for breaking and entering, if we could. After all, it was my word against the word of fleeing felons.

By the time Bert had finished telling what had happened, Hank had gotten us free and Bert and I were sitting side by side on the sofa, rubbing our wrists. Hank, of course, had not taken a seat. There was room on the sofa as well as several empty chairs, but you can't do the Disapproving Parent routine anywhere near as well if you're sitting. For maximum effect, Papa Hank chose to stand opposite us, hands on his hips, shaking his head. You could tell what he was thinking: *How on earth could you two be so unbelievably stupid?*

"How on earth could you two be so unbelievably stupid?" he finally asked.

What a surprise.

"Excuse me," I said, "but weren't you the one who

kept saying that Derek Stanhope was still alive? Wasn't that you? In the contest for most unbelievably stupid, I think you're holding your own."

Hank got that imploded frown look on his face again. Barry, however, who'd apparently decided to leave the Disapproving Parent honors to Hank and had taken a seat in the overstuffed chair to our right, simply smirked again. I couldn't decide which was more annoying—Hank's frown or Barry's smirk.

While we were showing Hank and Barry the computers and the deleted e-mail letters that had, in actuality, not been deleted on Lauren's computer, and going over the story for what seemed like the hundredth time, Barry's cell phone chirped. The police had indeed picked up Lauren and Nigel on I-64, heading east out of Jefferson County in her Mercedes. They'd been stopped for exceeding the speed limit—I'd bet they were going a hundred—and they were being brought downtown for questioning.

Hank and Barry immediately decided that Bert and I ought to take a trip downtown, too, to give our statements. I decided it was prudent not to point out that we'd just finished doing exactly that, and I followed Hank and Barry in my car to police headquarters, all the way into downtown Louisville. Bert at the last minute elected to ride with Hank and Barry. Which was just as well. I really preferred not to be in on that conversation.

At the police station downtown, Bert and I were immediately separated and interviewed in adjacent little rooms. My answers were taped for posterity by a truly humorless policewoman who was wearing the standard policeman's uniform: navy shirt buttoned to the neck, navy tie, navy slacks, and heavy black shoes and socks. She was probably a pretty woman when she wasn't wearing clothes that looked like a man's. I spent a lot of the time, as I repeated my story, looking at her very short haircut and wondering if the city paid her enough to dress like this.

The lady cop was just finishing and getting her recording gear together when Hank came back into the room. Ms. Cop gave Hank a quick nod and made for the door, just as Bert walked into the room.

Bert looked exhausted. Naturally, I felt another pang of guilt. Man, I'd really put her through the wringer today.

"Are you OK?" I asked Bert as she walked up.

Bert must've been too tired to remember that she wanted to clobber me, because she just smiled. "I'm feeling a lot better than I did a few hours ago."

I would second that.

Hank and Bert sat down across from me at the table. Next to Bert, Hank was scratching his head, looking confused. In other words, he looked pretty normal.

Then Barry sauntered in and sat down next to me. Wouldn't you know it, he was still smirking.

"It's like this," Hank said. "We've interviewed Lauren and Nigel separately, and, as you would expect, Nigel and Lauren are both claiming that the other one killed her husband. Problem is, they're both pretty convincing."

"We honestly don't know who to believe," Barry added.

"I'd personally go with Lauren," I said. "I think she killed him."

Barry looked over at me. "Why?"

"Because I really, really don't like her."

Barry's answer? You guessed it. He was going to be lucky if I didn't try to slap that smirk off his face.

"I'd vote for Lauren, too," Bert said. "Nigel really isn't that bad a guy."

I turned and stared at her. "Except for the way he ties people up and talks about murdering people, he's a prince."

Bert stared back at me. "I don't think he would've done any of this if he hadn't gotten involved with that awful woman."

"So she's his inspiration!" I said. "What's your point?"

Bert gave me a look. "Nan, I just don't think Nigel is the violent type. Not really."

Oh, for God's sake. Bert is just about my favorite person in the whole world. She is kind, she is sweet, but when she starts doing her you've-got-to-feel-sorry-for-the-bad-guys routine, I just want to scream. Bert actually thought that the Million Mom March was going to work. As if a few thousand mothers mad at murder would get people to stop shooting people. As if adding yet another law for criminals to break was going to end gun violence. When the whole thing had fizzled, she'd been shocked.

I shook my head. "I don't know, Bert, when some guy starts seriously talking about ending my life, I hold it against him. I just think he's not a nice guy. Call me oversensitive."

Hank held up his hand, clearly signaling that this discussion was over.

I hate it when somebody does that to me. I particularly hate it when the guy who's doing it is a cop who has every right in the world to tell me to shut up.

Frowning, Hank said, "Anyway, we're going to put Lauren and Nigel in the same room together and just let them talk. What we're trying to do is see if we can tell which one did the killing. I was thinking it might be a good idea if you and Bert listen to their conversation, just in case something either of them says is different from what they said with you."

"You want us to listen to their conversation?" I asked. Hank nodded.

"So you want us—Bert and me—to do you two a favor?" I asked.

I was simply trying to clarify the situation, that's all. I wasn't saying I was not willing to help out Louisville's finest, I was just letting them know that I understood what was going on here.

Hank, however, frowned again.

"Or we can always tie you up again," Barry offered.

It was, I had to admit, a point well taken.

Hank and Barry then showed us into a room so narrow, it seemed to be more of a closet than a room. The closet was dominated by a large window, in front of which was a line of metal folding chairs. Bert and I took seats on the two center chairs, and Hank and Barry sat down on either side of us, Hank next to Bert, of course, and Barry next to me. "This looks a lot like a scene from *Law and Order*," I whispered to Bert.

She nodded, but I could tell that she wasn't really paying any attention to me. She was trying to be subtle about it, but her eyes kept darting over to Hank about every five seconds.

I, on the other hand, was more interested in the window in front of us. Somehow I just knew that the room on the other side of that window had a large mirror on its wall, instead of the apparently clear window that we were all looking through.

"This is pretty cool," I whispered to Bert again.

"You don't have to whisper, Nan," Barry said. "They can't hear you, even though you can hear them."

"Thank goodness," Bert said.

Nigel and Lauren were both brought into the mirrored room by uniformed police officers, and were seated across from each other at the wooden table in the center of the room.

I couldn't resist. "Slimebags!" I called to them loudly. "Murderers!" The two didn't hear a thing, just sat there earnestly looking into each other's eyes. It was enough to make you sick.

Unfortunately, my companions did happen to hear me. Hank frowned at me, Bert looked startled, and Barry—well, you know what he did.

As soon as the officers left them alone, Nigel and Lauren reached across the table and took each other's hands. "Sweetie pie," Nigel said, patting Lauren's hand.

Lauren actually smiled at him for about a half second, but then apparently she had to revert to her lovable self. "Don't *sweetie pie* me, Nigel," she snapped. "I told you not to go over the speed limit, didn't I? Didn't I?"

Poor old Nigel really needed to get a new girlfriend. Once he was out of prison, of course.

Hank slipped out of our room, and in a second we saw him enter the other room with Nigel and Lauren. The two stiffened as Hank came in and sat down at the head of the table.

Hank clicked on a tape recorder that was in the center of the table. He then introduced himself, told the day and time and that Nigel Hampstead and Lauren Stanhope were there in the room with him. "Since both of you have told us that the other one killed Derek Stanhope, we thought you might like to discuss the matter with each other."

Lauren went white. Her eyes flashed as she turned to Nigel. "Excuse me? You told them *I* killed Derek?"

Nigel had yanked his hands away from Lauren, probably afraid she might use her fingernails on him. He shrugged. "Well, yes, I did," Nigel mumbled. "I had to. They said they found my fingerprints on the car that Derek's body was in." He looked up at Lauren, his expression sheepish. "And, after all, sweet pie, it's the truth. You did do it."

Lauren stared at Nigel, openmouthed. "What are you saying?"

"I'm saying you did it, sweetheart," Nigel answered. As he spoke, he sort of ducked his head, as if he were fully expecting Lauren to belt him.

Lauren looked as if she was considering it. Being in a police station where people actually get arrested for that kind of behavior must've given her pause. "You're a filthy liar!" She looked over at Hank in alarm. "I most certainly did not kill Derek. As God is my witness! I just helped Nigel hide Derek's body. That's all I did. I swear."

Nigel was shaking his head. "No, I helped *you* hide the body," Nigel said. "Derek was already dead when I got to your house."

"Because *you* had killed him!" Lauren yelled, glaring at Nigel. "Tell the truth, Nigel! You sniveling coward! You told me then that you'd killed him. You know you did! When you got to the house after that bitch-twin went away."

I glanced over at Bert, our eyes meeting. It was pretty apparent who Lauren was referring to as that *bitch-twin*. Lauren then had actually been in the house, watching me as I went over to Derek's car. She'd stood there, watching me bang on her front door and then run off to call the police. Her car, no doubt, had been in the garage. I remembered now that the garage door had indeed been closed. I'd been so rattled at having found Derek dead, I hadn't even thought to look inside to see if a car had been in there.

"I only came because *you* called me," Nigel said to Lauren. "Sweetie pie," he added. I was beginning to see what happened. Apparently, Nigel had arrived after I'd left to summon the police. While I was knocking on doors a street over, Nigel had driven Derek's car to the banks of the Ohio River to hide the body. Lauren had followed him in her own car.

Hell, I'd probably even passed Nigel's own car parked somewhere nearby, when I had been running around the neighborhood looking for someone at home. When I'd finally gotten back to the house, Nigel and Lauren had already left with Derek's body. Then she'd returned to the house in her own car, after picking up her daughter at day care.

In the opposite room, Lauren frowned at Nigel. "Don't *sweetie pie* me! *You* told me *you* killed him."

Nigel shook his head again. "No, sweetie lamb, I did not tell you I killed him. I told you that I was responsible for what happened. I was just trying to make you feel better about what you'd done." He turned to Hank. "She killed Derek because of our affair. Because Derek wouldn't give her a divorce."

As if *that* were a big surprise.

Apparently, it was a big surprise to Lauren. "I did NOT kill Derek!" Lauren shrieked. "Nigel killed him so that I would be free and he could be with me. I'm sure Derek made Nigel so angry that he didn't know what he was doing. Derek was like that—he could drive you crazy. Derek was just such an annoying—" At this point, Lauren seemed to realize that what she was saying about being driven homicidally crazy could also apply to her. She stopped in midsentence. "What I mean to say is," she went on, "Derek could make a person very angry. That's why Nigel killed Derek, I'm sure. Because Derek drove him to it."

Nigel just shook his head again. "Maybe Lauren doesn't even know what she did. She was hysterical when she phoned me, wanting me to help her get rid of the body."

"Because you'd killed him and left him in my driveway!" Lauren said. "Where the neighbors could see. Or Cissy!"

"I did not kill Derek!" Nigel said.

"You did, too!" Lauren said.

"No, you killed him," Nigel said.

"You did it!" Lauren said.

I stared at the two of them. That was the problem with relationships today—poor communication.

"You, you, you!" Nigel insisted, getting up from the table and leaning toward Lauren, as if his very size would convince her to confess.

Lauren bounced up, too, her palms flat on the table as she leaned toward Nigel. "You did it, and you know it." Tears were now rolling down her cheeks. "I can't believe you'd try to—to . . ." Her voice trailed off.

Me, I felt like applauding. The woman had talent, I had to hand it to her. The way she could cry on command was amazing.

Nigel did not look all that admiring. "But you killed him, Lauren. You really did." He sounded as if it really pained him to have to say such a thing.

I was beginning to think he had as much talent as Lauren.

Beside me, Barry moved restlessly in his chair. "Whoa, talk about reasonable doubt," he muttered. Wonder Boy was apparently still wondering. From watching all those episodes of *Law & Order*, though, I knew what he meant. Unless they could prove which one killed Derek, no jury would convict Nigel or Lauren. Both could raise reasonable doubt as to individual guilt by pointing at the other one.

Hank looked over at the mirrored window and seemed to be looking straight at us. It came as no surprise that he was once again looking confused.

# Chapter Nineteen

## Bert

After sitting there in that stuffy little room watching Lauren and Nigel for almost a half hour, I still had no idea which of them killed Derek Stanhope. I certainly had no idea how either of them could be proven guilty. What I did know was this: I was really tired of being in a police station. I was really anxious to get out of the viewing room, or whatever they called that tiny stifling room with the ugly metal chairs and the big window in it.

It seemed to take forever for Barry and Hank to finally get tired of watching the unappealing antics of Mrs. Stanhope and her untrained trainer. When Hank finally said, "Well, I guess we'll call it a night," I all but ran for the door with Nan right beside me.

Hank must have anticipated my abrupt break for the

door. He caught up with me in the hallway. Grabbing my arm and pulling me aside, Hank said, "Bert, before you go, I need to talk to you."

Nan came to a dead stop at my side. First she looked over at Hank—it was a drop-dead look if I ever saw one. Then she followed that up with a pointed look in my direction, which said: *"Do NOT, under any circumstances, speak to that cad.* He didn't trust you and got all jealous and has treated you like a complete jerk, and he was flirting with that Julia Roberts cop, so he isn't worth it and maybe you should just let him suffer."

Nan can put a whole lot of meaning into one of her looks.

Or maybe I was just projecting my feelings onto her.

"Hank," I said, "It's late, and I need to get home." I could feel Nan's approval. I started to pull my arm away, and then I got a good look at poor Hank's face. Goodness, he looked as if he had just earned a speaking part in *Les Misérables*.

I couldn't believe I was doing it—I definitely heard an exasperated sigh coming from Nan's direction—but I actually allowed Hank to pull me back into the viewing room. Once inside, Hank just stood there for a moment with his hands in his pockets, looking at the floor. Then he sort of rocked back on his heels. It was really kind of cute, like a little boy caught doing something bad. Unfortunately, he also chose to speak. "I think," he finally managed to get out, "that it is possible that I may have acted very poorly in all this."

I looked at him. Obviously, the remote idea that perhaps I'd been telling the truth and had never ever met the now-deceased Derek Stanhope in cyberspace or any other place was finally dawning on Hank. And it had taken only the fact that two other people had been sending Derek's e-mails to Nan and he now had the computer to prove it to finally convince him. Wow, did that make me feel special.

I cocked my head. "You *think* that it's *possible* that you *may* have?" I couldn't believe it. Did he actually think this was an apology? "Well, my goodness, Hank, anything is possible, isn't it?"

Hank blinked. "OK. OK. I *know* I've acted badly. I've been an ass. I really want to apologize."

I looked at him, still feeling pretty angry about his behavior. And yet, he was apologizing, wasn't he? "All right," I said. "Apology accepted."

"But mostly I want to do this," Hank said. And, before I could react, he pulled me into his arms. I noticed right away that his kiss was not apologetic in the least, but rather tender and insistent at the same time. I intended to be standoffish, to send him the message that I would not put up with the way he'd been acting, and yet before I really knew what I was doing, I'd slid my arms up around his neck and pulled him closer.

At the end of the very long, very wonderful kiss, I pulled my head back and looked up at him. "I thought you didn't make displays of affection at your workplace," I said.

His arms still holding me, as if he never meant to let me go, Hank smiled at me. "For one person, I make an exception."

Now that did make me feel special. I kissed him again.

When I looked up at him next, his face was very serious, his hazel eyes so dark, they seemed almost black. "You remember that thing I asked you to think about?" Hank asked gruffly.

My knees seemed to weaken beneath me. "Yes," I whispered, because I honestly didn't have the strength to speak out loud.

"I know this isn't the place to mention it," Hank said, his arms still around me. "But I'd really like you to think about it. So we can talk about it for real tomorrow night. Will you . . . ? That is, could you . . ." His voice sort of trailed off.

"I'll think about it, Hank," I said, patting his big chest. "I will."

I'm not sure how I managed to turn and walk out of that little room. Because the only thing that was going through my mind after that was something that made me shake inside. It was: *Goodness gracious, I do believe Hank Goetzmann has just pre-asked me to marry him. For the second time.* Only this time, oh my God, this time it had seemed much more firm. I felt a little numb as Hank and I left the little room.

Nan was glowering at me when Hank and I came over to her and Barry. Her look now said, "Are you a pushover or what?"

I smiled at her, wondering when I should tell her what had just happened. Hank wiped the lipstick from his lips with his pocket handkerchief. Of course, behind Hank's back, Barry was doing his smirking again.

That boy could be so annoying.

"So. Are you two going to hold Lauren and Nigel in jail or what?" asked Nan, her tone indicating that she expected both of them to be released immediately to wreak havoc on civilized society.

"Well, we can make a case for kidnapping and terroristic threatening," said Hank, "based on both of your statements to us."

"I understand the threatening part, but kidnapping?" I asked.

"Well, you two were being held against your will," Barry noted. "But, if that's the only case we've got and since no real harm was done to either of you, they may get off. After all, you were in Lauren Stanhope's home without permission. Their lawyer could probably make a pretty good case against you—claim the right of self-protection of personal property or something."

Hank was frowning again. "Not to mention, a good attorney would probably ask in court why you two didn't leave as soon as you realized no one was home. And he might wonder what you were doing looking through private files on Lauren Stanhope's computer."

Nan and I exchanged guilty looks but said nothing. There was no use opening that particular can of worms. At least, not until Lauren's attorney opened it for us.

"Of course," Hank added, "we'll have to wait on ballistics to determine if Mrs. Stanhope's gun was the one used to kill her husband. That'll take a day or so, depending on the backlog in the lab."

"Then you really think Lauren or Nigel killed him?" Nan asked.

Hank shrugged. "Most likely. They both had a motive. Although, if I were to have to choose, I'd lean toward the wife. After all, she was the one who had the most to gain from her husband's death—she'd end up with all their property and full custody of their daughter."

The daughter—I hadn't even thought about that pretty little girl. "Who's taking care of her?" I asked.

"Lauren said her sister had taken the little girl for the night."

I hoped Lauren's sister was prepared to keep her niece for twenty years to life.

Hank went on. "Lauren may have had other motives, too. Stanhope may have had a sizable insurance policy—we still have to check on all that."

"Probably the two of them did it together. And they just hit on a terrific way to get away with murder," Barry said. "To raise doubt, blame each other."

We left it at that. With any luck, Lauren and Nigel would be doing the rest of their personal training under a warden's watchful eye.

Nan drove me home. I had decided not to tell her about what Hank had said until I had a chance to think about it myself. I couldn't help but remember how she'd made fun of the last time he'd pre-asked.

As it turned out, it might've been better if I had brought the topic up. Just for a diversion. Because, after driving in silence for a few miles, with both of us pretty much lost in our own thoughts, Nan started doing a very bad thing. She started thinking out loud. Only it wasn't about Hank and me. It was much worse.

"Bert," Nan said, her eyes on the road but her mind farther away, "if Lauren did plan to kill her husband, why the whole ruse with the dating service?"

I glanced over at her. I'd been thinking about Hank, more or less getting used to the idea of getting married again, so I admit it. I resented her interruption. As far as I was concerned, the Lauren-and-Nigel episode was over. So why even bring this up? "I don't know and I don't care," I said.

Nan ignored me, going right on. "Lauren's signing Derek up with MySoulMate seems like she really was just trying to set up an infidelity cover for herself. In the event of a divorce. Don't you think?"

"I don't know and I don't care," I said again. I just wanted to go home and go to bed and think about Hank. And, of course, to pretend that I had never, ever in my lifetime been tied up with a gun pointed at me. The very thought of it still made my stomach hurt.

Nan pulled off I-64 onto Grinstead Drive. The traffic this time of day was light, one of the only perks I guess from spending a good deal of Friday in a police station.

"Do you really think those two could actually kill anyone?" Nan asked. "They were so lame. Lauren and Nigel actually argued over which one of them should kill us."

I shivered. "Don't remind me." But, now that she mentioned it, I did recall how uncomfortable they both seemed to be with a gun. I also recalled the strange look Nigel had gotten on his face when Lauren had told him to do what he'd done before. I started thinking about it, and then I shook my head. I wasn't going to get into it.

"I mean, wasn't their behavior pretty strange for people who'd killed before? And did you notice that the letters Derek sent to his brother and to Genevieve about his going away were not on his wife's computer? Not a one?" Nan asked, pulling up to a red light. "What about that?"

"I don't know and I don't care," I repeated, rubbing my still painful wrists.

"I mean, Derek really was dead when those e-mails were sent. So who could have sent them, if his wife didn't?"

I looked over at Nan, worried about where she was going with this. "Maybe Nigel did. Maybe Lauren used someone else's computer," I said. "She was on Prodigy." I took a deep breath. "Maybe I don't know, and for sure I don't care."

"But why would she do that? Lauren had a perfectly good system at her home, one that she'd already been using to send Derek's e-mail. Why change?"

"Ignorance and apathy, that's me," I said.

Nan glanced over at me, and then she did another really horrible thing. She made a U-turn, and suddenly we were heading right back the way we had come. It wasn't necessarily horrible because she had broken the law—although, of course, there was *that*. I do believe Louisville's Finest frown on U-turns right in the middle of a heavily traveled street. But what was truly horrible was that we were no longer going home.

I asked the obvious question. "Nan, where are we going?"

She smiled as she drove back up Grinstead toward I-

64. "There's just one more computer I want us to check out. It'll only take a sec."

I groaned. "Which computer?"

Nan smiled even broader. "You don't know and you don't care," she said.

I glared at her. No one likes a smart aleck.

# Chapter Twenty

## Nan

Bert was not in her most cooperative mood. But, hey, I really didn't blame her. That rather unpleasant episode at the Stanhope house with King Kong and his mate had left me a little shaky myself.

Although, if my twin vibes were reacting correctly, there was something else going on with Bert, too. Whatever it was certainly seemed to be weighing on her mind. If I were going to hazard a guess, I'd bet that her visit with Hank inside the viewing room was the reason for that odd look on her face. Still, even with a good portion of her mind obviously somewhere else, it didn't take Bert long to figure out where we were going.

"Derek's office," Bert said, turning to me. "That's it, isn't it? You want to take a look at Derek's computer. At his office downtown."

I shrugged noncommittally and took the ramp onto I-65 North, heading, oh yes, right back downtown.

"How do you think you can even get in?" Bert said. "His office will be locked up tight as a drum, or that Kelly woman will be there."

"I'll get in," I told her.

"You're not going to break and enter again."

"I didn't break the first time."

We were now passing a sign, BROADWAY EXIT, 3 MILES AHEAD. Bert looked rattled. "Just explain to me why we even care," she said. "I mean, you've been proven right, already. Derek Stanhope is really and truly dead. Let it go, for God's sake. Hank knows for sure that I wasn't picking up men on the Internet—"

"He should have known that from the start," I put in.

Bert went right on, as if I hadn't even spoken. "—and so we're out of it. Case closed."

"But the case isn't closed," I said. "The police seem to think it is, but I don't know. It just doesn't make sense. And, Bert, can we really stand idly by and let a murderer go free?"

Bert apparently didn't have to think about that one. "Yes," she said, nodding. "We can really stand idly by and let a murderer go free. Absolutely. It's not our job, understand? We're not in charge of Murderer Apprehension."

I hurried on. "As much as I would love to see Nigel and Lauren put behind bars for a very long time, I really do think it's only fair that they get convicted of a crime they really did commit. Besides, aren't you the least bit curious about all this?"

Bert looked at me. "I knew I never should have gotten you that cat. You've picked up some very bad habits."

I ignored her. "Bert, the police really could be arresting the wrong people."

Bert snapped her fingers. "So that's it. You just want to prove Hank and Barry wrong. Again."

I glanced over at her. Man. Was it possible that I really could be that petty?

The answer came to me in about a nanosecond.

I certainly could.

The Broadway exit loomed ahead, and for the third time in a week, I drove to the entrance of the Commonwealth Building. This time of day, late on a Friday after everyone had gone home from work, I expected to park easily right in front. Unfortunately, someone else already had the same idea. Several someone elses. The closest parking space was four cars up. I glided in, locked the car, and hurried with Bert through the Commonwealth's revolving doors as fast as my little feet could carry me.

I smacked the elevator UP button. Standing beside me, Bert was looking worried. "I really don't think this is a good idea," she said. Big surprise.

"This'll only take a minute," I said. "I just want to get a peek at his e-mail records. That's all." When the elevator ascended and the doors opened, I could see that the fourth floor was empty, too. Everyone was at home or at happy hour, celebrating the end of the workweek. Thanks to Lauren and Nigel, and Louisville's Finest, I'd had an unexpected holiday today.

Fortunately, my radio station always has a backup tape ready to play if, for some reason, a disc jockey can't make it. Whenever I'm absent or call in sick or whatever, WCKI plays a tape called "The Best of Nooners with Nan." Before anybody gets the wrong idea and thinks I'm responsible, I want to make it clear that "Nooners with Nan" is the name WCKI's program director picked to call my show. He said it would be "catchy." He was right. Every time I hear that name announced, my breath catches in my throat. I also want to make it clear that, in reality, there is no "best" of Nooners. There's just a stack of recordings of past shows that somebody grabs at the last minute and puts on the air. Today I'd be lucky if WCKI hadn't played a Christmas show.

As we approached the doors to Derek Stanhope, Graphic Design, we could see that there were no lights showing through the crack under the door. Bert turned to me and actually smiled. "See? I'll bet this place has been locked up tight. We might as well go on home because we're never going to get . . ."

Her voice trailed off when she saw the office key dangling from my hand—one of the three keys I'd removed from the Stanhope house earlier. The label on it had been difficult to read because the writing was nothing much more than hen scratching. But I'd finally made it out: OFFICE-DOWNTOWN.

"Drat," Bert said.

The key turned easily in the lock, and Bert and I slipped inside. Luckily, Kelly, the panic-prone girl Friday, was nowhere in sight. The poor girl was probably already at her therapist for a much-needed session on how to deal with irate clients.

"If we get arrested for breaking and entering . . . ," Bert began.

"We're not breaking, we're just entering. Besides, I have a key—"

"—which you stole," Bert finished for me.

"—which I borrowed," I amended. "I have every intention of returning it." I flipped on the overhead fluorescent lights, which seem to be the lighting of choice for every office in corporate America. Apparently, all business managers want their workers to look sickly green. The Stanhope office appeared sickly green and absolutely deserted. How very nice for us.

The key I'd used to open the outer office also fit the door to Derek's personal office. Once inside Derek's office, Bert flipped on more overhead fluorescent lights; then we both headed over to the large walnut desk in the center of the room. I sat down at Derek's desk and swiveled around to face his Compaq monitor on the credenza behind his desk.

Bert tapped her foot, looking around uneasily. "Just make it snappy."

I flipped the ON switch for Derek's computer and was rewarded with the gratifying hum of electronic machinery as it powered up.

Then I went through the same procedure as I had with Derek's home computers. As with those, I found I could log on to Derek's e-mail server easily; here, too, he'd saved his password. All I had to do was hit the ENTER key, and I was in. The computer supplied Derek's user name and password.

Man, don't you love high technology?

"Look, Derek's Internet provider here in the office is Prodigy," I said. "How much you want to bet we'll find those letters to Benjamin and Genevieve on this computer?"

With Bert looking over my shoulder, I clicked the computer mouse a few times and connected to Derek's e-mail program automatically.

I held my breath as I opened the on-screen file folder labeled SENT MAIL by clicking on its little picture.

The file was empty.

Bert must've been holding her breath, too, because there was a sort of *whoosh* next to my left ear as she exhaled. "OK, that does it," Bert said. "There's nothing there. We had our look. Now let's get outta here."

"Wait a minute," I said. I clicked on the other file folders that made up Derek's e-mail files. I need not have bothered. The password to get on the e-mail server seemed to be the only thing that Derek Stanhope had saved. Three of the little folders—SENT MAIL, RECEIVED MAIL, and OUTGOING MAIL—were all empty.

I looked at Bert. "The question is," I said, "did Derek himself delete the contents of these folders? Or did someone else do it for him?"

Bert's response was expected. "I don't know and I don't care. The real question is: How soon can we get out of here?"

"Get a grip," I said. "I'm almost done." I clicked open the picture of the little recycling bin on the screen. "Nothing," I said. "Either he emptied the trash before he died, or—"

"—someone did it for him," Bert finished. "Right, right. Let's go."

I began clicking on items in his e-mail program. The only thing that didn't look as if someone had purposefully deleted its contents was his address book. This was the list of the people and their e-mail addresses to whom Derek Stanhope sent e-mail messages regularly. By selecting all the people in an address book, he could automatically send messages to anyone in the book without having to physically type each of their e-mail addresses, a process that can be pretty time-consuming. In fact, by choosing all the persons in the address book, you could conceivably send a message to everyone Derek knew.

I noticed that despite her agitation Bert leaned closer to me as we quickly scanned the list. There was his brother, Genevieve, the secretary Kelly at her home, Derek's wife and his own home computer, his minister, some couples who were apparently in his church group, if you could believe the notation included on their listing, as well as the e-mail addresses of about fifty or so clients.

I stared at the list, thinking. It was such a nice long list of everyone Derek knew and communicated with. If Lauren and Nigel turned out not to be guilty, it was very probable that one of these people had killed him. The list gave me an idea.

"Well, that's it," Bert said, turning toward the door. "This has been fun, but it's time to go."

I began typing an e-mail message of my own, first clicking on the address book to prepare the memo to be addressed to everyone in Derek's address book.

Bert put her hand on my shoulder. "What in the world are you doing?"

I continued to type without looking up. "I would bet that the discovery of Derek's body has not had time yet to be on the early evening news. So a lot of the people he knows won't even know he's deceased. Except, of course, one person, who—if it isn't Lauren or Nigel, which is, I admit, a pretty big *if*—has got to be wondering what the hell happened to him."

Bert was obviously impressed by my amazing deductive ability. "Oh, for God's sake," she said.

I continued to type. "Since most of the time when you shoot a person dead, they pretty much stay in one place, Derek's shooter has got to be pretty damned puzzled." I finished my note and rolled back with the chair, allowing room so Bert could lean in and read my little epistle. "What do you think?"

Bert didn't even try to read the message. "I think that this is not a good idea," she said. "Sending the same message to several people at once on the Internet is known as *spamming*. I suppose you know that spamming is pretty much frowned upon over the Internet. Brian says so."

"That's for advertisements. Besides, murder is frowned upon, too," I reminded her. *"Anywhere."*

I read my note again.

> *To quote Mark Twain, the rumor$ of my death are greatly exaggerated. Like Mark Twain, I'm ready to tell my $tory. Unless you can give me a rea$on not to. If you want to di$cu$$ it, meet me at my office now. Derek.*

"Subtle," Bert said, now reading over my shoulder. "You're really not thinking of sending that, are you?"

I nodded, smiling.

Bert shook her head, frowning. "Nan, you might be sending an e-mail message to a murderer. To a person who shoots people, and leaves them to die in cars."

"That's the idea."

"Nan," Bert said, grabbing my hand, "you don't want to get to know somebody like this! You definitely don't want to correspond with them!"

I wrenched my hand away, blocked her with my shoulder, and before she could stop me, I reached over and used the mouse to click on the SEND button.

The computer hummed.

Bert gave a little shriek of alarm. "Aack!" she said. Really, that's exactly what she said. As if *aack* were a word.

"Get a grip," I said. "I just want to see who writes him back. Or who shows up. Probably no one. It's a long shot, I know."

Bert, however, apparently felt there was more of a chance for a response than I did. "You want to see if a murderer shows up here? Are you out of your mind?"

That remained to be seen.

# Chapter Twenty-one

## Bert

OK, it was official. Nan had gone crazy. I knew it would happen one day, and that day had finally come. Nan's mental train had slipped the tracks. I could not believe that Nan would actually take a chance on inviting a murderer to drop by.

Surely, though, the whole idea was ridiculous. The real killers of Derek Stanhope were his less-than-devoted wife and her-more-than-devoted lover.

Oh yes, the idea of it being anyone else was ridiculous. Please, God, let it be ridiculous.

I have to admit, though, as soon as Nan clicked on the little SEND button, I actually got a shiver up my spine. It suddenly occurred to me that anything was possible. And I really didn't relish another encounter like the one we'd had this morning.

As far as I was concerned, we'd been lucky to walk away from that one, and I really didn't think we should be tempting fate more than once a day. Come to think of it, once a lifetime to tempt fate would actually be my goal. The computer finally stopped humming, but I couldn't seem to tear my eyes away from the computer screen.

"What have you done?" I asked.

Nan looked up and actually grinned at me. As if all this was just one big joke to her. "I've sent e-mail," she said.

She obviously needed to be outfitted in one of those lovely garments with extremely long sleeves that wrap around a few times and tie in the back.

"Nan, what if this e-mail is successful? Have you even thought about that? Just look at us, we're sitting ducks here. We need to get away from here. And we need to do it right this second."

"Get a grip," Nan said.

Have I mentioned how very tired I was of hearing her say that?

The computer gave a little chirp, and both of us jumped like there'd just been a gun fired in the immediate vicinity.

"That's probably the sound Stanhope's computer makes whenever he receives an e-mail," Nan said. She turned back toward the computer.

I made it as plain as I could. "Nan, I want to go NOW."

Nan leaned forward, clicking on the RECEIVED MAIL folder in order to retrieve the e-mail message. A person called E. Blevins, probably one of Derek's clients, replied, *Hey, what kind of joke is this, buddy? I hope this doesn't mean your rates are going up. Ha-ha.*

Even as we read the thing, the computer continued to chirp, announcing more responses. When Nan went back to the IN BOX this time, there were five unread messages, all indicated by bold type. We opened the messages one at a time; they ranged from confused good humor to outright irritation. The last message, from a T. McClellan, inquired, *So, Derek, have you been drinking or what?*

While we read these, there were still more chirps, signaling the arrival of more messages. All in all, there turned out to be twenty-three.

I was really surprised to see how many people were writing immediate responses. But, then again, it was Friday night and still too early for dinner and prime-time television. In other words, it was exactly the time when those folks who have home computers sit down in front of glowing screens and start visiting chat rooms, paying their bills, or just surfing the Web. Not to mention, if you didn't have a real date on Friday night, then Friday would probably be the night you'd get online, trying to hook up with somebody as the weekend ahead loomed.

Nan and I read each e-mail message in order of arrival. Unfortunately, just as I would think that we were finally done and might get to leave, the computer would chirp again. Fortunately—or maybe unfortunately—none of the messages seemed the least bit murderous in tone.

Reading Derek's e-mail, I did get a glimpse of the man whom these people had known, a man who had really been little more than a name to me before. The Derek Stanhope these people knew had been well-liked, sociable, and respected in his work. He also seemed to be active in his church, since he got a couple of notes that began: *Brother Stanhope, what's this all about?* Some went on to mention something about the work he was doing for them, or to tell him a joke or anecdote. It seemed more than a little sad to think that the man whom all these people were writing was no longer alive, his e-mail server pretty much shut down for eternity.

I began to feel uncomfortable, as if we were reading someone's private, and very personal, letters. Which, of course, we were. It somehow seemed disrespectful of the dead.

"Nan, come on," I said, "let's get out of here, OK?"

When I glanced at my watch, I was surprised to realize how long we'd been sitting there. For God's sake, it had been almost a half hour. So far, there'd been no messages from anybody Nan and I had met, none from Genevieve or Benjamin, both of whom we knew had computers. "Nan, we've really got to leave," I repeated.

"We ought to stick around a little while longer just to see if anyone shows up." She stood up, looking around. "Come on, let's find some place for you to hide out in the hallway. Out there, you can see if anyone comes inside," Nan suggested.

I gave her a look that said what I thought of that idea. "And where exactly will you be?" I asked.

Nan walked over to the nearest door, opened it, and looked inside. "Looks like I'll be hiding in a bathroom."

I started shaking my head. "Oh no, you don't. If you think I'm going to leave you inside this office, all by yourself, you're crazier than you were when you sent that message in the first place."

All right, all right, I was beside myself.

Nan stared back at me for a silent moment, crossing her arms over her chest. "Look, Bert, I'm not stupid. I'm not going to confront the person. I just want to see who it is. Then we'll tell Hank or Barry. We need to do this."

"No, we do not need to do this. Both of us need to be getting out of this office," I said. I ran my hands through my hair. "I only wish that we'd never come here, and that you'd never been able to get into that poor man's e-mail."

Nan stared at me, her eyes getting larger. "Now that I think about it, that's right," she said. "We were able to get on to Stanhope's e-mail as easy as anything, weren't we?" She turned and headed back to the desk. Going around to face the computer, she said, "I just wonder—"

I followed her. "Nan!" I said, pulling at her arm. "We've got to go!"

Nan shrugged off my hand and reached for the telephone. "What do you think, do you suppose he has to dial nine to get an outside line?"

"Don't touch that phone," a woman's voice said. "I mean it. Don't TOUCH it!"

My stomach gave a sudden wrench. I'd been looking at the phone, but something told me that when I looked toward the door, I'd see yet another awful person holding a gun on Nan and me. This was really getting to be a horrible habit.

Sure enough, when I looked up, there was a handgun there, with a person right behind it. My heart seemed to drop to my shoes. It didn't help that the weapon was aiming directly at my chest. Naturally, with the thing pointed right at me, I saw the gun first. In fact, that piece of metal seemed to fill the entire room. Then I slowly raised my eyes to the face of the person holding that enormous weapon. I actually gasped when I saw who it was.

"Kelly?" I asked. Standing just inside the door, on the other side of Derek's desk, the poor girl looked awful—even more nerve-wracked than she'd been the last time we'd seen her. Her auburn hair looked as if she hadn't even combed it for the last couple of days—it hung limply on the sides, with the top portion looking oily and mussed, sticking up here and there like a punk rocker. The wrinkled suit she wore was the same one she'd been wearing when we'd visited this office last, but the wide run in the hose on her right leg was new. Her eyes were new in a way, too—they seemed to be lit from behind by a strange luminosity. I wondered when she'd slept last. And what she'd been taking to look that strung out.

I glanced over at Nan, as she slowly pulled her hand away from the telephone. From the look on Nan's face, I could tell that the sight of Kelly holding a gun on us was not as big a surprise to her as it was to me. Simultaneously, Nan and I slowly raised our hands.

"Hi, Kelly," Nan said, waggling her fingers. "Mr. Stanhope's secretary, isn't it?"

"Derek Stanhope's executive assistant," Kelly corrected, her tone haughty. She glared at us. "What the hell are you two doing, coming around here again? Being a pain in the ass."

No doubt, she meant pains in the ass. Plural. Or was it pain in the asses? I actually stood there for a moment, trying to decide. It's amazing what trivialities will go through your mind when you're absolutely terrified.

"Actually," Nan said, "we were just leaving. And we can explain what we're doing here. Really we can."

"SHUT UP!" The gun did a little dance in her hand as Kelly spoke. I really hoped she wasn't holding that thing too tightly. And that the finger she had on the trigger was resting there very lightly. It would be a real shame if she shot me and really didn't mean to.

Kelly looked slowly around the rest of the office, aiming the gun now at Nan. Having the gun pointed in Nan's direction was even worse than having it pointed at me. I could hardly stand to look at it, for fear a bullet would be emerging any second now. I didn't know how I could bear it if I had to stand here and watch Nan get shot. My mouth went dry.

"So where is he?" Kelly asked.

"Where's who?" I managed to say.

"Where's WHO? What do you mean, where's who?" Kelly said. Her voice really sounded borderline hysterical. "DEREK, of course. Who do you think?"

"He's not here, Kelly," Nan said. Her voice had suddenly gotten very soft, very gentle.

Kelly took that bit of information well. She fired.

The unbelievably loud sound of the gunshot seemed to reverberate inside my head as splinters from the top of the walnut desk sprayed around us. Fortunately, the desk must've been one solid piece of furniture, because the bullet didn't come through.

At the sound of the shot, Nan and I jumped together, like trained twin dogs in a circus act. My heart began beating so hard, it sounded like a drum in my ears. Unlike Nigel and Lauren, this was a person who was not at all afraid of pulling the trigger.

To make that point, she'd shot a neat hole in the front of Derek's desk.

Kelly leveled the gun at both of us this time, pointing the gun first at me, then at Nan. "OK, I'll ask you two again. Where the hell IS he?"

"He's at the morgue, Kelly," Nan said. "Don't you remember? You shot him."

I turned to stare at Nan. Kelly? Kelly shot Derek Stanhope?

Kelly frowned. In my opinion, it is not a good thing to see someone holding a gun frown. Especially someone as loosely wrapped as Kelly seemed to be. She shook her head, as if she were clearing away cobwebs. "But Derek sent me an e-mail from here. Just a few minutes ago." Her voice was a child's whine.

"That was me, Kelly," Nan said, her own voice very, very gentle. "*I* sent the e-mail. Just like you sent the e-mail from Derek to Benjamin and Genevieve."

Kelly looked at Nan, squinting now, as if she was trying to focus her eyes. "Well, I had to. I had to make them think that he was still alive so that I would have an alibi for the time of his death. I had to keep Derek alive while I thought what to do. I—I had to keep him alive." Her face crumpled for a second, as if she was about to cry. Then she seemed to catch herself. She took a deep breath and glared at Nan. "How the hell did you know I sent the e-mail?"

"I didn't," Nan said. Her voice was as soothing as lotion. "I just guessed, Kelly. Because you lied when there was no good reason for you to lie. You told us that you couldn't access Derek's e-mail because you didn't know his password. But we just found out that you didn't need to know it."

Kelly's chin went up. "Well, of course, I could read his e-mail. I was his executive assistant. I was important to him. I had to see who he was writing and who was writing to him. I had to. And then he up and fires me, just like I was nothing to him." Her eyes welled with tears.

I stared at her. Derek fired her because she read his mail?

And then she killed him because he fired her? My goodness, if that was a reason for murder, it would be open season on bosses all over the country.

"I'm really not a bad person," Kelly went on, brushing the tears away from her eyes with her free hand. "I never wanted to hurt anybody."

Having a gun in her hand as she said this pretty much destroyed her credibility, but I nodded anyway. "No, of course not," I said.

"Derek was the one," Kelly said. "He made me do it. Four years, that's how long I've been seeing him. I know I look a lot younger, but I'm thirty years old. *Thirty* years old."

Actually, today she looked more like fifty. "Wow, you look a LOT younger," Nan said.

"You sure do," I said.

Kelly shrugged. "Yeah, well, four years is a long time to devote to one man, girls. And I don't make it a habit to date married men, either, but you saw him. Wasn't he gorgeous? He was irresistible. God, how I loved that man. And he kept telling me, yes he did, he kept promising me that he was going to leave Lauren."

So Benjamin had been wrong. Derek had a girl-friend on the side, after all. I thought of what Lauren had said about all those late nights of his at work. Now that I heard it from Kelly, I didn't know why I hadn't thought of it before. After all, toward the end of our marriage, Jake had started spending a lot of late nights at work too—with his own secretary. Or, as Nan so in-delicately referred to her, his executive assistant.

Kelly looked over at me, that superior look on her face again. "Lauren was unfaithful first," Kelly went on, as if that excused everything. "For *years.* Eventually Derek couldn't ignore what was between us. He fell deeply in love with me." She said it as if she was trying to convince herself.

Nan was nodding. "Kelly," she said, "we girls have to stick together. Bert and I won't tell anyone about this."

I nodded. "Really, we won't," I added.

For an answer, Kelly fired the gun again.

The splinters of dark wood jumped around us again. And, of course, Nan and I did our circus dog act again.

Kelly really needed to stop shooting her gun. The smell of smoke was making me feel a little dizzy, and my head was starting to pound.

"This whole thing was all because of you," Kelly said to Nan. Her eyes were looking strangely luminous again. "Or maybe it was you." She used the gun to point at me. "I don't know. It was one of you."

I wasn't about to help her decide.

"Whichever it was, if you hadn't shown up at work that day, everything might've turned out different. But no, you had to come up to us and flirt with him while we were standing waiting for the elevator. So, naturally, I just wanted to know who you were. That's all. I just asked Derek a few little questions when we got up to the office, and he gets all weird on me. All at once, he's like somebody I don't even know. Yelling at me, bawling me out. Going on and on about how sick he is of my being jealous all the time."

I recalled seeing her at the elevator. She had turned to ask Stanhope something as Nan walked away. Now that I thought about it, Derek had looked a little put off by her question. Kelly must have pressed the issue again when they got back to the office. In fact, I had a feeling that what Kelly was saying now was not a totally accurate description of what had gone on.

Kelly hurried on, her eyes looking stranger and stranger as she talked. "Then Derek says that he thinks he's going to make up with his wife, but even if he doesn't, it's better that we make a clean break. Then he actually fires me. Just like that. For nothing!"

I glanced over at Nan, knowing that she was thinking the same thing as I was. Derek had not fired Kelly for nothing. This had not been the first time that Kelly had made a scene about another woman. Derek Stanhope had obviously decided that he'd simply had enough.

Kelly said, "Derek tells me he's going home for a

while, and I am to clean out my desk while he's gone, like maybe I'm just his maid or something. Well, I'm nobody's fool. I heard what you said to him at the elevator. One of you, anyway. You said 'MySoulMate.org.' That's the Web site you mentioned. So as soon as Derek leaves, I get on the Internet in here, and I look it up."

I exchanged another glance with Nan. Good Lord. What Nan had said to Derek Stanhope had gotten him killed. Just like that.

Kelly hurried on, her voice getting more and more agitated as she kept pointing her gun first at Nan and then at me. "And I see his profile on MySoulMate. I see it and I know. He was just getting rid of me so he could look for another girlfriend—that was what he was really doing."

I wondered what Kelly would say if we told her that it was his wife who'd listed him on that service, not Derek Stanhope himself. Something in her frantic behavior, though, told me that she wouldn't believe us. It also told me that Kelly was winding down her story, and when she did, she would have to do something about us. I began to look for something to use as a weapon. There was only the massive desk between Kelly, her gun, and us.

Let me see, there was a computer, a monitor, a keyboard, and a mouse. Not exactly your arsenal of weapons. The heaviest thing on the desk was the monitor, but I do believe Kelly could easily shoot me before I had a chance to pick it up and throw it at her. Not to mention, I wasn't at all sure if I could throw a monitor very far. The computer itself was lighter, but I'd have to be moving at lightning speed to throw it before Kelly could shoot.

"I was so mad. I wanted Derek to know what I'd found out, so I followed him out to his house," Kelly was going on. "I got there just as he pulled into the driveway. I certainly wasn't planning to shoot him."

*Except that you brought a gun with you,* I thought. *So what was that for? To make sure you got his attention?*

"I just wanted to get him to listen to me, that's all. But Derek wouldn't listen to anything I had to say. He didn't even act like he was interested." Her voice was getting that hysterical edge again. Not a good sign. "He actually *waved* me away. Like—like a servant! Said for me to stop bothering him. Well, I couldn't let him get away with treating me like that. I had to *show* him."

What she showed him was a few bullets. Heading rapidly his way.

Kelly's breath was now coming in broken gasps as she remembered what she'd done. "So I left him there. And then, *nothing happened.*" Her voice took on an eerie quality. "No one called to say that he was dead, or that he was shot, or anything. His wife didn't know where he was, his brother, nobody. It was just as if he'd *disappeared.*"

Nan glanced over at me again, and I knew that we were both remembering Kelly the day we'd met her. We'd thought she was panicking over Derek not coming in to work, but she was going crazy because she thought no one had found his body. She wasn't taking phone calls, because she was terrified.

"OK, so I keep thinking maybe he's all right, maybe I

didn't do what I think I did, but then I think, well, even if he's alive, it can't be OK, because he *knows* what I did. I keep waiting, I keep thinking that they're coming to get me, or worse, that *he's* coming to get me." Her voice was shrill with panic again. "It was awful, you know?"

As she spoke, I stared at her wild eyes, her straggly hair. What could it have been like for her these past few days? My God, she must've been going crazy. Literally. I might've actually felt a little sorry for her, except, of course, I got the impression that she was telling us all this just to make sure everybody in the room understood that it really wasn't her fault that she was being forced to kill us. I hated to tell her, but it was going to be pretty difficult to get Nan and me to see her point of view.

On the other hand, considering what was clearly coming next, she was welcome to try to convince us for, oh, the next several years. In fact, I really wished that she would.

Kelly's eyes hardened as they started doing the familiar Twin Bounce, looking first at Nan and then back to me. Her face pale and drawn, she was not a pretty woman at all anymore. "You know something else?" she asked. "You really should have stayed away from Derek," she said.

She raised the gun and pointed it straight at me.

# Chapter Twenty-two

## Nan

I gasped as Kelly raised the gun toward Bert.

"Drop!" I yelled, grabbing Bert's arm. I pulled as hard as I could, dragging her with me, as she and I dropped to the floor behind the desk. The only thing that stood between us and this nutty homicidal woman was Derek Stanhope's huge mahogony desk. It had already taken a couple of bullets, and they had not passed through its massive bulk. I was counting on it to keep its record going.

When we dropped out of sight, Kelly let out a little yelp. "No!" Her voice went as high as a little girl's. "Get up, get up, get up!" she yelled. For emphasis, apparently, a bullet slammed into the paneling behind us. When the gun went off, Bert and I flinched in unison.

Other than putting another hole in the paneling, though, the shot seemed to do no other damage.

I pointed to the kneehole under the desk, the huge size of which made it actually possible that we could both fit in there. Bert immediately nodded. She backed butt first into the kneehole, getting down as far as she could on her hands and knees, and motioning me to follow. I hesitated.

"Stand up, you two. Right now!" Kelly had to be kidding. She must've been high on something, because anybody sober would've realized by now that there was no way we were showing ourselves again. Unless we had to.

I couldn't be sure—since I couldn't see her—but judging from the sound, I think Kelly actually did stamp her foot as she sent still another bullet slamming into the paneling above us.

I looked at Bert, her face a pale oval in the shadows of the desk, her hands now frantically motioning me inside. Lord, she had to be folded up in there like a Japanese fan. She'd called us sitting ducks before. We'd really be sitting ducks in that kneehole waiting for a crazy woman with a gun to find us.

From the other side of the desk, I now heard Kelly's high heels on the move as she started around the desk. My heart leaped to my throat. On my hands and knees, I quickly scrambled around to the other side of the desk, gauging my progress with the sound of Kelly's heels. One thing about being on the radio, you acquire an acute sense of hearing from constantly training yourself to listen critically to the quality of the sound you're producing. Not only that, but you get a really good sense of time, of just exactly how long it actually takes to do something. I figured I had about the time it takes to play two radio spots to get us out of this mess.

As Kelly came clipping on her heels around the back of the desk, I scooted backward on my hands and knees, moving silently on the plush carpeting. I made it to the side of the desk, just as the sound of Kelly's heels came around the back on the other side. I huddled there, listening.

I could hear Kelly grunt with annoyance when she saw no one behind the desk.

Now she would either come the rest of the way around, gun at the ready, and I was a dead woman; or she would stop first to take a quick look into that knee-hole. I prayed she would not let that darkened spot go uninvestigated. I heard her heels take a step or two and then stop. The split second the sound stopped, I forced myself to peek around. Kelly was turning her back to me then and beginning to lean over to look into the kneehole.

The radio commercials were almost over.

I sprang to my feet and ran around to the back of the desk again. In one fluid motion, I grabbed the keyboard of the computer, yanking it free from its connection, its cords hanging loose. Kelly had certainly heard my approach, but she'd been facing the other way, leaning down, preparing to look under the desk. As she stood back up to face me, she had to turn her whole body toward me, along with that terrible gun. It took her no more than a split second, but it was all the time I needed. I pulled the keyboard back and backhanded her with it, keys side up, as hard as I could, right in the face.

I think I heard Kelly's nose crunch. I know I saw her reel back, clutching her nose with her free hand. She fell sprawling on the top of the desk. Blood was running out of her nose, and I could plainly see the imprints of computer keys on her cheeks and chin. Even with all this, the woman still managed to hold on to that damn gun.

Bert had scrambled out of her hidey-hole and started tugging at the handgun with both hands, careful to keep its barrel pointed away from us. The gun went off again, taking out the computer monitor in a shower of sparks.

Smoke filled the room as I brought the edge of the keyboard down again, this time on Kelly's wrist. Kelly squealed and finally let go of the gun, jerking away her injured wrist. You'd think she'd give up, once the gun was gone; but, as I believe I have mentioned before, Kelly was nuts. With a snarl, she grabbed a fistful of hair on the side of my head with her uninjured hand and twisted. It felt like she was trying to tear off the entire side of my head. I screamed, and Bert lifted the gun, holding it now in both hands.

I really didn't want Bert to have to shoot this bitch. So I turned toward Kelly again, her hand twisting in my hair, and used both of my own hands to slam her with the keyboard edge on the side of her head. Hard. Really hard. In fact, as hard as I possibly could.

Kelly staggered back, fell across the desktop, and

then slid to the floor, her mouth open, her nose dripping more blood. I stood above Kelly's slack form, holding the keyboard aloft, mentally daring her to move. She didn't.

As I backed up, panting, Bert came closer, training the gun on Kelly. "My goodness," she said. "Are you all right?"

Before I could tell Bert that I was fine except for the excruciating pain on the side of my head where Kelly had, no doubt, removed a hunk of my hair, a male voice from the doorway said, "Wow. Catfight."

It was Barry. Who else?

Hank came in right after him, mumbling about the lack of parking this time of night.

When he caught sight of us and the smoking computer, he didn't seem to know what to say. "What on earth?" His words seemed to dry up when I moved to one side so he could get a good look at Kelly, lying unconscious on the floor. Then, of course, he spotted Bert in the corner with a gun in her hands. His eyes got so big, he looked like a giant Pokémon.

Needless to say, Bert and I spent the following few hours at the police station, enlightening Hank and Barry about Kelly and her murderous, jealous rages. Hank, of course, spent the following few hours shaking his head. And Barry, well, let's just say he became the Smirk Champion of the World.

According to Hank, he and Barry had started thinking everything over, and they, too, had come down to Derek's office to take a look at his computer.

When she came to, Kelly found herself strapped

down on a gurney and on her way to the psych ward for a little mental drying out. Her trial doesn't start until next year, but it looks as if she is going to be behind bars for a very long time.

It didn't help her case any to appear on WHAS-TV news and say that she hadn't really meant to kill anybody. That it was all Derek's fault. "If he'd treated me right, I would've treated him right."

It made perfect sense to me. Kelly also had a couple of episodes at the Jefferson County Jail, yelling and screaming and trying to punch that young cop who'd been talking to Hank outside the courthouse that day. Shortly after that, from what I read in the paper, that young cop resigned from the force. She was quoted in the paper as saying, "I knew I would be dealing with criminals. I just had no idea that I'd have to deal with crazy people, too."

Kelly did look not at all well on the evening news, hyperventilating and wild-eyed, and talking on and on about Derek. Sometimes, to hear her talk, you'd have thought the man was still alive. I suppose killing someone and then having them disappear into thin air for a few long, long days could really send a person over the edge. I have a feeling, with Kelly's history of jealous tantrums, she never had been any too tightly wrapped in the first place.

It's amazing after all the things that happened, how quickly life can still return to normal. No doubt, it's a testament to the resilience of the human species. That Friday night, after we'd spent far too many long, long hours at the police station and we'd finally gotten home in the wee hours of the morning, this particular example of the human species fed my cat, fixed myself some soup and a cheese sandwich, and then crawled into bed, thinking I would sleep for about a week.

But the next morning I was up at my usual time. I drove to WCKI, did my Saturday shift, making up for my absence of the day before, just as if no one had recently held Bert and me at gunpoint. Twice.

Bert seemed to bounce back pretty quickly, too. A day or so later, my head had finally stopped aching, and I'd just settled down when the front doorbell rang. When I answered, Hank and Bert stuck their heads in my door. Hank was actually dressed in a suit. Not a uniform, but a real suit. I wasn't sure if I'd ever seen him dressed up before. Bert was dressed up, too, in a black wool dress and matching coat, high heels, with hair pulled back into soft waves held by a black velvet bow. It was obvious the two of them were on their way out to dinner.

Hank had his arm around Bert's waist, but the guy still looked like a cop to me, suit or no suit. I barely remember dating the guy myself, so I don't know what we had looked like together. However, every time I see Bert and him together, it always looks to me as if Bert is under house arrest.

Hank wasted no time in getting to the point. "Bert told me that you'd want to know that the gun you two took from Kelly Putnam was tested by ballistics. It was the gun that killed Stanhope, all right."

I tried my best to look surprised. "No kidding," I said.

"Lauren and Nigel are out on bail. We skipped the case involving you two and charged them with Illegal

Disposal of a Corpse. We thought about Littering and
Water Contamination, but then there's the current condition of the Ohio River to contend with. Might be hard
to prove any damage. You can still press charges for
their holding you all, but I'd advise against it unless you
want them to countercharge with breaking and entering. Could be messy." Implicit in his tone was something akin to: *You deserved what you got.*

I shrugged and glanced over at Bert to see how she
was taking all this.

Tucked into the crook of Hank's arm, Bert was looking idly around my apartment while Hank was speaking. I stepped in front of her, trying to block her view
into the apartment, but it was too late. She'd already
spotted what I was hoping she'd miss.

At the far end of the room, my computer screen
glowed like a beacon on my desk. She looked first at it,
her eyes widening, then at me. One look at my face, of
course, and she knew.

Damn. Have I mentioned that it's rough being twins?

"I can't believe it! You've listed yourself on the
Internet again!" Bert said.

I shrugged, waiting for what I knew she'd say next. I
wasn't disappointed.

"Are you out of your mind?"

"Now, Bert, this time I'm just listing me. My profile,
my information, that's all."

"I repeat, are you out of your mind?"

"No, I am not," I insisted. I looked over at Hank, who
was busy looking at his shoes. He wasn't stupid—he was
staying out of this.

"Look, I think I have as good a chance finding a nice person on the Internet as I do in the real world."

Bert raised an eyebrow.

"All right, look at Derek Stanhope. He hooked up with Kelly of all people, and he'd been talking to her face-to-face every single day."

"I repeat," Bert said, "are you out of your mind?"

I tried another approach. "OK, let me ask you something—have you talked to your daughter lately?"

Bert eyed me suspiciously. "I haven't been able to get her on the phone. Besides, what's that got to do with it?"

"The reason you haven't been able to get in touch with her is that she's having the time of her life. Ellie has met several men through MySoulMate, all of whom she's been going out with. One's a pilot, one's a marketing manager, and one's an attorney." I saved the best for last. "Oh yes, and one's a doctor."

Bert's eyes widened as a tiny smile formed at the corners of her mouth. "A doctor?"

I knew I had her. What mother doesn't want her daughter to marry a doctor? For the life of me, I've never been able to figure out why. Maybe they're hoping for free health care. Whatever the reason, Bert stopped asking me if I was out of my mind, and instead went on to dinner, with only one worried look over her shoulder before she left.

I, on the other hand, went back to my computer. I clicked on the MySoulMate.org Web site, typed in "Country MusicTwin" and then my password.

The way I see it, one bad experience doesn't make

all Internet dating bad. You just have to use some common sense. You don't run off to meet some stranger alone. You also have to tell the truth about yourself. Bert had been right. It's not a real good idea to start off any relationship with a lie. And you have to have a little patience. I had been expecting to find a wonderful guy in about ten minutes.

It probably wasn't going to work that way.

The Web site had finished loading. And, what do you know, a little heart was now pulsing in the middle of my computer screen.

Goody! I had mail.

# Chapter Twenty-three

## Bert

Two hours after leaving Nan's duplex, Hank and I were feeling pretty mellow. We'd had a wonderful meal and now were just sitting, sipping an after-dinner wine that our waiter had recommended. Around us, Jack Fry's restaurant all but hummed with activity, but noticing that intense look in his eyes, it seemed to me as if Hank and I were all alone.

Ever since we'd first started dating, I'd known that Hank Goetzmann was not a man given to showering a woman with compliments. He was a no-nonsense, meat-and-potatoes kind of guy who felt as if compliments weren't really necessary, so when he leaned closer and whispered, "You look beautiful," I almost teared up.

Back in high school, if a guy had ever said such a thing to me, I would've said right back, "Are you nuts?

Have you had your eyes checked lately?" Nowadays, at the ripe old age of forty, I am most happy to accept any compliment sent my way. Rule Number One these days is: Never, *ever* argue with a man who uses the words *you* and *beautiful* in the same sentence.

"Thank you so much," I told Hank. I smiled at him. And, of course, I continued to wait for what I'd known was coming when I first saw him at my door earlier this evening. All night long he'd seemed slightly preoccupied, as if what he had to say to me had been constantly going through his mind, distracting him.

Hank took a long sip of his brandy. He was either fortifying himself before he spoke, or maybe it was just that his mouth had gone dry. "Bert?" he finally said. "Have you thought any more about . . . well—you know, what we talked about?"

What an incurable romantic.

And yet, I wouldn't want him any other way. My ex-husband, Jake, had proposed to me in front of Nan and what she often refers to as the "entire fam damily." Oh yes, old Jake had gotten down on bended knee at a large Thanksgiving dinner hosted by my mother and attended by every relative I knew and some that I didn't. Jake had taken my hand in his, presented with a flourish a garishly expensive diamond ring, and asked me to become his blushing bride in a voice that seemed at the time to be loud enough to echo off distant mountains. Jake had said the words easily, and what do you know, years later it was apparent that our wedding vows had meant little to him.

I'd much rather have a man who thinks the issue is

so serious that he can hardly bring himself to say the word out loud.

I met Hank's gaze. "Yes, I've thought about it a lot."

Hank's eyes seemed to darken as he looked at me.

I smiled at him. I really hoped I was about to give him the answer he wanted. We'd had such a difficult time being together since the *m*-word was mentioned. At times, during the last week, Hank had seemed like a different person from the man I'd been dating for over a year now.

That's right. For over a year now.

You would think that by this time, Hank would know me like he knew his right hand.

And yet, if Hank could actually believe, even for a moment, that I'd be talking to him about getting married at the very same time as I was listing myself on a dating service, then he still didn't know me.

He certainly didn't know me well enough to marry me.

And I didn't know him well enough, either. I'd finally admitted to myself that what I'd felt when I'd first seen Hank talking to the young policewoman out in front of the courthouse that day had been jealousy. And suspicion. And a feeling of betrayal.

All because he'd talked to another woman!

Obviously, I still needed to heal the damage that my marriage to Jake had done. I needed to learn to trust again.

In fact, Hank and I both needed a little more time— for both of us to be absolutely sure. Hank and I needed to learn to completely trust each other before we walked down the aisle together. For one thing, how could you fully commit to someone when you weren't even sure he would be faithful to you?

Hank reached for my hand.

"So what's your answer, Bert? Will you . . . ?" His voice was actually shaking, his hands ice-cold. He swallowed and tried again. "I do love you, Bert. Is your answer *yes* or *no*?"

I smiled at him, squeezing his hand. "I love you, too. My answer is *maybe*."

Hank seemed to start for a moment, searching my eyes. "*Maybe*? What kind of an answer is *maybe*?"

I began to explain it to him.

I was scared to look at him when I was finished, but when I did, I found that he was actually smiling. "OK. *Maybe* works for me," he said. "But the next time we talk about it," he added, "*maybe* won't be an option."

"That's fair enough," I said. He seemed all right with everything, but I wasn't sure. Was he just saying what he knew I wanted to hear? Did he think I was just trying to let him down gently?

"So how about tonight? Do you want to spend the evening at my place?" Hank asked. "Or is that a maybe, too?"

I shook my head. "No," I said.

His face fell.

Apparently, he'd taken my answer differently from how I meant it. "No, Hank," I said, "what I mean is, no, that's not a maybe." I smiled at him. "That's a *yes*."

Hank was smiling, too, as he signaled the waiter for our check.

# Grab These
# Kensington Mysteries

__**Hush Puppy**       1-57566-600-6       **$5.99**US/**$7.99**CAN
by Laurien Berenson

__**Vanishing Act**       1-57566-442-9       **$5.99**US/**$7.50**CAN
by Barbara Block

__**Splitting Heirs**       1-57566-365-1       **$5.99**US/**$7.50**CAN
by Rick Hanson

__**Killer Calories**       1-57566-521-2       **$5.99**US/**$7.99**CAN
by G.A. McKevett

__**The Frightened Wife**   1-57566-603-0       **$5.99**US/**$7.99**CAN
by Mary Roberts Rinehart

__**Hanging Curve**       1-57566-656-1       **$5.99**US/**$7.99**CAN
by Troy Soos

__**Flesh And Stone**       1-57566-273-6       **$5.99**US/**$7.99**CAN
by Mark Miano

---

Call toll free **1-888-345-BOOK** to order by phone or use this coupon to order by mail.

Name_____

Address_____

City _____ State _____ Zip _____

Please send me the books that I have checked above.

I am enclosing                $_____

Plus postage and handling*       $_____

Sales tax (in New York and Tennessee)   $_____

Total amount enclosed         $_____

*Add $2.50 for the first book and $.50 for each additional book. Send check or money order (no cash or CODs) to: **Kensington Publishing Corp., 850 Third Avenue 16th Floor, New York, NY 10022**

Prices and numbers subject to change without notice. All orders subject to availability.

Visit our website at **www.kensingtonbooks.com.**

# Your Favorite Mystery Authors
# Are Now Just A Phone Call Away

__Buried Lies                    1-57566-168-3    $5.50US/$7.00CAN
  by Conor Daly

__Skin Deep, Blood Red           1-57566-254-X    $5.99US/$7.50CAN
  by Robert Skinner

__The Murder Game                1-57566-321-X    $5.99US/$7.50CAN
  by Steve Allen

__Twister                        1-57566-062-8    $4.99US/$5.99CAN
  by Barbara Block

__Dead Men Don't Dance           1-57566-318-X    $5.99US/$7.99CAN
  by Margaret Chittenden

__Country Comes To Town          1-57566-244-2    $5.99US/$7.99CAN
  by Toni L. P. Kelner

__Just Desserts                  0-7860-0061-7    $5.99US/$7.99CAN
  by G. A. McKevett

---

Call toll free **1-888-345-BOOK** to order by phone or use this
coupon to order by mail.

Name_____

Address _____

City_____ State _____ Zip _____

Please send me the books I have checked above.

I am enclosing                          $_____

Plus postage and handling*              $_____

Sales tax (in NY and TN only)           $_____

Total amount enclosed                   $_____

*Add $2.50 for the first book and $.50 for each additional book.

Send check or money order (no cash or CODs) to:

**Kensington Publishing Corp., 850 Third Avenue, New York, NY 10022**

Prices and numbers subject to change without notice.

All orders subject to availability.

Check out our website at www.kensingtonbooks.com

# The Classic Mysteries of
## *Mary Roberts Rinehart*

| | | |
|---|---|---|
| __The Album | 1-57566-280-9 | $5.99US/$7.50CAN |
| __The After House | 1-57566-651-0 | $5.99US/$7.99CAN |
| __The Bat | 1-57566-238-8 | $5.99US/$7.50CAN |
| __The Case of Jennie Brice | 1-57566-135-7 | $5.50US/$7.00CAN |
| __The Circular Staircase | 1-57566-180-2 | $5.50US/$7.00CAN |
| __The Door | 1-57566-367-8 | $5.99US/$7.50CAN |
| __Episode of the Wandering Knife | 1-57566-530-1 | $5.99US/$7.99CAN |
| __The Haunted Lady | 1-57566-567-0 | $5.99US/$7.99CAN |
| __A Light in the Window | 1-57566-689-8 | $5.99US/$7.99CAN |
| __Lost Ecstasy | 1-57566-344-9 | $5.99US/$7.50CAN |
| __The Red Lamp | 1-57566-213-2 | $5.99US/$7.50CAN |
| __The Wall | 1-57566-213-2 | $5.99US/$7.50CAN |
| __The Window at the White Cat | 0-8217-5794-6 | $5.99US/$7.50CAN |
| __The Yellow Room | 1-57566-119-5 | $5.50US/$7.00CAN |

Call toll free **1-888-345-BOOK** to order by phone or use this coupon to order by mail.

Name_____

Address _____

City_____ State _____ Zip _____

Please send me the books I have checked above.

I am enclosing $_____

Plus postage and handling* $_____

Sales tax (in New York and Tennessee only) $_____

Total amount enclosed $_____

*Add $2.50 for the first book and $.50 for each additional book.

Send check or money order (no cash or CODs) to: **Kensington Publishing Corp., Dept. C.O., 850 Third Avenue, New York, NY 10022**

Prices and numbers subject to change without notice. All orders subject to availability.

Come visit our website at **www.kensingtonbooks.com**.